Praise for *A Grandmother Begins the Story*

A *Library Journal* Best Book
2023 Atwood Gibson Writers' Trust Fiction Prize Finalist
2024 Thomas Raddall Atlantic Fiction Award Winner

"Michelle Porter's *A Grandmother Begins the Story* blows the doors off the typical family saga. This novel's five Métis generations intertwine in wild, thrilling patterns, like the music that sustains them. Beautiful and daring, this book carries the weight of history lightly and is full of surprises and shifts. The story's striking voices resound long after the final page."

—2023 Atwood Gibson Writers' Trust Fiction Prize Jury

"[A] searingly captivating debut . . . The tender, tough, funny, and heartbreaking voices of the characters will seep into readers' souls."   —*Library Journal*

"*A Grandmother Begins the Story* will leave you forever charmed and soulspun. What a vision. What courage to blow a hole through all expectations of what a story can be and how it's told, and what a masterwork from a voice I'd follow anywhere. This is why we read and this is why we write: to discover places and voices and visions like these."

—Richard van Camp, award-winning author of *Godless but Loyal to Heaven* and *The Moon of Letting Go*

"This singular and visionary debut spectacularly reimagines the epic family saga novel. Touching, evocative, and kaleidoscopic."

—*Ms.* magazine

"In this lyrical book, we follow five Métis women confronting the wounds in their relationships with one another . . . Their many voices shine through in snippets of a few pages at a time to build a family chorus . . . This choir really drives home the point that no story stands alone, even when an individual storyteller might feel like no one is listening."   —Shondaland

"I totally fell in love with Porter's masterful storytelling . . . Told with the unique musical cadence of a Métis jig . . . A Grandmother Begins the Story is a stirring ode to the rhythms of generational exchange."   —Audible

"Through lyrical, spiritual storytelling, we see five generations of women in Carter and Allie's family determined to maintain the thread of their connections to each other and grow their legacy into the future."   —Book Riot

"A weeping birch grows in front of my house. Its leaves hang down on long, thin branches that, leafless, look like hair. When the sun is out and the winter air stirs, the sun's rays passing through these branches break into shifting patterns of shadow and light over the house. When I was reading A Grandmother Begins the Story in my front room, that moving light passed through the prismed edge of the front door window and broke into rainbows across the page, and they danced with each other and the darkness between them over the writing. I don't need to find the words to tell you that a story can change the way you belong to the world. Nature and Michelle Porter have done that for me. And they will for you, too."

    —Richard Harrison, award-winning poet and author of
On Not Losing My Father's Ashes in the Flood

"Michelle Porter's novel, *A Grandmother Begins the Story*, is charged with huge blasts of imaginative force—magical in every way. In this novel, divided families come together, there are wise bison and dogs with opinions, [and] an Indigenous family history spanning generations. Here is heaven and then, what the rest of these vivid characters must contend with, life on earth, with all its splendor and heartbreak. Porter is sometimes knee-slappingly funny, sometimes wry, poignant, nuanced, and gleefully irreverent. But this novel is full of reverence for the most important things: music and stories. Porter's characters are tough and tender, courageous and flawed, and so true to life you'll go back to the beginning as soon as you turn the last page, because you can't stand for it to be over. Michelle Porter's voice is unique, uber-alive, utterly gorgeous. Just *wow*!"

—Lisa Moore, award-winning author of
This Is How We Love and *Caught*

"[A] beautiful and affecting debut."　　　　　—*Shelf Awareness*

"Heavy ties of interdependent energies run through these characters, both human and more-than-human, simultaneously. These are exciting stories attached to the land with identifiable characters that could be one's family members, and it's the land that holds the story and hand of the grandmothers who lead the herd and hold space for life and story after them."

—Marilyn Dumont, award-winning poet and author of
The Pemmican Eaters and *A Really Good Brown Girl*

"[Porter] expertly weaves together voices and stories like a master."　　　　　　　　　　　　　　　—*Debutiful*

"Michelle Porter weaves an intricate story out of sparse, inter-locking poetic fragments in her fiction debut . . . [A] beautiful meditation on the interconnectedness of spirit, land, and family."
                                                            —*BookPage*

A
GRANDMOTHER
BEGINS
THE
STORY

ALSO BY MICHELLE PORTER

Scratching River

Approaching Fire

Inquiries: poems

A GRANDMOTHER BEGINS THE STORY

MICHELLE PORTER

ALGONQUIN BOOKS OF CHAPEL HILL   2024

Published by

ALGONQUIN BOOKS OF CHAPEL HILL
Post Office Box 2225
Chapel Hill, North Carolina 27515-2225

an imprint of WORKMAN PUBLISHING
a division of HACHETTE BOOK GROUP, INC.
1290 Avenue of the Americas
New York, NY 10104

First paperback edition, Algonquin Books of Chapel Hill, August 2024. Originally
published in hardcover by Algonquin Books of Chapel Hill in November 2023.

This is a work of fiction. While, as in all fiction, the literary perceptions and
insights are based on experience, all names, characters, places, and incidents
either are products of the author's imagination or are used fictitiously.

Library of Congress Cataloging-in-Publication Data
Names: Porter, Michelle, [date]–author.
Title: A grandmother begins the story / Michelle Porter.
Description: First edition. | Chapel Hill, North Carolina : Algonquin Books
of Chapel Hill, 2023. | Summary: "The story of the unrivaled desire for healing
and the power of familial bonds across five generations of Métis women and
the land and bison that surround them"— Provided by publisher.
Identifiers: LCCN 2023022891 | ISBN 9781643755182 (hardcover) |
ISBN 9781643755205 (ebook)
Subjects: LCSH: Métis women—Fiction. | LCGFT: Novels.
Classification: LCC PR9199.4.P67545 G73 2023 | DDC
818/.603—dc23/eng/20230807

LC record available at https://lccn.loc.gov/2023022891

ISBN 978-1-64375-519-9 (paperback)

10 9 8 7 6 5 4 3 2 1

First Paperback Edition

For my grandmother, Estelle

Light the smudge, breathe deep, from this sacred tobacco, cedar,
sweetgrass, and sage, burn all jealousy and hatred from this earth.
O sacred smoke, make the world and us whole again; we women,
this is what we do: sew and smudge, make the ugly, beautiful.

—from the "Mending the Violence of Men" aria,
Li Keur: Riel's Heart of the North, by S. M. Steele

A
GRANDMOTHER
BEGINS
THE
STORY

Mamé's afterlife is a fiddle

I had my choice down there, didn't I? Eve, she chose the apple. That's the story they tell, the story they told us all. At the school and at the church on the Sunday that was oh so holy. I didn't want the apple, no. I went and I chose him, the one with the fiddle, the man who put all his restless self into his songs and who made people's feet dance in their moccasins on the dirt floors and in their fancy shoes on the dance hall's wooden floors, move in ways they'd never before, step so quick and light they'd wonder who it was that had touched their feet. It was him. Every time.

Dee hears a rumor

Dee heard a rumor spreading though the herd, leaping from cow to bull to calf. The herd would be divided. A truck and trailer would come and load up the chosen. Some of them would be moving on. She had to ask an auntie, What did moving on mean?

Carter negotiates her fee

So my grandmother—my grandmother who I never met, by the way, because my birth mom refused to get us together saying her mom was a piece of work—called me up to ask if I'd help her kill herself. Which isn't helping; it's doing it. I said sure, I'm a part-time assassin. In my spare time. But can you afford my fees? I'm good and I don't come cheap, I said. She said be serious. I am, I said, dead serious. Then she called me a cunt and a few other things, I didn't catch them all. Okay then, I said, what's in the will—you got the money to pay? She hung up. I didn't even get to ask how she got my number. I'd think I made the conversation up, but my phone logged the call, tells me I talked for five minutes with someone named L Goulet. What does *L* stand for? I don't know, she never told me her name.

Like I said, I never met her before she dropped this on me. And she didn't have the guts to ask in person. It was fucked.

Geneviève forgets

She couldn't take the old organ with her where she was going, that was for sure. All morning she'd been poking about the main floor, searching for the things that made up her sputtering life, the things she always forgot: reading glasses, cellphone, her father's old sash, the little statue of Mary that had belonged to her mama Mamé, an old book of piano music that her sister had marked up. So many things to forget and then she thought of her piano and it came over her all of a sudden that she couldn't bear to live away from it, not even for twelve weeks. And what was she going to do when she up and died? They said that was going to happen before the year was up and she should get around to telling people as soon as anything, say her goodbyes, but instead she went and booked herself into rehab, stubborn old hag that she was.

She put her hand on the spinet organ's faded wooden frame. Geneviève didn't know how the organ got to be so old. The spinet was small and a bit frail now, but the old girl still had a strong voice and she still responded to Gen's touch, still created music beneath her fingers. Velma had socked away as much as she could of her performance earnings and competition winnings to pay for it, had been so proud to bring it into that log house their father built. And every once in a while it was just like it was when Velma was there, standing near the end of the piano, emptying her bow and her fiddle into every song, telling Geneviève with a glance when to wait and when to rush ahead. Been a long time since anybody was there to tell her to hold back on anything. Long time.

Mamé and the crookedness of time

Tonight's a party.

We're celebrating those of us who just got here.

Even if it took a long time.

Well, by the standards of the earth, we just left. Which isn't the way to count time up here. Bob's always telling me that. Time's all crooked up here, he says.

Bob's going to make the music for everyone. Him and his band.

Soon, he'll be walking through this tall grass with his bow and fiddle. Soon as the sun starts to settle into the grass for a sleep, soon as the light starts to slip away and the whippoorwills start to sing. He'll play in that old cabin.

Everybody's coming to hear Bob play. I'll see everyone I haven't seen since the old days.

What about my girls? I ask him. Velma and Geneviève.

Bob says, Mamé, don't worry about that, the spirit world isn't the place for worry. They'll be here eventually.

Everyone comes here eventually, he says, and he makes me laugh.

He's right.

And yet I want to look.

I'm new here but Velma's been in the spirit world a while now. Bob says he's heard that she plays down at the dance hall but he's never been to a show. Says she only wants the music for company and that she doesn't come around this way much and when he says not much he means never.

And could I just for a moment see Geneviève's face again?

Still getting the hang of things here.

Anyway all these stories began with me, got started that first time I heard Bob's fiddle.

It's not about me, not anymore. It's not like that. Up here the stories are us and we are the stories, every single one of them. Took me a long time to make my way here and now it's almost my turn to be the stories—or to *tell* the stories, as we used to say before we passed.

They say everyone does it different.

Some tell late into the nights, some gather in the morning. Summer or winter, around fires or wood stoves, in cabins, tee-pees, or outside, whatever.

When it's my turn, I'm going to bring everyone around an old wood stove, smell of a stew bubbling on top, the heat making our faces pink as the stories unwind. Can't get enough of the telling. Which is a good thing, because if there's one thing we've got here, it's time.

Dee fills up on grass

Auntie said that moving on would happen before the bluebonnets flowered in the time and space humans called March. Dee's mother had been gone for months by then and Dee worried. Did her mother know about the moving on? Would her mother miss them? The aunties worried. They bellowed and shook their great heads until their beards dusted the earth and the starlings and brown-headed cowbirds they carried on their backs scattered. In the days after the rumor arrived, the aunties who had invited Dee to their milky teats began to refuse her, to feed only their own calves and each other's.

Mockingbirds flew in long arcs from bison back to bison back, singing the phrase that'd been moving through the herd, Moving on! Moving on!

Hunger gnawed at Dee, began to eat her up.

She'd dream of milk and the scent of the herd's mothers would fill her nostrils and she'd wake suckling air. Then she'd rise in the dark to find the part of the fence her mother had broken through. She'd stand near that mended section of fence until the first streaks of morning showed.

After the rumor, the elders took her away from the rest of the herd to graze but she couldn't get enough to satisfy her tight belly. The milky smell of the other calves needled her, made her angry.

The moving on would begin before the flowers, the elders said. Dee counted ahead. Her first molar would be nearly out; her hump would be higher; her horns would be pushing out. She would be seven months old then.

Carter makes room in her schedule

Gramma called back not too long after—like about a week or something. I knew she would. You don't call someone up to ask something like that if you're the shrinking violet type.

So bio gramma called back and she said, I want you to get me pills. I know you know all about drugs. Sure, I said. Of course, I said. The drug that's in the news, that's killing people, you know it, right? There's a few of them now, Gramma, you got to be more specific. The F-one, you know it! Yes, I said, I heard about it.

Get it for me, she said. I put on my business voice. I don't know, Gramma, I got a schedule, you know, it's packed. And let's see now, I could maybe fit you in for a pre-consult? You know I like to meet the people I'm going to kill. Real customer service, me.

I didn't ask you to kill me, she said. I want to kill me.

Anyway, Gramma, drugs aren't my method. My creativity goes in another direction. Drugs are cowardly, don't you think? My instrument is the knife. And then I got ways to get rid of the body. There's where improvisation comes in.

Gramma got mad, as far as I could tell on the phone. She said, I'm wanting to kill myself and this is what you say to me? I said, You're asking me to kill you and then taking away my creative control? I don't work that way.

She hung up.

But this time she called back right away.

Please, please, I'm begging you.

Gramma, I got to meet you first, I said.

That'll take too long.

What, you got a meeting with the ancestors?

I'm going to heaven.

Word is Jesus doesn't let you in if you kill yourself.

That's not true.

You so sure about that? You want to gamble?

I looked into it. That's only if you're Catholic.

You're Protestant then?

It doesn't matter what I am. The Lord is calling me to do this.

The God bit got to me, how Gramma could use God to purify what she was doing, as if there was nothing else God ever wanted her to do that she should have done, as if what she was asking me was okay. I said, What, God never wanted you to ask my mom about me before now, before you wanted to die?

I didn't—

And now that you want to die so suddenly, God wants you to give me a phone call?

It's not—

I'll come see you. Make sure it's you calling me, first of all.

Who else would it be?

How do I know I'm talking to you? I mean you could be someone setting me up to kill you. You could be my mom. You're not my bio mom, are you?

Shut your mouth.

And then I'd go to jail. The headline would be weird: "Adopted-out granddaughter returns to kill gramma she never met."

You're being a shit.

We can explore that further in person. Or fuck off. Your choice.

Geneviève curses

John shook his head and said, Don't go, babe.

Geneviève looked over at the old man in the old recliner, said, You'll be here when I get back?

Don't know.

Why you've got to be like that.

Just being honest.

John had always liked watching Geneviève.

She still knew how to walk into a room and suck the breath out of everyone, even when she was only wearing an orange muumuu and slippers. And she'd find the thing to get a laugh and she'd spread that around a bit.

The radio was on and he'd been watching how she moved one of her hands with the music but now the newsreader's voice cut in and she dropped her hand back to her side.

The newsreader talked about the number of days they'd been without rain. The radio was at the far end of the living room on the old spinet organ that was right next to her upright, the one she'd bought with the winnings from a scratch ticket ten years ago, the only time she'd had that much money in her hand at once. She turned her back to John and crossed the room to turn off the radio. There on top of the organ she found everything she'd been looking for: her glasses, the piano music, the sash, Mamé's statue, and the jar of ashes. She'd been planning to leave her tarot cards behind because all her readings had been coming out the same these days, ending with Death, but all of a sudden she had to have a deck of cards with her. From the half a dozen different decks next to her bed, she wanted the cards painted by that little Michif artist from Saskatchewan. The colors were muted and comforting. Maybe she'd left them in her side table drawer, there in a tin container with the artist's name printed in green over the top, *Audie Murray*. She picked up the tin but it was larger than her hands and she dropped it, knocking the cover off and a card fell out, face side up. Staring up at her was Death, a painted skull surrounded by plant life.

You didn't have to do that, Gen said to the cards.

She had to get on one knee to get the card and return it to the deck, pressing the lid back on tight. She scooped up another deck too, a faded pile of cards held together with an elastic, the Rider-Waite-Smith deck that she'd had since her mother passed on. Back on her feet again. Everything into her shoulder bag, and then she zipped it up.

She said to John, Don't want you to be gone when I'm done with this.

Just take a seat here on my lap.

Can't.

You always liked it.

I'd never get back up.

With one hand she gestured to the car she could see through the front window. It was packed and ready, waiting. Said, Out there I've got the rest of my life to live.

You're eighty-one, babe. Not a lot of room for what else.

The radio came to life again. Geneviève frowned and her eyebrows pulled together because she was sure she'd just turned it off. Some low-pressure system moving in. She crossed the room again and pulled the cord from the outlet.

John leaned his head against the back of the recliner like they had all the time in the world. His woman bragged that she had the firmest bosom of any woman her age because she never took off her bra, said the support kept her going. She could switch from English to French to Michif and still remembered enough Cree to get by and she was a woman who wore heels around the house because, she said, she needed a boost sometimes, never mind if they made her feet ache. And him, sitting there in the chair, an old man who hadn't been on a trapline in half a century, a man having trouble moving on even though the ancestors were calling him back home, a man who wasn't sure he could wait around for her anymore.

You just better be here when I get back, John.

Got no control over that. It's all you.

She looked hard at him, said, You hate that. Said, Ever since you started coming around, you hate that I'm the one that's in control of this.

He said nothing. He damn well knew she hated it when he started with the silent treatment.

Useless to say anything to the man, so she sat down to the piano to play something he hated, an old show tune that always reminded him of his first ex-wife. He kept a straight face but she knew she was getting to him. He shifted in his seat and she had to stop playing to laugh at the both of them. One hand was in her lap, but the other hand kept fussing with the keys, just touching and not asking anything of them. She saw the twist of a smile beneath his beard, said, You'll take care of my piano?

You don't have to go, he said.

You'll dust it every day. Maybe clean up the bottles, maybe.

You're just fine, baby.

Don't call me baby.

Baby—

I'm an old woman.

Okay but what about the dogs, he said.

Already in the car.

You don't have to do this, that's all I'm saying. You always liked drinking. Nothing wrong.

I never left them in a kennel before.

You always been good times.

I met you when—shit, I want a drink.

Geneviève sat down on the sofa.

Just one, said the man in the recliner.

I should.

Not a crime to feel good at your time in life.

Oh, listen to you talk.

Look at the sight of you. You're shaking.

Just one, to steady my hands.

You won't make it to that place without a drink. Nothing wrong with it.

There was a half a bottle of something on the side table and a glass holding onto signs of drink from the night before. She reached for it. She poured herself a drink. She tipped it into her mouth and her eyes closed. She sighed, relaxing against the sofa back.

Oh God, I needed that. I couldn't face all this without just one drink.

You don't have to stop at one, babe.

I know.

It's time to get to the car, she said. Can't leave Perkins and Lottery for long.

She stood up. The drink helped her put one foot in front of the other. At the front door she stood all quiet. She was a woman who knew how to stand in a silence that was louder than most people could shout.

John called out to her, Stay here with me.

She turned her back to the door and leaned against it. She said quietly, And me? What about my life?

He said nothing to her. The silent treatment again. Anger made her chest burn and her head spin. She repeated, What about my life? He said nothing.

She faced the door and gripped the handle. It opened and then she was outside on the concrete step and the door was closing. The sun beat down on her. The latch clicked. She let go of the handle but took hold of it again a moment later and opened the front door. She pulled the jar of ashes from her bag and leaned into the house as far as her hips and knees would allow. The whole time he didn't say a single word to her and his silence pissed her off more than anything else. She placed the jar on the floor, just by the boot mat. Fucking asshole, she muttered. She cursed him out in English, French, and all the Michif she'd been given before her mother and father died and then she closed the door one more time.

She stood a full minute with one hand resting on the knob before she could bring herself to turn her head and look through the front living room window. The recliner John had been sitting in was empty. Only then, on that front step, could she admit that the recliner had been empty for eleven years now and she was still pissed with him about it. There was no way she could bring him with her.

She walked down the steps and up the concrete path to the car by the curb. It was a hard walk. With every step she wanted to turn back, and if not for her fury at John's giving her the silent treatment, she would not have had strength enough to make it the whole way.

Mamé checks on her girls

Bob's not here yet so I stick my nose into my girls' business the way he told me not to.

I can't help it.

Velma's up here in the spirit world and I shouldn't have to think about her at all. But even though she's up here, even though she's telling stories with her music, she's trying to forget. You can make yourself do that here for a long time, if you really want. So right away, I'm worrying about her.

More than I worry about Geneviève down there. Geneviève, now, she's finding her way. Look at her now, she's traveling down south in the direction of her healing. Isn't it funny how we all think we know why we do a thing? She thinks she's doing this for herself, but really it's for Velma.

And then there's Geneviève's girl, my granddaughter, Lucie. Oh my.

I see what she's doing and I could fix it all up for her and arrange to have her move on to the spirit world the way she wants right now. But things up here don't ever work out the way you think they will when you're dreaming of it down there—and anyway she's got to help Carter now.

Carter, my great-great-granddaughter. She doesn't understand what that means yet, partly because I was gone before she was born, but I think she'll do what she's got to do. And maybe she'll help her mom, my great-granddaughter Allie.

Maybe. It's a lot to ask. There's a lot on Carter's shoulders and she wasn't even raised with her own family. But she's got the ability to burn, she does. I had it too. But only small fires for me.

Carter, from what I can see up here, she's the one who could burn it all down, who could make things ready for the new growth to come on up, all green and tender again.

There are others I could check in on but I have to wait on that because here comes Bob over the knoll out there, across a spread of prairie grass and I know he'll say not to poke around in these things, that it'll never do any good. He'll tell me that all my girls—*our* girls—will be just fine and they'll figure everything out in good time. You're in the afterlife, he'll say. They'll be here with you soon enough. Sometimes I think what does he know about these things anyway—he's an old man, even up here, and his life has only ever been about the music.

Oh but he'll waggle his eyebrows and his eyes will spark in that way that always makes my legs turn to butter and he'll say, Let those girls down there alone, Élise, and come make music with me.

He knows I'll go with him.

Bob doesn't want to fool with the stories down there. Not his way. He travels around the spirit world from the bison trails to the teepee camps to the dance halls and to all those log houses, all the time carrying his songs in his chest and playing his fiddle crooked. Even up here they all want to listen all night long. And night lasts as long as you want here.

He's coming to pull me away from looking below.

Here comes my Bob Goulet, and here am I, ready as ever to hear him tell me stories with the dance of his bow, and you know what, I don't want to jig right now, I just want to set myself down in that old cabin over there.

They've all dragged most of the furniture outside to make room for the dancing. Only left a couple of chairs inside. People have walked here from all over, all kinds of families coming to gather, so many of them it will be packed tight from wall to wall. Me, I'll find a chair right by the wood stove and wait for my Bob, get my ears ready for the tune of what he's got to say.

Dee kicks up dust

Before her mama left for good, Dee would ask to hear the story of her birth. Her mama would tell it sometimes on clear nights when she let herself forget about the fences for a while, during those hours when Dee was allowed to press herself against her mama's strong chest and press her muzzle into her cape. This was back when the days were getting shorter, before Dee's first winter, before the buds of Dee's horns had appeared, in the days when Roam had milk for her.

Roam always started by saying how she had walked her girl into life, how nine months pregnant and ready to birth, Roam tore through the fences and trotted all the way to the calm of the canyons. Dee would sigh and flick her tail and shift closer to her mother, wait to hear more. Roam would say that she'd found herself pregnant later in the season than anyone else, that all the other cows had birthed their calves already and that Dee was the last and, for that reason, the most important. Roam would say Dee began her journey into the world the moment they reached the shale and sandstone cliffs and how quickly Dee had slipped from her mother's body, landing solidly on the earth.

It was midafternoon, Roam might say then.

The hottest time of the day? Dee would ask, wriggling a little in anticipation.

You wouldn't stand up.

I wasn't in a hurry, right, Mama?

Some calves get up right away but you? No way. You scared me.

I kicked the dirt.

You sure did kick up dust. I watched for coyotes. And bobcats.

You said, Get up, Dee? Right?

Uh-huh. And I thought about the fences here that would have protected you.

I liked dust, right?

You liked dust from the moment you were born. The way it sparkled in the sun, I think.

At this point in the story Dee would usually roll and kick the earth beneath them but if the story was being told late at night there would be no rising dust because the grass that was their bed held the dirt close.

I was safe, Dee would say.

The buttes and the monoliths all kept you safe.

You too, right? You kept me safe.

Yes. For an hour. An entire hour, my child. There was this magpie that started swooping over your head, so I stood right over you. I wasn't going to let that bird peck your eyes out.

A magpie would do that?

I haven't seen it but I've heard stories, little one. You weren't worried though—you didn't get up until a quail started calling across the canyon.

I wanted to see the quail?

You were curious, yes. You only got to your feet to greet the quail.

And that's how I came into the world?

And that's how you came into the world.

Sometimes that would be the end of the story. Other times Dee would prompt more telling and say, And then the humans came.

Then Roam would tell how they'd been together for two days before the humans showed up, separated mother from daughter and led Dee back up the trails out of the canyon to the truck.

I followed you out of the canyons, Roam would say.

Why? Dee would ask every time, just to hear the answer.

Because I'm your mother, Roam would say.

For Dee, memory began at the end of that short truck ride from the canyons to the herd. These memories came in flashes: the scents making their way into the truck before the door slid open; the first sight of fences from the truck, the way they cut things up into boxes; the flat earth that walked all the way into the blue sky; the bison everywhere in shades of earth, their great heads and horns, how their eyes were fixed on her, their friendly faces, their solemn faces, their stern faces, their ancient faces, their curious faces; the red calves who ran after each other, breaking the silence by calling out to each other and daring each other to call her a baby; and the elders who hushed the calves; the aunties calling out comforting snorts; and the birds calling out welcome songs from the solid backs of the herd. Her mother urging her down the ramp with low grunts, telling her to go where the humans asked, everything would be okay. The panic of her first fences. She stood right up against her mother's big flank as each member of the herd welcomed her. The old ones saying, She's the biggest calf born this season, and one of the aunties saying, This will settle Roam down.

Dee didn't understand what settling meant but she felt her mother tense and thought it must be a bad thing. She pressed herself against Roam's udder even though she didn't want any milk.

It turned out the aunties were wrong about Dee's mother. Nothing settled Roam. Dee couldn't say how soon her mother got back to the work of breaking free, but she remembered watching her mother tear at a post with her horns and there was snow on the ground and her body was so little and she was shaking. The humans put an electric shock in the outermost fence, but that didn't stop anything. Roam would take the shock, go through the fence.

Roam would say not to worry, that she'd be back when her udder filled tight with milk. But Dee always waited against the fence, trembling with the fear her mother would never return, straining for the smell of her and then the shape of her in the distance or the sound of the truck on the other side opening to let her mother out. Dee asked Roam why, and Roam said, You'll follow someday, my baby, when you're brave enough. Dee didn't believe she'd ever be as brave as her mother.

The struggle with milk began as the days became warmer and the herd spent more time in the shade of the trees. Dee knew Roam would leave after feeding her, so she refused to eat. If she didn't eat, her mother wouldn't leave, she thought. Dee lost weight. So much weight that three of the other mothers invited Dee to feed along with their own calves. Full teats didn't stop Roam from leaving but her milk slowed and then it stopped. Dee noticed how the smell of canyons had replaced the sweet scent of milk, how her mother smelled different from the others.

One winter night Roam woke Dee, said, Come.

Dee followed her mother to the farthest part of the fence. She watched as her mother tore through with her horns, her massive head taking the shock without flinching. Roam stepped over the wreckage. She turned to her daughter and said, I want you to come with me.

Dee's long legs went weak and the shaking came into them. She didn't remember being on the other side of all the fences, couldn't recall a time a fence wasn't within sight. The aunties told terrible stories about the other side of the fence and so she had only her mother's stories about a better place to hang onto but those were short and rare and filled with words she didn't understand, and once when she'd asked her mom what language those words were in, Roam had flicked her tail and said it was the language of the free. Roam had promised she'd translate and even teach it to Dee one day, but the right time never came and now Dee couldn't make her tongue speak the language of the other side and she was afraid. But neither could she face letting her mother go and so her

MICHELLE PORTER

legs were like the grass in the wind, wobbling this way and that and when she opened her mouth to answer her mother Dee's terror came out as laughter, it just bubbled up, nervous and high-pitched and then her legs became steadier, could hold her up again.

Roam said, Come on.

What was this brightness inside? Dee had never laughed before and she had never heard anyone else laugh either. She wasn't afraid of this. Laughter made her feel the way suckling at her mother's teats used to. How could Dee produce more of this new milk? She took a few steps forward, as if the new light inside could carry her over the fence and out into the open world.

She thought of watching the other calves playing chase and how their excited snorts were the closest thing to laughter she'd ever heard, how one had slipped in the mud after a rain and the others had gathered, capering and prancing and squealing around their fallen friend and how she had been drawn near as well, the youngest of the calves, the one born outside of the fences. Looking directly at her mother she lifted a hoof to step over but then dropped to the ground, rolling over and over. Dee moaned as if in pain—but as her mother leaned closer to look, Dee couldn't suppress a giggle. She wanted more of that flash or glow or blaze or whatever it was that got inside her when she laughed.

Roam stepped back and looked at her daughter with one big eye. And then she tossed her head and laughed too. Dee never forgot that sound. It was like a thousand hooves galloping for the joy of it, like the deep rumble of an earth drumming the ecstatic rhythm of all their quickened heartbeats, like all the fences in all the world crashing down, crumbling into nothing but rubble so her mother didn't have to leave.

And how long did that last? Dee would never know, only that way too soon her mother shook off the laughter and scratched at the dirt with one hoof. Come with me, daughter.

Dee stopped rolling and playing, stood up again. She moved forward and nudged her mother's flank. And will your canyons grow milk for me?

Roam said a few words about all the things a bison had to leave behind for freedom, how nothing would stay the way it was before you left it, how there would be no coming back. Dee didn't want her to talk. She wanted more of that laughter. She pressed her little body against Roam's neck and said, Mama, I know a joke. Wanna hear? Old Bark told it to me. It's about a bull.

Roam stepped back. She turned to look at the land behind and said something about how far she had to travel before the humans noticed the fence. She said, I have to go.

That's okay, said Dee. You can take the joke with you.

In a small voice, Dee began. Roam stood to hear the beginning of the joke and then she walked into a night so cold it made her shiver. Roam never heard the end of the joke, but she laughed when she thought the time was right, when her little girl would have delivered the punchline and would have been waiting for her mother's approval. Dee finished that joke and began another. When she finished that one she stood until light appeared in the sky, until a magpie landed on her back and asked permission to feed on her ticks, until the herd stirred and one of the old ones, taking an early walk to ease the joints, found her there. The old cow just stood beside Dee, shoulder to shoulder, looking at the broken fence. Four old starlings flew over and landed in a line on the old one's back. They hopped around and shifted her fur with their beaks hunting for ticks and fleas. I know a joke, Dee said after a bit. Want to hear? The cow nodded and the four black birds stood still and Dee began with the one about the bull. She never finished the joke though because she was interrupted by the lactating cows, who called for her to take her turn at their teats.

Carter regrets her curiosity

Carter got to thinking how she had to quit with the curiosity thing. It kept getting her in over her head. Cause shit, here she was, planning to meet the gramma she'd never met.

Why'd I insist? she asked herself. All she could come up with was curiosity.

She did a surprising number of things because of curiosity. College, for example, where it turned out she didn't belong. What a relief it had been to quit that place after two months and go get on a plane to Europe instead. And Slavko. She'd been curious about him, hadn't she? His time growing up in the former Yugoslavia, the war that had divided him from his family for years. She'd gone so far as to marry him, ha ha. It's just that she always wanted to know how things would turn out.

Her bio mom had warned her. Said Gramma would stab you in the back if she could. Said Gramma never got over the fact that she'd had a girl and not a boy, that she'd stuck her bio mom with the name Allan and then refused to call her Allie the way everyone else did. Said Gramma had sent Allie off to live with one of Gramma's ex-shrinks when she was fifteen, had said to him, take her, she's ruining my marriage. The ex-shrink was in his late twenties and interpreted Gramma's offering as an arranged marriage of sorts. He was excited having Allie in his house, him being an awkward nerd who'd been unable to maintain a relationship with any woman longer than five days. Didn't take him long to convince the very lonely, very young Allie to go to bed with him and then they were inviting Gramma for dinner once a month. Allie said it took her way too long to figure out how to get out of that toxic relationship.

Gramma'd been married a few times. Didn't seem to take much to ruin her marriages.

Carter had once said to Allie, Gramma's an old woman, isn't much harm she can do anymore, is there? Allie made a noise that reminded Carter of a horse and said, You'll think everything's okay and then you turn around and she's a witch.

Yeah, Allie was that kind that said witch instead of bitch. Wouldn't tell you not to swear but couldn't bring herself to say what she was clearly thinking, to say motherfucker or shitshow or cunt, none of it.

Sure, curiosity got her hooked when her bio gramma called, but now she was like a fish on her grandmother's line. There was no way she could get herself off that line before her grandmother reeled her in, no amount of flipping or flopping would do it even if she wanted to. When she was a kid she'd daydream sometimes, like in the middle of math class she'd picture what her bio family was like and how they'd react when they saw her, how proud they'd be, how happy to finally meet her. In her imagination her bio grandmother had always been wearing an apron and was always holding a cookie sheet fresh from the oven and she had big soft boobs that took up half her body and her hugs were squishy as hell and she smelled of love and happiness and chocolate. Now she thought about it, the grandmother she'd created in her mind was totally white and totally rich. This one who had called her up was not that imaginary grandmother, not even a little bit.

Carter figured she didn't have any history with the old woman, the way her bio mom did. Carter figured she was safe because she didn't want anything from the old woman. Anyway, Carter was going to go through with this thing, whatever it was.

Who knew, maybe she'd like her bio gramma so much it'd be a pleasure killing her.

Perkins and Lottery in the passenger seat

Geneviève was pressing her foot heavy on the gas and gripping the steering wheel too tight, just like she always did. But even so, Perkins was worried.

She had rolled the passenger window all the way down to let Perkins's nose out into the open air. The wind blew through his short hair, teased at his sensitive ears. Not a cloud in the sky.

Something was off, he could tell. But the sun was just the right kind of hot and they were going somewhere and he was getting ready to belt out a song, one from the old days.

He looked back at Lottery on the seat behind him. How could she sleep?

That sky went on and on and he was getting that feeling he got sometimes and it made his legs restless. His nails were a bit overlong so he made something like music whenever he shifted his paws. Shuffle, scuff, scratch. He began to relax.

Beneath all that blue was the ribbon of road and the conversation of vehicles, revving, turning, and blinking. An old song was coming to him, one created by his ancestors, and he was waiting for it to arrive complete, whole, and ancient. Shuffle, scuff, scratch.

Geneviève wasn't telling him to stop and he was feeling like—wait, why wasn't she telling him to stop? He looked back at her.

This isn't right, Geneviève was muttering.

She wasn't using her dog-loving voice, no, her voice was like an old house in a storm and Perkins realized she hadn't looked over at him since they'd left their street. A burst of anxiety hit and his music faded away.

Geneviève said, No, no, no—I can't do this.

That was it, his song was gone. Perkins tried to swallow back his growl, but out it came anyway. It was always that way. Some made music with their troubles, but not him.

He pulled his head back into the overheated interior of the car and nudged Lottery with his snout. Didn't work. He circled and aimed a firm kick to her belly with his back right foot.

Lottery opened one eye, rolled over before the kick could land, and said, Quit worrying.

Something's going on, Perkins whined.

Lottery shook the nap out of her curly hair and limbs. Her tags jangled in a way that almost put the music back into Perkins, but not quite. Lottery sat up. She said, Nothing you can do about what's going to happen anyway, you know that, right?

Gen lifted a hand off the steering wheel and banged the dashboard with her palm. Why am I doing this? Gen asked.

It was as if she was arguing with somebody, Perkins thought. He looked in the back seat just in case, but no, there was no other human in the car. He lifted his nose in the old woman's direction and sniffed.

She smells different, said Perkins.

Humans are like the weather, Lottery said.

Perkins thought he'd try sitting pretty—that always worked. He got in position. He whined just a little. Then he looked over at her—had she noticed? She hadn't. That really got to him, hit him hard.

The old lady's different today, Perkins said.

The sky never changes, said Lottery. Did you know that?

Humans are always changing every goddamn minute, Perkins said.

Could be she's taking us to a park, Lottery said.

No, Perkins said, I know that route and this isn't it.

The vet, then?

Geneviève slowed, switched on the turning signal, and

turned off the road. She let the car roll to a stop. She pushed open the driver's side door. The smell of gasoline flooded in. The old woman pulled herself out of the car and gave her attention to the gas cap and the fuel pump. Whatever that woman does, she does with passion, Perkins thought with pride. When the car door opened again and she lowered her weary self into her seat and reached for the seat belt, she didn't greet the dogs.

Perkins and Lottery jumped up onto all fours to get her attention and their tags jangled. The old woman started, looked at them, and then blinked, frowning. Oh my God, she said, and then she repeated it, but in that angry tight voice.

She smells of surprise, said Lottery.

Not a good one, said Perkins.

Geneviève banged her left palm against the steering wheel.

I forgot, she said. I fucking forgot what I was doing.

She started the car and backed up a little, then paused.

Perkins whined, low and quiet.

Well, shit, guys, the old woman said out loud, I gotta turn this car around.

She switched on the radio and moved slowly to the turn. She flicked on her turning light so one light flashed and then she flicked it so another light flashed. Then she flicked it off.

Okay, she said. Which way do I go? Right or left? What do you say? Perkins? Lottery?

Perkins whined.

Lottery said, Now I remember what's going to happen.

The dogs jumped up and wagged their tails. Their tags jangled again. This time Geneviève looked at them. This is a good sign, Perkins thought.

Lottery stepped over the cupholder, climbed onto Gen's lap, and butted her head against Gen's hand. Gen rubbed a sensitive spot behind Lottery's ear.

Gen said, Maybe a drink would help. What do you think, Lottery? A drink? Just one. Would you wait for me in the car?

A horn blared loud behind them. Startled, Geneviève swore and pressed the gas pedal. The old station wagon jolted forward and then skidded to a stop as she slammed on the brake. Lottery's head hit the steering wheel before she tumbled down to Gen's feet. Perkins landed in the water bowl on the passenger-side car floor.

Oh God, Gen said, as she helped Lottery up to her lap and checked that Perkins, who was already back on the passenger-side seat, was all right. She opened her window and waved her arm to say Go ahead. A red truck rolled up and the driver paused to give her the finger. Gen put a manicured hand to her lips and blew him a big kiss. Fuck you, the driver said and screeched ahead. Gen laughed and switched on the hazard lights. She put both hands back on the wheel and said, What do I do what do I do what do I do?

I think she needs a song, said Perkins.

On the radio a sad country ballad played out its first notes. Perkins broke into a series of yips and yaps, warming up for a round of deep, soulful barking. He threw a bit of his own rhythm into it and Lottery joined him to smooth out the rough edges. Anything to help Gen, Lottery thought. Hey, hey, cooed Geneviève. She switched off the radio and reached over to scoop Perkins into her lap beside Lottery. Another car drove around them and Gen pressed her face against each dog's head. How many times do I have to make this decision? she asked.

A yellow hybrid blared its horn repeatedly before pulling into the other lane and passing the old station wagon. The driver gave Gen the finger as he passed, but Gen didn't notice because she was staring at a sticker in the corner of the rear passenger window. Stuck to the window was a reproduction of a tarot card, a nude woman in the sky with a cloth covering her genitals. It was the World card.

Well, if that's not a sign from above, I don't know what is, Gen said.

Lottery leaned over to lick Gen's face. Gen turned off the hazard lights and put some pressure on the gas pedal and then they were moving down the highway again.

It'll all be okay, Gen said to the dogs. But Perkins thought her smell said the opposite and Lottery agreed, so they kept up the barking all the way to the kennel.

Gen parked the car in front of a set of glass doors and lifted Perkins and Lottery off her lap. She hauled herself out of the car and shut the door on the dogs. Lottery hopped onto the driver's seat and lay down. It was warm.

She left us, said Perkins.

She's handling it, said Lottery, stretching her back legs one at a time.

It smells of guilt in here, doesn't it?

You're only, what, a couple hundred years old? What do you know about guilt?

What do you think she feels guilty about? asked Perkins.

Whatever's about to happen.

Oh my God.

No need for that. Just call me Lottery.

Shut up, said Perkins. He shook himself so his tags rattled. This is serious, he said.

The glass door in front of the car swung open. A man held the door as Gen stepped back onto the sidewalk. The man and another woman followed Gen to the car. Gen opened the trunk and pulled out the dog carriers.

Perkins barked and barked. I knew it, he said. It's the vet.

Lottery yawned. She said, She smells like fear now.

Yeah, she does, doesn't she?

Never smelled her like this before.

The woman opened the driver's door. She picked up Lottery. Perkins barked as loud as he could.

No, no, no—this is not the vet, said Perkins. The woman reached in to get him, but he jumped to the passenger seat and growled. When she reached for him there, he jumped into the back seat. They went around like this a couple of times.

Lottery said, You're making it worse.

Making what worse, barked Perkins.

Our old lady. Smell her.

Perkins stopped barking. Yeah, he said, panting.

Gen was in the doorway now. She reached out for him. He stepped onto the driver's seat and licked her hand. Good boy, Gen said.

I think we gotta let this happen, Lottery said.

For Gen, I'll do this, said Perkins. And so when the man reached in Perkins let him scoop him up, wagging his tail for Gen to see. He let himself be shut up into the dog carrier and he let himself be carried into the building.

Perkins craned to see Gen through the gaps in the carrier. I can't see her, he said.

Use your nose, Lottery said.

Perkins pressed his nose through a square in the wire door. He sniffed, trying to catch Gen's scent before they went inside. There it was. She's a little calmer, Perkins said.

The woman placed Lottery's carrier on the floor. Her nose was flooded with the smell of so many dogs. Her ears perked up.

The man brought Perkins's carrier over and left it beside Lottery's.

A change is coming, Perkins said.

Lottery pressed her nose against the carrier door and sniffed. She couldn't smell Gen anymore. Now you can bark, Lottery said.

And man, did Perkins ever bark then.

Dee steps into the light

Trouble arrived on a warm afternoon before the flowers bloomed, the way the aunties said it would. The revving of the trucks, the clanging of doors, the rattling of gates, the blowing of whistles, the yelling of men, the jolt of the electric prod.

Dee raced around the perimeter of the pen and joined the other calves who had all bunched in a group in the farthest corner from the gate. One of the humans climbed the fence directly behind the calves and reached out with his electric prod and another came close from the other side, making menacing noises. A mockingbird swooped over them all and then dive-bombed the humans, flashing the white of his breast and using his beak as a weapon. One of the humans broke away from the commotion. The bird darted after him, calling out, Moving on! Moving on!

Dee ran and kicked and how it happened she couldn't tell but all at once she was separated from the others and closed into a paddock by herself. She watched as five of the herd's bulls were brought into the paddock next to hers. That gray mockingbird landed on Dee's back, eating bugs from her fur and intermittently calling out, Moving on! Moving on!

Dee watched as the aunties whispered nervously behind their fences and it came to Dee then that the aunties had given her up to the humans. They'd selected her for this separation by taking their milk from her. She felt a hot dark knot form in her belly, a feeling so new she had no words for it. She longed for the comfort of an udder. All she could do was lie down and roll in the dirt as if the craving was an itch she could scratch. She watched the dust rise again and again and then settle onto her flank. She was the extra, the hanger on, the one who mattered least.

The humans began shouting to each other and slamming doors again. They brought one bison at a time through metal corrals, pushed needles and drugs into them, all the bulls and Dee. They loaded the bulls into the back of one livestock trailer and Dee was coaxed into another. The door slid shut and aluminum walls stood between Dee and the herd.

She was alone for the first time in her life.

Dee skittered over the mesh trailer bed and pressed an eye against one of the long narrow slits to see all that she was leaving behind. The narrow openings boxed her old world up and nothing looked the way it had before. The fences and pasture were all broken up. She couldn't see the whole herd. She could only see bits of flanks and tails, the tops of so many humps and the worried eyes in the upraised faces of the aunties, the ones who had fed her milk after her mother left. They were there on the other side of the fences, as close as they could get to the trucks. She stumbled from one slit to another, desperate, trying to get one more look, trying to put the pieces of the herd back together into something whole again. But she couldn't find the right spot.

An old bison lifted her grand head and bellowed as loud as she could, You're going to the land my grandmother was from, you're going north. Another one called, Find another auntie and stay close, she'll teach you.

The engine roared to life again. Dee moved from one slit to another, as if she could stop what was happening just by looking, just by seeing another piece of her home from another angle.

The truck lurched forward.

Dee looked and looked until the truck turned away and there weren't any pieces to see anymore. Then Dee lay down on the hot trailer bed.

Dee did not move for a long time.

From the vehicles: revving, honking, screeching, and braking. From the humans in the world outside: swearing, shouting, laughing, singing, and jeering.

Dee couldn't understand any of it.

The air became thick with exhaust and diesel fumes that choked Dee. There were other smells from beyond the truck, frightening scents that sent a blaze through her body. At night, light flashed into the trailer and beams of light ran over her back and sleep would not come.

During the day Dee would make herself stand and press an eye to one of the slits. How could there be so many trucks in so many shapes with so many humans in each of them, as far as the eye could see? All the buildings rising up like slumbering monsters. She would pull away from the sight and stagger back to the middle of the truck, her heart beating like one of the little grassland birds, so quickly she was sure it'd give out, and then she hoped it would just stop.

The truck drove on and on.

One cold day a wind blew and a thin snow swirled around the truck. It wasn't long after that when the truck stopped and the door slid open.

Light and air flooded the back of the trailer. Dee's nose was overwhelmed as she lifted herself back to her feet. The smells of this new place numbed her senses. A ramp appeared. There was no other path to walk. She wanted to stay in the back of the murky trailer. No, no, she wanted to laugh at it all, and she almost did. But she was alone, there was no one to hear her, no one to join her, not in the truck and probably not anywhere ever again. She swallowed and snuffed all laughter out, set her jaw in a hard line, and stepped with steady legs into the light.

Carter on dying

There's something about dying people, right? Used to work part-time in a hospice. The stuff you see. People get themselves ready to die. They start going through their memories and bringing out their stories one by one as if there was a photo album in their head and they've got to get through it before leaving. They want to move those stories around, make them mean something. They want it all to mean something. For some people, they can't stand the meaning of their lives and they think they can make up for it real quick at the end. It's like they reach out to grab what isn't theirs to take.

Geneviève crosses the river

Geneviève forced herself to turn her back as two kennel employees coaxed Perkins and Lottery each into their own crate and carried them inside. The barking was enough to break her, almost made her decide to take them back and drive home, sit with John the rest of her life, and she leaned on her car as they disappeared into the building and the doors closed behind them. Sometime after that she found herself back behind the wheel, driving to a river near the border between two countries.

From Memorial Drive, Gen turned onto Deerfoot Trail and then drove south, crossing over the winding Bow River a couple of times before she was out of the city. From there, the road was straight and the sky was clouding over and her emotions were a pressure system about to burst and in between songs the radio was talking about the drought—will this be like the one that dried up the Milk River two decades ago? And this all got to Gen because the rehab center she was driving to was on the Milk River and here she was near as old as the river and shit if she wasn't heading to a dry river to dry out. She laughed until her belly hurt.

Next she caught the bit about how by the middle of summer most of the water in Milk River came from another river through a canal built in the last century, and how that fed the river system all the way down into Montana.

And the canal's broken, of course, Gen said to her car.

Shit, me and this river understand each other, she said, and the pull of the dying river was so strong that just south of Claresholm Geneviève stopped on the shoulder of the road. She put her hazard lights on and she mapped out a route that would take her across over the cracked old riverbed. She still had the map in her hands when another man on the radio said how canal repairs were almost done and water would flow as soon as the two countries signed some agreement. Ha, said Gen. Good luck with that.

And then she was on the road again and she drove south to Whiskey Gap and then east a bit into a nature park where she slowed way down as she crossed the bridge over the near-dry Milk River. She rolled down her window all the way. Hello river, she called out, I'm going to dry out too! She wanted to stop, but she was getting the shakes just a bit and the rehab center was near another part of the river, a bit farther northeast, so she kept on.

Prairie so dry the land couldn't hold onto color and then on the horizon a mirage of green that Geneviève didn't believe in at first. It couldn't be true. And yet the closer she got the more the green unfolded itself into groups of trees and bushes, a perimeter of green that marked out the boundaries of the rehab center, made a sort of island out of it. She turned down a gravel road marked by a parade of trees on either side and drove to the parking lot and buildings at the center. She turned off the engine. She reached over to the passenger seat to pet Lottery or Perkins but her hand found only the bulk of her black shoulder bag. Shit, she said. Okay then. She pulled the bag into her lap and unzipped the front pocket where she usually kept a flask, a nip of something. The pocket was empty. She reached into the main part of her bag and groped for the jar of ashes. She knew she'd decided to leave it behind, but she kept searching with her hand just in case memory had failed her.

Where the gates open for Mamé

Everyone's coming over, saying tanshi and boon swayr. Wrapping their arms around me, telling me how good I look and smell and how long it's been and how short it's been too.

We're in the cabin and dusk is falling. They've lit a smudge by the front door. Bob's waiting for the third and fourth in his band, the piano player and the second fiddler.

I've got my moccasins on my feet. I'll be here when the music begins.

I didn't come straight here. No, it took me a long while to walk here from where I found myself, by those Gates, right after I passed on.

Dying doesn't take long.

It's the journey after that can fill a night of stories.

That's how it was for me.

One moment I'm in bed and the next I'm standing barefoot in complete darkness. I stand for I don't know how long. And then there's light.

I turn and see that the light is coming from twelve pearly gates—the ones they always talked about down there. They look like they've come right out of a Bible verse, lined up in a giant semicircle two by two. Behind that a golden city rises up, out of focus no matter how you squint.

Am I shocked to find out that it's true? That there are pearl gates after all? Yeah, I am. I am disappointed too. Shouldn't there be more to the entrance to heaven? Shouldn't there be something unexpected, something that hadn't been described in a book?

From a distance the gates are immense and yet up close they seem to shrink to a more human scale, a little less than twice my height, I'd say—and I'm not a tall woman.

Whatever their size, I can tell these are the gates with a capital G and a capital H, the Holy Gates, you know. The ones you feared would be denied you when you were quaking in the confessional when you were twelve.

I hadn't been to tell a priest my sins since I made my choice down there. Not once, so it doesn't make a bit of sense to me that I have an invitation to walk through those gates.

All that time I was dying, I wouldn't see a priest, wouldn't let anyone anoint me. But here are the gates. I can walk through them if I want. I don't know what else is out there. I don't know how to get to the spirit world where my husband's ancestors are. I don't know any of this but oh yes, I have to make the same choice all over again.

And then there on the other side of one of those gates, there they are: the family I was born to, all of them calling out to me.

MICHELLE PORTER

Dee, in between fences

In the hours after Dee walked down that ramp, three cows pressed their faces against the fence that stood between them. The smells of the place told more stories than Dee could take in all at once and those cows kept talking to her, telling her about the place where she'd arrived, as if she cared. When one stopped, the other rushed ahead into the silence. It was as if they thought Dee was afraid of quiet. They told her she'd come to the Facility, that the old bison name for the Facility had been lost. They said that many of them had come from somewhere else too, and had been in her situation. She'd get used to it, not to worry. It was a good place, they said. She'd like it, they said. As if, Dee thought. They told her the Facility had been built as a temporary place, a holding place for bison who were supposed to be transported to their next home, but then bison just stopped moving on and some of the families had been there for generations and didn't remember living anywhere else. They'd been waiting so long that waiting had become home.

The cows offered their own names but Dee just flicked her tail and turned away. She stopped listening. They asked Dee for her name, but Dee didn't answer. That didn't stop the cows though. Not to worry, the aunties said. She'd be alone just for a few days and then they'd take her around and make sure she got a proper welcome. One of the cows said that by the smell of her she'd come from down south. There were others who'd come from the south but probably not from the same herd. She's big, isn't she, one said. But look at her horns, said another, small as a calf's. She's a baby still. Must be scared. Oh, sweetie, don't worry we'll take care of you.

Dee clenched her jaw hard and muttered under her breath. She flicked her tail again and walked to the part of the paddock farthest from the cows to wait for them to find something better to do than ask her stupid questions. Eventually they did and she was alone again.

The sun was just going down when a breeze carried the musky scent of a bull over the fence to Dee. She turned to watch him approach. He took his time. He swaggered. He stopped to graze, turning so she could see him in profile, admire the rise of the fine hump above his shoulders, the ripple of the muscle beneath his coarse woolly brown fur, the perfect angle of his horns, and the length of his beard.

He walked right on up to the corner where Dee had retreated in search of relief from the cows. At first he didn't look at her at all. He looked over the fences, he looked at a group of cows grazing a ways off, he looked back where he'd come and she burned for him to see her. When he lowered his eyes to her, he looked slowly, one feature at a time across her body until she felt a heat in places she'd never felt before. And then he was done and his eyes were on everything but her, the grass, the sky, the other cows, until she fidgeted and squirmed with the desire to have this bull look at her like that again. He said, You'll be a yearling this summer. She couldn't speak so she nodded and even though he wasn't looking at her he must have seen the nod because he went on. I'm Jay, he told her. He lifted his head higher and gazed into the horizon, striking a philosophical pose. He said, You know, we don't have to live this way, there's a better way, you know. Dee's eyes widened and she didn't mean to, but she nodded again as if she agreed with him even though she had no idea what he was talking about. His words were sparks, little bursts of light in the dark hidden parts of her. He shifted a little so she could better see the strength and the heft of his impressive flank. He asked for her name, and because of that flicker and because she was so dry, like so much unburnt kindling, she couldn't help herself, she gave it to him.

Carter asks for help with beading

Allie beaded so tight she warped the cloth.

I was thinking I'd tell her about Gramma today, get it over with, but it would be like ripping out the threads that held her together. They were fraying anyway so what the hell but I didn't want to see that sort of hurt look on her face, the way she got when she tried to hide that something was making her sad.

She kept peering over at my little piece to see if I was pulling the beads as fucking close as she wanted me to. I wasn't. I left big loops of thread showing.

Allie lives like she beads, as if the tighter she tacked those beads down the longer she'd keep away the bad things, the mess, anything that wasn't good. As if the beads were going to get loose and she'd be left on her hands and knees groping behind the couch in the corner.

She looked over at me the same way she did the first time we met.

Met my bio mom the first time at a coffee shop.

She sent an email out of the blue. In three lines she wrote who she was, that she wanted to meet me if I was interested. I deleted it. Thought it was shitty she didn't call me. Didn't she want to hear my voice? I'd always wondered if a bio mom sounded different from an adopted one, like if you felt different when you heard her talk to you. The drip drip drip of the question was tor- ture—what did her voice sound like? So eventually I fished her email from the trash. I wrote back, Sure. The next week I walked into the coffee shop she'd chosen, twenty-two minutes late to meet my bio mom for the first time.

It was a place that roasted its own coffee beans in the back and there was a line of people waiting to order. I looked around at all the people in the little coffee shop. What the hell did my bio mom look like? We hadn't exchanged pictures. I guess I didn't want to need a picture of her. I wanted it to be like I'd recognize her anywhere, that I'd just know who she was.

There were two women alone. One in line to order, wearing jeans and a cute jacket. She looked elegant and had a reassuring air, like you could bring your problems to her and she'd sort it all out. Her dark hair fell to her shoulders and was going gray. When she turned to scan the room for a free table, I saw that she had dark brown eyes. The other woman who was there alone was already sitting at a table. She sat still, like an animal listening for prey, but she was watching me over her glasses. She slumped a little in her chair. Her hair was lighter and pulled back from her face, and her neck and chin folded against each other. She wore a loose gray T-shirt and jeans. It's got to be the other woman, I thought, and I walked toward the dark-haired woman in line. Excuse me, I said. She turned to look at me and I had the urge to take her hand as if I were a five-year-old who'd found a safe grownup in a crowd. I asked her if she was Allie. She smiled and shook her head. No, sweetie, the woman with brown eyes said in a voice that I wanted to be my mother's. When I turned around to scan the room again, the other woman was on her feet. She waved at me. My bio mom.

Her eyes were light. They weren't brown, like I was expecting, like mine. The chair scraped against the floor as I pulled it out and sat down. She sat back down without making any sound at all. She said hello and she said my name and she told me her name in case I'd forgotten I guess, and her voice was a bit gravelly and a bit crunched up and I didn't feel anything except I wanted to throw up. Closer up I could see her eyes were a pale sort of gray. I must have said something or she could see me looking because she rubbed her forehead and told me lots of Métis had light eyes. And skin, she said, reaching out to touch my arm, my pale skin. Those eyes are your dad's, she said. Then she clammed up like she was surprised she'd said so much. That was how I found out she was Métis. That I was Métis.

It's stupid that even when you don't expect anything, you can be disappointed. I was eighteen. I was in a bad place. I couldn't sit still. Got a stir stick. Got a couple of creamers for the hot chocolate. Got a water. Ordered another hot chocolate. My bio mom was so still that first day. Looking at me. So much looking I could hardly stand it. She didn't drink her coffee, even. I couldn't wait to get out of there.

Suddenly I wanted to call my adopted mom and say something bitchy, but I couldn't. I hadn't even told her I was going to meet up with Allie. Couldn't take the yelling, or the lecture that she'd launch into. Knew what she'd say to me, could hear her saying, *I* raised you, *she* didn't. She'd be so mad she'd lose it and tell me she wished she hadn't adopted me. I was eleven the first time she said that, a sucker punch that knocked me over for a while. Got a few years on me since then so I know she doesn't mean it, not really. But I didn't want to deal, you know? So I couldn't tell her about it, not right away, not until I was ready for the onslaught.

So I went straight for the jugular. I asked my bio mom, Why did you give me up?

That was the one time she looked away from me. She looked out the window and then at her hands. I was alone and I was scared, she said. Then she said, We can talk more about that later.

She wouldn't answer any questions about my bio dad. Not today, she said, and it's never been the right day since. She said his name once. I don't think she knows she said his name. But I remember it.

Neither of us was much for small talk that day. It was me looking away, at my phone and at that other woman there, that comforting dark-haired woman, and it was her looking way too long at my hair and my face and staring at my hands as I fidgeted with the mug and the stir stick and the empty creamers. It was as if she were trying to memorize me, as if she might not see me again. Things got real quiet after a bit and then she took a big breath in and said, Well, now that we've met, I'll let you call me when you want to see me next. I don't want to crowd you.

She left her coffee there for the waitress to dump out. No milk, no sugar.

Didn't call her back for years, not until just before I left Slavko.

Allie was brewing tea. The pot was in the middle of the table. Her other two daughters were there too, keeping their beads neat and tight like they were taught. They're like that, my bio sisters. Bio half-sisters, technically. They've got light eyes too, except theirs are pale green, both of them, matching pairs. I'm the odd one out.

Oops, I said, I got my thread all tangled again. Allie, would you pull it out for me?

Allie's lips got all thin and tight, but she took my design and pulled at the threads. First project she had me do was a simple flower design on a piece of felt. She said everyone began that way. This time she'd said I could choose what I wanted to bead and so I brought a design that would piss her off. She was so quiet about it though, tried not to show it. She removed a couple of the beads and explained again what I've got to do.

Maarsii.

That word still felt out of place on my tongue. I'd showed up to a few language classes, just enough to pick up a few words of

Michif, enough to make Allie so fucking proud that I had to quit. Anyway, I didn't belong there with those other Métis: most of them had grown up with their parents in their culture, only the language was lost. There was one other girl there who, like me, had only just learned her family was Métis, but she talked about her mom a lot and we didn't talk to each other at all.

Allie sort of smiled and said a few words in Michif I only half understood.

That was enough sucking up for me.

Oh no, Allie, I said. I did it again. Look at the knots I made. Oh no.

Then she was telling me how to hold my needle so that I don't make a rat's nest of it all. She spoke slow and clear.

I'd done it four times already and every time she'd put down her own work to pick up mine, pulling the threads apart and unpicking my stitches. She'd been so fucking eager and it was cute how she was pretending not to be annoyed.

The woman needed to be so good, you know? To make up for what she did maybe or to make up for being alive. Fucking painful to be around, if I'm honest.

If Allie would let herself swear, she might be a little less wound up. The only thing she said out loud was Make sure you hold your thread over here away from the needle, like this, see?

Instead of aggressively tacking down another poor, helpless bead, she got up out of her chair and filled the kettle with water, set it to boil. She said it was to *refresh* the teapot. She opened a tin and laid out some cookies on a plate and dropped it in the middle of the table. Went back to check the kettle. Drummed her fingers on the counter as she waited.

One of my bio sisters said, Where's our nephew today?

I wanted to tell her to fuck off.

Yeah, said the other. Where's Tucker?

Before I got a chance to say anything, the first one asked, Wait, isn't he turning four soon?

I stabbed the needle through the cloth and yanked the thread through, pulling two white beads close to the material. I hadn't told them anything about the mess of my life, not about why I left Tucker's dad or my adopted mom, not about my depression, not about having a hard time holding down a job. I said, He's with his dad. I said, He'll be four in two months. I said, Where's your boyfriend today?

And that got them off my back and they were chattering on about boys as if they invented them or something. I didn't know which one was talking when because I was studying the back of my beading.

Took me a long while to agree to meet my bio sisters after the weird coffee shop meeting, after I finally called Allie again, after Tucker was born. What the fuck were they supposed to mean to me? Only thing they were good for was to remind me that my bio mom didn't raise me and that I wasn't part of any of the stories they told.

They hadn't met Tucker, but they always asked about him as if they were super interested in someone else's kid. Made me throw up a little in my mouth every time. They used to ask about Slavko, too, only Slavko was never interested in meeting my bio family. They're *your* family, he'd say, his eyes on whatever video game he was playing. Then he'd shrug and ask, What do you want me to do about it?

Allie had met Tucker once. She'd trembled so much I thought it was better if I didn't bring him round anymore. This thing we got here—it's about me and her. My kid didn't need to get caught in her knot.

Oops, I got the thread all tangled again, I said. I looked up at Allie. Would you pull it apart for me again?

MICHELLE PORTER

My bio sisters watched.

Allie came over, repeated herself. Make sure you hold your thread over here away from the needle. That way the thread doesn't get all jammed up and the flower will come out strong and even.

Okay, I said to her with a smile that she ate up.

Then I added, O-fucking-kay.

She winced. The kettle boiled.

Geneviève and one more goodbye

That was a good drive, that was, just the two of them, her and Bets. That river back there—when they crossed it Gen felt Bets's engine shaking everything beneath her, as if she felt the same thrill Gen did. Gen thought how long it'd been since that kind of shaking happened when she was in a car. A real long time. She wanted to keep her ass there in the seat and have a long comfortable talk with Bets.

Gen remembered how an auntie used to say that your spirit could rub off on things and make them halfway living. She said some thought the old river carts had a life force. That drums were alive and teepees and even the little cabins they'd build for the winter. She said the needles the women used to bead with were alive and that some beadwork held the spirit of the aunties and grandmothers who created them, spirits that needed to breathe and dance. The fiddle comes alive too—at least it did in her papa's hands, and her sister's too. Lots of times when Gen played the old songs on a piano it felt like the piano was more alive than she was. The tarot cards felt like that too, like they had a life of their own, except they always wanted to be ornery.

And her Bets, this old Volvo wagon? She's been with Gen so long it was like she was breathing with Gen sometimes. This car was the last thing she'd say goodbye to before she walked through those doors up there.

The grassland speaks to Dee

There's an art to setting fire to things.

She was just a calf and maybe she'd never seen a fire, but she knew the word and it heated her up. She was lying on me, wallowing around and waiting for things to happen, and I got to thinking she was the calf to talk to about fire.

She stopped playing in the dirt, perked up, listened harder.

It's been a long time since the last fire burned around here.

She repeated the word, Fire.

I'm waiting for it, I said to her. And I've been thinking that while I'm waiting, might as well take some acting classes.

The calf let herself giggle and kicked up some dust.

Just kidding. I'm more the nurturing type.

She kicked again. It was a hot day for this time of year and my ground's quite dry in places.

And then Dee said, You going to make fire?

That's not my work. I wait for the fires and then I let them take everything I have.

She was real quiet then but I could feel the excitement in her body; she spoke it with her restless limbs and the way her heart jumped a few beats.

I said, I'm getting old. The next fire will really give me that get up and grow, feed my dirt. Used to be the people took charge of this. The setting of fires. The ones that come between lightning strikes.

I saw lightning once, the calf said. She was so young she really liked to make everything about herself. Then the young one said, You *want* fire?

Yeah, I said, speaking right up into her bones, I think I can do some good with it. Make stronger relations between me and the other ones who live with me here, the grasses that root me, the birds who come to nest and to dance, all the furry ones that use the earth for dens, all of them.

The calf rolled around on me a bit, then asked, What do my people do?

The buffalo? Don't you know? You come in after the fire, help with the healing, make the grass grow.

Don't know anything about it, she said. She stood up, put more distance between us. But her hooves were sinking in deep and she couldn't get away from that.

Child, I said, the treaties tell us there has to be burning. There's some that act as if the treaties expired. As if forgetting about them means you got no responsibility for them. That's its own fire, and not the burn-it-down-so-we-can-regenerate kind of fire.

She was walking around, pretending not to listen to me. But I was still there.

I said to her, Everybody has treaties they're responsible for.

She jumped up onto a metal container the humans put there for their own use. Then she wasn't touching me at all but I could wait. She had to come down some time.

My bones felt so old. I was so impatient to feel the roots of the echinacea and the fireweed and all the other things that grow after a fire. I wanted to feel them creep around my mineral joints and fungal tendons and ease the aches and pains. It was hard on my dirt to try to give what all the flowers and grasses around here need, not without a good fire now and then. When you're a giver, you've got to take the time to care for yourself. We always knew that. The time after the fire, that was my me time.

Eventually she jumped down from that big old container. She said, I don't care about fire.

I laughed and she felt it in her feet. It surprised her, made her run around in circles until she was out of breath. When she was

MICHELLE PORTER

still again, I told her, Oh, you would care about fire if you'd been there after one, a nice big one you could see for miles.

She harrumphed and stomped a hoof.

Oh, it's true. Used to be there was an agreement with the humans who belong to this land, your people, and me. If they burned the prairie one season, I'd grow so much beautiful new grass in the ash that all your people would come to me and ask to eat. I'm like a mother in that way.

She lay down then. She rolled a bit and said, How do I make fire?

I laughed again. You don't, I told her. You wait.

That was when I noticed it, that slight scent that said so much, that she was changing. I reached out to the other cows who were grazing on other parts of me and understood that the other cows had smelled it too.

As if she knew what I'd been thinking, this calf lolled over onto her back and asked, Can a bull be like a fire?

Carter moves out

What happened was my adopted mom went off on me and Tucker, yelling and shit, so that after she left for work I called Slavko, said, Come get Tucker. He showed up eventually and I took Tucker's bag out and strapped him into his seat. And then Slavko and I got into it. I needed to shout at someone and there was my ex, giving me a good reason. After he left I went back down to the room I rented for cheap in my adopted mom's basement, the one Tucker and I had been staying in since I left Slavko.

I didn't get up that day or the next. I was out of work so I didn't have reason to. Took my adopted mom a couple of days to come downstairs and knock on my door, all Where's my grandson and stuff.

The fight we got into isn't worth the time it'd take to tell you about.

Back to bed again. I didn't want to be alive anymore and I thought about my gramma and I thought how I understood her then and I didn't think I wanted to understand her at all, not that part of her.

Then this chick I used to clean with last year texted me back finally, said if I still needed a job they had one for me, didn't pay much though and the hours weren't regular. Whatever. Yes, I texted back.

The morning after that I kept to my lair in the basement until my mom went off to work and then I transferred my last chunk of cash to get this cheap little Airbnb for a couple of months, just long enough until I could go get Tucker—because I still planned on doing that, eventually. Well, I planned on going to see him at least. I felt guilty because it wasn't like I had any sort of life o offer him. I mean, nothing like my ex's parents, who'd spoil him like crazy, give him his own room, teach him their language and culture. Which is good, right? I mean I knew fuck-all about my own.

I crammed all my stuff into black garbage bags, because I didn't want my adopted mom saying I stole her suitcases, and called a cab. I gave the cabbie the new address. The key would be waiting in the mailbox.

Going home? the cabbie asked.

None of your fucking business, I thought. But I kept my mouth closed. That anger, it kind of jumpstarted me, burned away some of the numbness. It was like I felt something for the first time since—well, I'm not talking about that.

Of course when my bio sister asked about her nephew, I didn't tell her any of that. None of her business. I changed the subject.

I'm good at pivoting.

So that's how I got out of my adopted mom's house. For good, I told myself as the cabbie turned off our street. I thought, This time I'm all the way gone.

Geneviève and the ruins

Geneviève pushed the car door open, set her running shoes on the concrete, and grabbed onto the edge of the roof to haul herself out. God, her bones ached, didn't they. They were still good bones for eighty-one, except for what the doctor could see in his MRIs, but she wasn't about to define herself by that. Slammed the door closed and leaned against the old Volvo, looked around. She knew that behind the trees, farm and grassland were laid out in regular rhythms, but from where she stood she couldn't see them at all. It was as if the prairies weren't there. For a moment she thought she could see an old buffalo walking behind the trees among the bushes, but of course there wasn't a buffalo. There weren't any buffalo here.

She knew she should look over at the two old buildings at the front of the parking lot and she tried to make herself see them, but she couldn't bear it, couldn't hold the weight of what was going to happen, not when she was here to do this thing she didn't think she could do.

So she shifted herself to face the scatter of ruins to the right of the buildings. These she could look at and she decided to walk closer to them to ease the stiffness in her hips and unravel the knot in her gut.

On the site of the crumbling foundations, she felt strange. It was as if she could sense the ghost of the old structure. The old bricks rose up and light shone around drawn curtains and shadows passed from window to window. Then it all fell down and she was standing among the ruins again. She sat herself down on a decaying section of wall and hoped it wouldn't fall apart beneath her.

It wasn't until she heard a voice that she noticed the man there in the length of long grass between her and the parking lot.

A tall skinny old man. She put her hand up to her forehead to block the glare of the sun. Had he been speaking to her? He walked toward her, along the length of what used to be the side wall.

Gen shivered and her pulse raced a little faster than normal. She shook off the feeling and called out to him, asked, When was the old building torn down? A smile flickered across his lined face and then he was there next to the section of wall she was sitting on. The same deep calm voice answered, Oh, that'll be before the center even bought the land and everything here. Of course, now they're raising money for a new building, right where you're sitting. And before Gen could ask about the new building, he was answering, It's for traditional healing, the indoor sweat lodge and ceremonies and the like. We got a sweat lodge on the land right now but it needs rebuilding after any weather. Couple years back we had a flash thunderstorm, took it right out.

The sun was behind him still so Geneviève had to squint to look up at him and couldn't really make out his face, but she thought it was grizzled a bit and she asked, They have a sweat lodge here? He pointed it out to her. There in the trees, he said. It's made the traditional way, like out of trees but with canvas instead of skins.

She thought he must have had better eyesight than she did because she couldn't see it.

What's your name? she asked.

Gabe, he said and then he dipped his head and asked hers and she offered it up.

Gen's pulse had returned to normal and his talk and name had chased away her shivers.

Well, said Gen, getting back to her feet, it's nice to meet you, Mr. Gabe, but I've got to get to my car and get a few things before I go on in.

He nodded. When she started walking he joined her, shortening his stride to match hers, told her how they were supposed to get rain any time now and what a relief that would be.

When they got to her car she patted its hood and said, This is my old Volvo, Mr. Gabe; it's my constant companion. She wanted to ask him if he'd come with her to get a drink, just one before she went on in. Instead she opened one of the back doors and took out a pair of red dancing shoes. She leaned against the rump of the car, took off her sneakers, and slipped on the heels. She reached into the car again and pulled out a delicately embroidered long coat, the one Mamé sewed for Velma before she passed on. Gen slipped the long coat over her shoulders even though it wasn't coat weather and she told Gabe, It's as good as the day Mamé made it. She was that good with a sewing machine. Gabe nodded. Looks good on you, he said. It'll last forever, said Gen. It'll last longer than me.

What she didn't say to Gabe was that the coat didn't fit her, that she couldn't even begin to button it up, and that right then she'd trade the damn coat for another night back home with a bottle. Didn't matter, she could swagger in that coat anyway and she could stand tall, all her five foot four inches. She was the kind of woman who wore a coat like this, the kind of woman whose coat flared and swirled around her shapely calves and a woman who still knew how to wear her old dancing shoes. She smiled at Gabe, said, Will you take me in? He held out his arm and she rested her hand inside his elbow. She thought how lightly she stepped beside him, well as lightly as an old woman can step when she's eighty-one and only wants another drink, she thought, and when she laughed at herself Gabe noticed how her laugh sounded big and broad as the prairie sky above them.

Afterlife and the temptation of Mamé

I won't say I wasn't tempted.

That heaven there is white and bright and it smells like all the best days you've had all wrapped up together and tied up in one of my husband's best sashes. Yeah, I want to go in.

And that being the holy place, I can feel they were going to forgive me for everything too. They'd all forgive me for living my life in the way I did. For my choice. They would forgive me, too, for the price I paid—ha, for the price they made me pay.

I don't think you ever forget anything in heaven. I'm not going to kid myself. I don't believe they'll stop sneering at me or my husband's relations. But there, on the edge of the kind of heaven the Bible tells about, it feels like it might not matter so much.

It's heaven, right? Now I understand it's different for everyone but for me it's like this. From where I stand everything on the other side of those gates—that big shining city and all those angels in glowing white robes—is like those pills they gave my daughter back on earth, the ones for her depression. Things aren't exactly better or gone, and you still got your memory, only you're okay with all the judgment and you're okay with the pit of fires the gates are built on; you're okay with the people being sent below and you're okay with all the animals that are made dumb. Seems to me there's a soft edge to everything, even sharp things, a sigh, a fuzziness.

And then I see Maman just inside those gates. Oh, she is beautiful to see. The whole family arranged like a picture: my father there on a chair and everyone standing around him. Maman is straight and stiff as she can be, by his side, a hand on his shoulder.

I'd been a young woman the last time I'd seen her.

I'd learned from Maman how to make a fine dress. I learned how to just look at a man's shoulders and create a coat that would fit well enough, as she would say, for the noblesse d'épée. For me, she'd defied Papa's instructions and stayed in my room with me when a sinner's fever almost stole away with my childhood. After, a sister told me that Papa raged and Papa threatened and Papa threw things and Papa pounded on the door, but she remained by my side, day and night, until my fever broke. When I had grown and wanted to see the world instead of marry the man Papa selected, she held me out of the way of father's wrath, spoke the words he wanted to hear, and arranged for me to travel with the nuns who were going to bring more Christian education to the lands in the west.

She repented that bitterly. The last words she'd written to me had been in anger. I won't repeat in this place what she wrote about my marriage.

And yet, how I want to run past those gates and to kiss Maman on her cheeks, which are fatter and younger than I've ever seen. I want to see up close her round face and her dark hair, that simple bun she'd always wear, to see her dark eyes and hold her soft hands. Her nose. We all of us have long noses, except for Maman, and Papa's became larger and sterner the older he got. But Maman's nose had been touched by the angels, our aunts used to say, compact and turned up at the end, just a little. When he was in a lighter mood, which wasn't often, Papa might say that he had married our mother for her nose, that he was sorry its shape hadn't been passed on to any of his daughters.

And to smell each of them again! My father's pipe, his choice of tobacco; my mother's rose perfume, how it lingered after she left a room; the lilac scent shared among myself and my sisters, the way it rose into the air as we combed each other's hair before bed. How I long to be among those homey aromas once more.

MICHELLE PORTER

That's the only thing. You can make a decision, and there's always the thing you leave behind, the thing that aches in the joints of your fingers when you play the guitar for the dancing people who belong to your husband and now belong to you because you chose him, the thing that lets you feel sorry that you had to turn your back on the family who hated the husband you chose, who looked down on him and his People. But regret is worth nothing because you can't be walking all the paths or you wouldn't be walking any path at all.

Dee, the biggest cow

Dee learned how to slip into Jay's paddock, waiting for the humans to leave a gate open or forget to mend a post. She told Jay how sometimes she felt she knew the dust here, that it made her calm, that sometimes she thought she could hear the land speaking through her hooves. She told him how much it bothered her that she couldn't tell if this was the land her ancestors had walked on. Jay had a way of listening, just standing there quiet and nodding, that made her feel like she could sprint the length of the paddock and back a hundred times if she wanted. The humans would always bring her back to the other side of the fences.

She could always count on a tongue lashing. The aunties told Dee that no good would come of making too much of any one bull. They said she'd upset the balance of things if she wasn't careful. They said he smelled like any other bull and that'd be plain obvious to her if she'd get her head out of the sky. They said she was too young to be chasing bulls. Dee pretended she couldn't hear.

You don't know anything about me, Dee thought. I don't belong here, she told herself. The aunties' words were no more than another fence she had to get around.

As the first crocuses came up and the world warmed, the herd moved out of the winter pasture to the next set of fences that would be their home. Little white stars dotted the greening prairie grass and golden beans had come up bright and yellow when the humans opened the gates and brought in Jay to live full-time with the rest of the herd.

The coming season would be her second full summer and she had grown into the largest heifer at the Facility. She was taller. Her shoulders were thicker and her hips took up more space. Don't get a big head, the aunties told Dee. They said there were cows larger than her outside the Facility, that she wasn't the biggest thing on four hooves.

Didn't matter: Jay stayed close to Dee. Jay told her how much he loved the size of her, that he'd never scented so much pent-up laughter, a buffalo who held so much back. The prairie filled up with color, the bright yellows and oranges, the purples and pinks, and the soft violet of harebells and coneflowers and asters and yarrow and goat's beard and clover—and all of them crawling with the ones who came in search of nectar. When the change finally came to Dee and she was ready for a bull, she and Jay went together to an empty end of the pasture. He couldn't get close enough to Dee. He kept other bulls at a distance. She had never felt so whole. Panting, he raised himself against her haunches again and again and Dee thought how much he smelled like the earth and all that dust that rose when the herd ran.

They were inseparable for a full moon cycle, until it was clear she was carrying a baby—until the elders came for her.

There were four of them in a line, shoulder to shoulder, and they stopped a few feet away. Dee refused to greet them. She moved behind Jay, thinking he'd drive them off like he had any bull who'd strayed too close.

It's time, the cows called out.

Time for what, Dee muttered.

You're pregnant, the elders said.

So what? Dee said. She kept Jay between her and the cows, just as she had for the past fourteen months.

You'll need the teachings, they said.

It's our job to pass them to you, they said.

Don't need your teachings, said Dee.

You need the other mothers, they said.

Dee looked to Jay.

He stepped over and pressed his forehead against Dee's belly.

You've got to go, he said.

I don't, she said.

Jay breathed in her scent and closed his eyes for a moment and then he stepped aside. He nodded at the elders.

Go on, she's yours to teach now, he said.

They walked forward and surrounded Dee. They were almost as close as Jay had been.

Come, said the oldest one, whose name Dee remembered then. It was Solin.

Dee stepped away from Solin, but another of the elders flanked Dee's other side.

Jay said, Go on, Dee. It's time for you to have a baby.

Dee felt a fire burn through the grass of her heart. She looked out over the horizon, looked directly into the sun. She wanted to scream at Jay, to run at him, to batter him with her horns. She set her jaw in a hard line and put out that fire until there was only smoke in her chest. On steady legs she followed the cows where they led, even though she knew nothing would ever feel good again.

Geneviève arrives

Somehow I'd forgotten I was on fire but they reminded me when they asked me to empty my shoulder bag and line up the bottles of pills along the counter. They'd called a nurse to come talk to me, and she was so young it hurt my coochie to look at her, as if she'd just come out of me and I'd just been stitched up. This newborn told me her name and she looked over the bottles and she took note of the pharmacy addresses and she said, We'll have to contact your doctor. I told her how young she was. I told her, You're such a baby, look how beautiful you are, and she looked at me for the first time and there I was, older than the universe and as far as that nurse was concerned I was already dead and she wasn't wrong, so I said, You're not far off, sweetie, and I lifted an arm and shook it to show the newborn nurse how loose my skin was, how much like crinkled crepe paper and the bangles on my arm jangled, and the baby nurse's gorgeous brown eyes went a little wide and she smiled at me like you'd smile at a toddler and she said in a voice that was louder than necessary—I wasn't deaf—she said, I like your bracelets.

I threw my head back, which was not easy at all with my stiff neck and the little hump in my back, but I did it anyway. I threw my head back and I laughed. No, no, sweetie, I told her, I'm not two years old. I'm two thousand years old. She was a little uncertain, I could tell, and I wanted to put her at ease so I reached out and held her chin in my manicured claw and I told her that she only needed a bit of makeup to bring out her features and I'd teach her all she needed to know if she came by my room and anyway that led me to the question, Where is my room? She asked how to pronounce my last name and I told her Goo-lay but she could say my name whatever way sounded good to her,

I didn't care, and she frowned and pressed her lips together and I noticed they were so smooth that you wouldn't bother asking to bum a cigarette from this one and she said, We'll have to contact your doctor and she said, We'll have to confirm your prescriptions. You already told me all that, Pamela, I said and she looked at me again but this time more closely because she was surprised I got her name right.

I didn't say what I was thinking because I knew this baby couldn't handle my coochie, as far as she was concerned I didn't have one, did I? I patted her hand. It's okay, I said to her, I remember everything even though you wouldn't think so, would you. Everything—it's my sister who forgets, the lucky asshole. I laughed and my bangles jangled again and the music pleased me, and Pamela couldn't help but smile for real this time.

She crammed the pill bottles against each other in a box and she said, We'll have to hold on to these, and she said, The day nurse will make sure you take your pills. I looked around for another face but it was only Pam there now. I asked, Who's the day nurse? She was shutting the box, locking it shut, secure as the braided black belt that was tight around her tiny waist and she said, Well, there's Greg, too, but honestly most days that'll be me. And the way her lips pressed against each other anyone could see she was locked tight as that drug box there.

Dee, walking away

The chickadees knew what was coming so they flew out of the pastures to find the food and company they liked elsewhere. The starlings had been getting ready for their great murmuration but they'd held off a bit later in the season than they wanted for this day—and now that it was here, they covered the backs of the herd like a fluttery blanket, hopping from one bison to another, chattering and waiting for the run to begin.

Dee said she would not run with the herd. So what if they had moved into their new winter pastures? It was embarrassing to run around like that, wasn't it? The aunties told her again and again that it was a ceremony to mark the change of seasons, to celebrate the move from their spring and summer enclosures to their fall and winter home. They'd do it again in the spring, when the humans moved them back.

We didn't do that where I came from, Dee said. It was the same thing she'd told them each time they'd invited her to the running before.

It's a celebration, the aunties said, and then they left her alone.

I don't feel like running, Dee muttered as she rubbed her back against a fence post on the far side and stared into the distance. She hadn't seen or scented Jay in days, not since the humans had taken him away.

The herd gathered first in a pool and together they eddied, spiraling restlessly in place as they gathered their energies, slipping the calves to the edges to give them room to spin and leap. They were vibrating, trying to stay still and yet constantly moving. The ground opened up to the bison's hooves and the thin layer of first snow melted. The starlings whistled and trilled.

The tension heightened. Dee could feel it from where she was. The fur on her hump stood on end and she could feel her blood pumping, as if her entire body had become a thick throbbing heart. The elders drummed their hooves against the softened earth. They beat a slow, steady rhythm. The calves joined in, and then the aunties, and then the bulls. And when finally the earth joined in, thumping back into their legs so that even Dee could feel it, the starlings rose from their backs as one, twisting and swirling and singing. Then one of the elders nodded to the aunties—it was time.

Dee watched as they flooded over the land, churning and frothing at the edges of the enclosure. She moved a couple of steps closer and craned her head to see as they shifted and poured in another direction. Her muscles hurt with holding herself back. Too soon they were over a rise in the land and out of sight. A family of magpies dropped onto the mud and dirt the herd had just torn up, hopping here and there to feast on the exposed bugs. Dee could still feel the running in the beat of the earth she stood on. Her hooves burned.

The winter paddock was so large you could see neither the beginning nor the end of it. The magpies darted up as the herd ran back, past the place where Dee stood. They were a roaring river. The noise of them untethered Dee. She felt the ground rumble and she heard the snuffs and grunts and the music of so many hooves and it wasn't as though she made a decision to join the herd, no, it was that she was already a part of them and then she, too, was running deep into the far end of this new enclosure.

Oh and they were stunning, all of them together. They were spilling around trees, flowing around the corners of fences, lapping at the boundaries to see if the fences really would hold them all in.

MICHELLE PORTER

Dee had never run like this. She'd never felt like this. She ran until she couldn't anymore, until they all stopped, gasping and leaning against each other, holding each other up. There were cows pressed against every part of her. The starlings dropped back down to cover their backs. She looked up and saw a flock of geese in a V-formation winging it across the sky. I know how they feel, she thought.

The herd began to pool and eddy once more, readying for a second round. The starlings called to each other, singing about their next rise into the sky. A breeze came to cool them and Dee lifted her face, closed her eyes, and leaned into it. She inhaled deeply. And then just like that she tensed and opened her eyes again: she'd caught Jay's scent. She pushed through the herd, pulled herself away from the cows. She left them as the elders started to drum the earth; she left to see if she could reach the scent's source. The rhythm trembled up her legs as she walked away.

Geneviève takes the elevator

The elevator opened wide and I took a step as if to walk in but Lord oh Lord didn't one foot get all tangled up between the old hardwood planks on one side and the carpeted little elevator. I was too stiff to catch myself and so down I went, face first. I landed right in the middle and the elevator door didn't know what to do. Good thing I wasn't too shabbily padded but anyway I took a moment there on the floor to get my breath back and to check if it felt like I broke anything anywhere, and Pam dropped my bags right there and pushed the doors wide, crouched over me, fussed at me. I said, Well, could the earth swallow me up? Then I was shaking all over and gasping and Pamela raised her voice and said she'd get help but I said, No, no, and I said, I'm fine. And then she saw I was laughing and she tried not to but she just couldn't help it, she'd been so scared for me, she sat on the floor in relief and just let herself go, fell into giggles and tears and snot like she'd wanted to for years. The doors were trying to close again. Maybe it's a sign, I thought, and this got me to laughing some more.

I was still on my stomach but when I got a few calming breaths in I said, We'll be good friends by the time my stay is over. I reached out and patted her leg with one hand, then I said, Come round to talk to me whenever you have time. I'll read your tarot for you, well, unless you all lock up my cards in that safe box of yours.

I didn't feel like getting up just yet and I said to that nurse with the beautiful skin and the hair pulled back in a ponytail that the only thing else I wanted was if I could forget a little bit more, you know, like my sister could. My sister had the talent for forgetting and that was why she'd been my hero all my life, and I said,

You remind me of her a little bit even though you don't play music, do you? I can tell. Your hands aren't the kind that get a fiddle going. No offense to you, little girl, because lots of good, kind people don't play music and you look like that sort. But the people I love most, the people I am at home with, they do play music, you got to know that. The best? They play the crooked tunes. I don't play the fiddle, but maybe one day I'll forget I never learned. You think I'll ever learn to forget?

I was done talking, I guess, and she was blowing her nose and then I was up on my hands and knees. She said, Let's get you on your feet.

No, I said, I'll do this.

Oh God and Oh Velma, wouldn't you just die to have seen me? Pam held the door open and I did it, Velma, I crawled into that elevator and the doors slid shut and up we went.

Carter finds a crow's nest

There was a note in the mailbox that said the key would open the door at the top of the fire escape at the back. Up three flights of wrought iron and steel stairs, hauling my two ugly garbage bags. Kind of freaky to see everything falling away down below.

I opened the door and stepped into the tiniest little attic room you ever saw, only one little window that I could see. Smelled like cigarettes and weed and the floor was sticky with what smelled like spilled beer and the place hadn't been cleaned since whoever was here last and there was a clear vase propping up a dozen wilted roses and I could feel the tension lifting off my shoulders after just a couple of minutes in this place.

First thing I wanted to do was piss but I got distracted by this narrow window above the toilet. Sitting on the ledge on the other side of the window I saw a damn crow. I didn't really believe my own eyes.

I took a step closer and it cocked its head to look at me and cawed. The window was closed so I felt safe taking a closer look and when I pressed my face to the glass I saw a nest tucked on a crumbling cornice just below and there were three fledglings in it.

The second parent swooped in, eyed me.

My phone buzzed.

I looked at it. Gramma. I declined the call.

I pissed, then got out of the bathroom.

The place was furnished but bare. I poked around a bit to get my bearings and right away I found three small bags of weed, one in the drawer beside the bed, one in the veggie compartment in the fridge, and one pushed halfway between the couch cushions. I dropped them on the kitchen counter. I was all set.

I opened my garbage bags right off, started putting things away. I can live anywhere, just about. But could I bring Tucker here?

No.

The place was smaller than that crow's nest out there. A kid needs space, right?

But—and this was maybe more important—could I kill my gramma here?

I looked around the place once more.

It was about the right size for a murder.

My phone buzzed again. I answered but instead of saying hi or whatever I cawed three times and hung up. I'd call her back later.

Geneviève lays a card

Pam dragged the suitcase ahead of Gen into the room and from the hallway she could see a single bed and a narrow brown dresser and a window. For some reason she'd thought she was going to be bunking with some other soul but here she was with a room all to herself. Pamela was already getting out her forms and checklist of things she had to explain to Gen. Through the window Gen thought she saw that buffalo again, but it was far away and a bit out of focus and her eyes were old.

It's dangerous to forget you're burning so that tiny nurse got to reminding Gen right there. She started to line up the medication Gen was allowed to keep in her room and she said, I want to let you know that there's a chance you'll miss a couple of doses because withdrawal might make you too sick to take them or you'll vomit them right back up. Now a doctor will make rounds and talk to you about all that tomorrow but I wanted you to have time to think about it because it could impact your long-term recovery.

Gen thought how Pamela'd forgotten about the laugh they'd had back then. Pamela was all business.

Gen walked in as if she belonged there and sat her ass right down on the bed.

Come here, Gen said, all quiet so Pamela moved closer and leaned in to hear better. They were so close Gen's forehead almost touched Pamela's and Gen said, Oh baby girl, you know I'm dying, right? You know? Pamela's face kind of closed up then but she held Gen's gaze hard.

Sweetie, Gen said, these meds, all they're for is to keep my motor running until I'm done here. We didn't even bother with the chemo so all this hair is mine, it's not a wig, even though

72   MICHELLE PORTER

when I got the diagnosis I went out and bought three new wigs, one a blonde wig because I always wanted to know what that was like, and one's red and so curly it's like a new perm because I always wanted to see how that felt on my head. My hair straight as it is would never take to a perm, it'd break off rather than take on those tight perm curls, and now I have the chance because I bought them before we decided the chemo was no use. So don't put those wigs in your lock box, okay? I want to wear them.

Gabe came into the room then, all quiet and shy. An ache was blooming on Gen's hip where she fell and Gen knew there would be a big old bruise, but she didn't say anything to Pam, she just smiled and nodded to Gabe.

Did she want water? Pamela asked.

No, no, Gen said, just pass me my tarot cards. They're in the front pocket with the statue of Mary.

Pamela fished both decks out. Gabe pointed at the cards with his lips, pulled his eyebrows together, said, Been a long time since I seen a deck of those cards. Gen took Audie's cards out of their box and got to shuffling. Audie had painted each card in quiet colors, nothing screamed at you, and they felt like they were part earth. Gen knew what the cards would say to her but she didn't care, she wanted to talk with the cards. Gabe, well, he stepped around Gen's legs and past Pamela and was out of the room before you could ask anything about anybody's uncle. It made Gen laugh. Some people are like that with the cards. Pamela's phone buzzed and she checked it and said she had to go, said to Gen, We'll finish up later.

Gen put her mother's Mary on the table beside the bed and settled herself down there on that mattress and shuffled those cards. She thought how she needed a big spread, one that'd take a long time to read because she didn't want to think about should she tell Lucie she was here and she knew that's just what she was going to do, but a big reading would take her mind off it. Gen was always turning over Death these days, first thing, and she was expecting it again when she turned over the first card. Death, Death, and more Death. Sometimes she thought the cards were hurrying her along to the end and Gen got a laugh out of it. She was prepared for that laugh but it wasn't Death she turned over first: it was the Empress. Gen didn't turn over another card that whole night. She couldn't.

Carter drinks tea

Do I want milk and sugar in my tea, Allie asked.

Just milk, I said. I had to come out with it, that I was going to see her mother, my bio gramma. I didn't know how.

She'd just untangled my beading again. Next she was fixing my tea. Poured milk into my cup until it was a caramel color. Funny thing was, I didn't take milk in my tea anywhere else. Just with her.

It was a bit Freudian.

Both of my moms felt guilty because they wanted me to suck milk from their tits. Neither of them ever got over it, if you ask me. It's all about the boobs.

My bio mom had soft little boobs she kept strapped back in these maximum support bras, as if they were going to jump off her chest if she gave them the chance. My bio sisters had the same boobs as her, except, you know, younger. Sure as hell I didn't get my boobs from her.

Mine were big. I didn't think my bio mom was comfortable around them. Like she had got to get out of their way or something. She never said anything, but she wanted to sometimes, especially when I wore something that let a person actually see them. Which I did a lot around her because it was a laugh to see her struggle not to tell me to cover up.

They lost me my job at the hospice back when Tucker was a baby, my boobs did. This patient died, but that wasn't the trouble. They're all dying. They're all on the edge, looking to the other side, trying to see where death is taking them, trying to know ahead of time what'll happen next.

The trouble was that this patient who died left me his money. Wasn't much, but it was everything he had.

His family didn't like it. It wasn't like I asked him to leave me money. Honestly, he left the money to my boobs. Fuck knows, they've caused me enough trouble. I mean, the girl with the most developed tits in junior high? That's hell.

Richard's the name of the old guy who left me money.

I had two more beads to tack down before I called it quits. The bio sisters were stitching away and talking about stuff that never interested me in my whole life. They were all about homework and dance classes, about drama club and memorizing lines. One of them would blurt out a line they knew, like from a book they both loved or a movie they'd watched a hundred times, and the other would say the very next line and they'd go back and forth like that until they started giggling and the scene fell apart. My bio mom was cleaning up the counter, washing the dishes from afternoon tea and cookies and whatever was left from their Sunday breakfast.

Richard used to like to sneak a squeeze. That's how the whole thing started.

You liked it, didn't you?—that's me accusing myself. And I thought how that was the first time I ever thought about liking it or not liking it. Richard never asked me if I liked it.

Right there, when I finally asked the question of myself, I thought, No, I don't think I did like it.

But who gives a shit? He needed it, didn't he?

He never said anything about money or anything. It was just that he needed me. That first time my milk leaked out into big wet circles on my shirt because I was still breastfeeding Tucker. Richard reached a trembling hand out and pressed his palm against my left boob, said, Get them out and let me drink.

A bit of softness in his life, a bit of the tit, you know? We all want it one way or another and I had it to give and, I don't know, even though I was shocked and went totally still, even though I thought about the best way to tell him to get his hand off me, after a few moments, I figured, Well, why not? I washed in the employees' washroom after each time. Paper towels and hot water at the sink at first. After it became a regular thing I brought my own soap and cloths and showered if I could, which I usually couldn't, there being so many patients who needed my attention.

Once I let him breastfeed, that's what he wanted on the regular whenever I was assigned to him.

I had plenty of milk then because my boy was always on a growth spurt.

Richard could tell it skeeved me out a bit, so he always made me laugh. He had that. He could get a girl laughing so she didn't think too much about getting her tits out for him. For a while I kind of liked him. Richard was headed out to his own ancestors pretty soon and he was an old guy who could talk a mile a minute about heaven and hell and confession and sin and what was going to happen to him after.

But then instead of just letting go and leaving everything behind for the living, he really wanted to take something, to steal from someone who was going to go on without him. And one day I walked in and there were my tits all full of my baby's milk.

I got myself assigned to another group before he died. I was gonna keep my tits to myself at work after that. I had other things to do. He got pretty weak after I was reassigned, not because of me; it was just his time. He died not long after.

Never got my money though. The man's family said they'd fight it and I didn't want what wasn't mine anyway.

Not too long after that I got fired. Which is how I got my start cleaning other people's houses. I left Slavko, which I should have done a lot earlier, but whatever. Tucker and I ended up moving into my adopted mom's basement and I got so depressed I couldn't get out of bed and couldn't keep the stupid cleaning job either and it kind of turned to shit all at once.

Anyway, the more I thought on it, I didn't like what Richard did. It was like he was sucking up the stuff that was meant for my son.

When my son drank from me it was different. I was tired most of the time and impatient to get on to something else, but lots of times it was nice, too, when he looked up at me. I could see my boy needed me, but not like the old man did. Tucker's need was something else. It was a light that led me somewhere else, down another trail to a future I wasn't sure I deserved, wasn't sure I could fucking handle. My marriage was shitty and I wasn't on speaking terms with my adopted mom. I hadn't called my bio mom for another meeting yet and I hadn't been able to look in a mirror in years. What did I have to give my kid? Only milk.

Tucker didn't need all that from me now. No milk left in me.

Allie sat back at the table and picked up her needle.

Well, I said to everyone at the table, that's it for me.

Allie slipped her needle right into a black bead on the table. She bit her tongue, squinted, and got these ugly lines on her forehead that showed her age. I mean otherwise she looked pretty young, especially if you knew that she was a grandmother.

She wanted to teach me how to pick up a bead with a needle, but I didn't really want to learn.

I picked up my half-full half-empty cup, carried it to the sink.

Allie picked up my beading and ran a finger along the beads. She said that you were supposed to let mistakes into your bead design. She said, It keeps you humble.

My lips twitched. That's me, I thought. I was the mistake she couldn't unpick or redo. I was keeping her humble. I just about burst out laughing.

My cup was in the sink. I turned around. It was time to tell her.

I took a deep breath and opened my mouth and one of my bio sisters spoke up. How long was Tucker in—where did you say he was?

I couldn't let her throw me off. I was supposed to pick him up in a week, but I hadn't even booked a ticket and I didn't want to talk about it.

I'm going to see Gramma, I said.

Allie looked at me with hard gray eyes, her lips thinner than ever. My bio sisters looked from me to Allie and back again.

I wouldn't do that, said Allie.

She called me up, I said.

Your grandmother won't do you any good, Allie said.

She wanted to meet her granddaughter, I said, lying through my fucking teeth. What's wrong with that?

Don't fall for it, Allie said. She's toxic.

She might play me a song, I said.

A song? That's what you want out of this?

Allie put down the beading now and said she'd be right back. She left the kitchen and we heard the door to the bathroom down the hall close.

One of the sisters said, We've never met her.

Well, said the other, I met her once when I was five.

Oh right, said the first. And Mom told me she held me for, like, thirty seconds before she had to go. I was six months old or something.

Never met our great-grandmother either, the other one said.

We're such a close family, aren't we?

She drinks a lot, like a lot, and Mom says she won't see anybody.

We have Kokums though.

Yeah, like at the Métis community center.

And aunties.

I left the sink and packed away my beading, got my bag. There was a silence but then one said her birthday is coming up and would I come to her birthday party. Some escape game they'd booked. I already knew there would be no drink or drugs. I said sure, send me an email, but I knew I wouldn't be there.

I didn't tell them Gramma wanted me to kill her.

I could only play one escape game at a time.

Dee asks questions

Her teats hurt, was that normal?
Why did she feel off balance on her own four hooves?
What was going to happen next?
Where would she give birth?
How could a bison be this hungry all the time?
Did they really believe this birth would change the world?
Had they changed the world?
How much longer would she be pregnant?
Where had Jay gone to?
Why did they act like they're related to her?
Why did they go on about the days when the cows
were the herd's leaders?
What about the bulls?
Why couldn't she go off by herself?
Anyway it didn't matter. Hadn't they noticed that
the fences changed everything?

They told her about their own swollen udders,
about the cracked teats and engorged milk bags.
What did she mean? Was she ill?
She would mother, that was all and that was everything.
The winter pastures had trees that would offer places
for birthing, near one of the ponds would be best.
Not to worry, she could eat all the hay she wanted. The
humans would bring more.
Could she ask again later? They were with the calves,
teaching them survival skills for the coming winter.
Didn't she remember her first winter storm?
She would birth in late spring, because she

and Jay had waited.
The aunties said bulls would come and go and
it was best not to think too much about them.
The aunties told her Jay wasn't reliable
and wasn't supposed to be, that Jay
would always be off chasing his own tail.
You think aunties are only about blood?
Here's how to search for
the bit of grass beneath the winter snow.
Here's how to find the first spring greens.
Everyone knows it's the cows that hold the sky
on their humps.
What about the bulls?
Where was Dee? Gone again.

Perkins and Lottery at the kennel

Perkins walked to the other side of the cage and nudged Lottery's forehead with his nose. We could leave any time we want, he said.

We could.

He flopped down in pretty boy position. But then who would entertain all these dogs?

I'm already tired of this conversation.

We're helping them wait for their people.

It's always should we stay or should we go.

What? What do you want me to say? God, it's like—

I'm not God.

I know.

How many times with that. You and me, not gods.

I know.

Then quit with the—

More me than you though.

What?

I'm more godlike than you are. Admit that.

Lottery lay down and stared at the wall. Sure, she said, you've been at it longer.

About a thousand years longer.

Lottery huffed and closed her eyes. When they heard a door open down the hallway Lottery opened her eyes and Perkins jumped back up to all fours, his whole back end wagging in excitement.

Calm down, said Lottery.

It's this dog body. It just feels so good. See my tail?

I see your tail, said Lottery, closing her eyes again.

It's glorious, Perkins said. He chased his tail around and around and then stopped and posed. What a body, eh?

You know something's got to be wrong, right?

Perkins walked back to the cage door, pressed his nose through a small gap, and whimpered.

I wonder what's taking her so long, muttered Lottery.

Afterlife, where Mamé can ask for forgiveness

And then I am walking toward those gates and closer to Maman.

I don't mean to. My feet betray me.

Maman's shoulders are high and tense as she calls out to me. She says, Come. She says, It's time.

She moves a few steps in my direction, away from the family, and she becomes the young woman she must have been before I knew her. She is barefoot now too. Her hair is free from the pins and combs—when I was a child she would have called it an unholy mess.

I've never before seen that my mother also had this thing that I possess—the potential to come apart. I can see that what I treasured and nurtured, she had thrown away.

Then her name is on my lips. I call out, Marie Élise.

She stops halfway between me and the family. She waits.

My older sisters hold each other's arms. The brother who'd gone to meet the Lord as a baby is now a handsome young man in a well-cut suit and his hand rests on our father's shoulder. My two aunts exchange glances with raised eyebrows.

And there is my father, Papa, sitting in his chair with a newspaper in his hands.

Would he see me? Oh, I feel like the girl I'd been all over again. Papa, I say, and he looks at me the way he'd always done when I'd displeased him. He is a man who looked only to remind himself of a person's faults and in his eyes I can see how many blemishes I carry and how heavy it is to be this sinner, this woman, this self.

His glance commands me to come to him, to humble myself at his knee and confess my shame for the scandal I'd caused. If I do this small thing, his eyes might look at me softly once more. At least until he found another shortcoming.

How sick am I at the part of me willing to do anything to gain his favor. And yet how can I ask his forgiveness for loving my fiddler?

I look for a long time at Marie Élise, my mama as the young woman I'd never known. She is fierce. Her feet are planted like thick roots. Even as I watch, her body becomes a trunk and her arms become branches bearing small red apples, hard and sour.

The grassland sees Dee's path

I'm always here. So it was easy, when Dee slipped away from the herd, to offer a bit of myself to hold her up.

Nice of you to visit, I told her.

The aunties got to lecturing. Not my scene.

Well, wallow a little. You'll feel better.

She hunched her shoulders, said, I'm fine.

I wanted to laugh but I just shrugged a little beneath the tree roots and told her that I know the aunties could be a bit much for her.

She said, You're telling me—I left them talking at the calves.

Dee lay herself down, stretched out so her belly was right up against me. Even through two inches of snow I could hear the heartbeat of the little one she's growing. I breathed with her a few beats.

They're trying, you know.

They stink, she said.

They all smell just fine to me.

No, you smell good, she said.

She cleared away the snow with her head so she could press her nose against the frozen mud of me. It tickled a little and I shivered. I offered her a bunch of meadow brome grass and she took a mouthful and chewed slowly.

Not far off a grouse pushed its way out of the snow and scanned the area. There was a snowberry bush nearby so the bird left its snug tunnel and clambered up into the branches. Another grouse appeared at the entrance of the snow tunnel and followed the first into the bush.

Dee watched for a minute and then said, I don't know why the aunties bother.

They're trying to work with the treaties. They don't know how, mostly. They don't know that trying's the point.

Whatever, Dee said, and she rolled onto her back and kicked her feet into the air.

I was annoyed with her now. I said, You're on protected land, you know.

She dropped her feet to the ground so she could hear me better and raised her head. She said, What do you mean?

This bit of me here, it's what they call protected. Do you know what they do to the land in other places?

No, she said, and she was quiet after.

Big swaths of land are smothered in chemicals that kill everything except one plant, the one the humans want to grow. Could be anything, really, corn or canola or wheat. And that's all you see for as far as you can see, and as far as you can travel. They pretend they don't know about the treaties.

Is there a treaty I can make with a bull?

The one between the bison, the prairie dog, the fire, and me—that's what I'm talking about. Your people—I mean the ones who carry two names, like you, bison or buffalo—disappeared after those treaties were ignored.

She stood up. She said, You're going to talk about that?

Do you know what it felt like when there were no bison? Any idea?

She started pawing at snow then. She said, Well, no.

I remember the first day bison were brought back right here, on top of me.

She snorted. Said, Must have made you feel better?

Oh, I was in pieces before your people's hooves returned.

Don't you think that's a bit dramatic.

All I know is the prairie dog came back and I could breathe

again and the rain could reach all the deep places and I drank it up. I felt better than I had in a century, really.

You're old.

Ha ha. And no, you can't make a treaty with a bull, not the kind you're thinking of.

I'm not thinking about any kind, she said.

Anyway, you don't know what your people mean to me. When those first bison came off that truck and walked through the gates, when I felt their hooves sinking into me, I shuddered. Just ten of them at first, but theirs were the first bison hooves I'd felt in a century. And when they wallowed I thought, Maybe there's a future. The first rain came and filled up the wallow and the birds came to it. I don't know. I had something like hope for the first time.

Drama queen.

You don't know yet. Hope can be a lie. It can be an awful thing, in my opinion. But this wasn't a false hope. This was real.

What's wrong with hope, Dee asked.

That's for another time. The point is that your people, the ones who carry the names of bison and buffalo both, have healed me every place you go, so I owe you a lot.

She was paying attention then. She said, I know how you can pay me back.

I can't pay you back. That's the point.

You can watch over my calf after, you know, after I do the birthing and stuff.

I watch over the whole herd, Dee. What do you mean?

And you can show me where the fences are weaker.

I don't know, child. Used to be all of you would all tear down fences all the time but now hardly any one of you takes the trouble.

You know about fences, right?

Your people learned that the land on the other side of fences swallows whoever leaves and they don't come back.

Dee pressed her hooves into me because she knew how much I liked it. Jay said it can be different, she said.

I've heard some say that the time of wide-open spaces is over.

My mom wasn't afraid of fences, Dee said.

I know your mom, I told her. Well, I think you'd say knew. I knew your mom.

She got jumpy. Don't tell me, she said. I won't listen to it.

I turned back into myself, reached deep into my dirt, and listened to the whispers of the roots, fungus, and minerals.

Anyway, if I wanted a lecture, I would have stayed with the aunties, she said.

She headed out toward the part of the fence that gave her the best mix of breezes to carry any news of Jay to her nose.

I sighed in a way she didn't feel. I knew what was going on. This young one thought the bull was the path. Oh, I'd seen this before.

Allie texts Carter

Sorry I didn't get to say
goodbye
Love your beading
Really coming along

No worries
Had to get going

You really going to see
my mom

On my way now

Oh

What's her first name?

She was great when I was a
little kid
But she's not that anymore
She'll try to use you
Be careful

She never said her name

She could try to use you to
get at me

Weird
Didn't ask her name either

Lucie

Can't use me

Be careful

Not an addict or anything
is she?
Nice name

I don't think so
I haven't talked to her in

forever
A decade
Just to men
She's addicted to men

Geneviève sees a ghost

Near midnight and someone knocked at Gen's door. A trembling knock, a stuttering rap on an old door in an old building and Gen was spooked. The wind had picked up and the rain kept getting carried away in the gusts and then falling all at once against the window in a shudder. She was in her nightgown already, under the blankets, and she didn't want to get up so she called out some-thing—she didn't know what, but some noise left her throat—and the door opened and there was Gabe, looking just as he had when he'd walked Gen to the front doors.

Right away Gen told him to come in. Didn't know you worked nights, she said. And he smiled and made his way to the comfy seat near the bed, sat himself down. Don't you go home at night, she said but then she saw he was staring at the cards on the bed-side table. There were two of them because that morning she'd taken out her second deck and pulled the Empress again. She'd stashed the rest of the decks away in the drawer, so it was just the Empresses and Mary side by side by side. The first Empress, Audie's Empress, was standing tall by a prairie stream, all these medicinal plants growing high around her, everything done in soft earth watercolors. The other Empress was sitting on an orange throne wearing a crown with twelve stars, regal and sure of her power.

Used to be Gen sometimes did readings for people, not a lot, only friends and family. When she did readings for Velma, Gen'd tell her to pick a card that represented her. Every time Velma picked the Empress, one of the most powerful. The Empress is protector and provider, shield-maiden and mother, life, death, and rebirth. Velma always knew what she was. Gen never knew which card to pick for herself until now, when she was always turning Death. Anyway, the way Gabe looked at those cards made her ache for her sister and her whole family, made her want to talk.

I've got one sister, but she's in the spirit world, Gen found herself saying to Gabe.

Gen didn't stop there, she kept on going. And then there's my mother up in the spirit world. Promised she'd contact me after she passed if she could, but I haven't heard from her and I always thought it was because I started drinking. We called my mom Mamé for so many years, but her name's Élise. And my papa's in the spirit world too. Bob. They're the ones who knew me before I started drinking. And there's those who are living. The ones who are needing a different me, the one I used to be or maybe could have been. I don't know how I can be now what I could have been. Anyway, there's Lucie and her girl Allie and Allie's girl Carter and Carter's boy Tucker. And I haven't seen anybody. Not in so long.

Gabe stood up and walked behind the chair to look out the window. Come here, he said. Look.

Never mind her nightgown, Gen got out of bed and went to stand beside him. She could see the rain falling on the cars. She knew her car was down there somewhere. She couldn't see the prairie, not for the trees that had been planted. There were tall lamps standing among the trees that lit up their branches. She leaned her forehead against the window and her breath made a little circle of condensation.

Over there, Gabe said. He was pointing toward the buildings and the ruins on the left.

Gen had been in the other building earlier, for her first group meeting. Met everyone. Learned how to say she was an alcoholic. After, she'd said to Pam, I'm not very good at it— saying it, I mean.

Gabe said, Used to be that building was a sanatorium.

Gabe said, After that it was a rail station and the trains would stop right close to here. The nearest town still has a train station. Used to be busy bringing things and people through but it's a ghost town now. I don't have to tell you that before all that this was Blackfoot land.

Seemed to Gen she could see it all out there, just the way it was.

Gabe shuffled his feet a little, looked at Gen and then back out the window. The rain said everything that needed to be said, Gen thought. Way off in the trees behind the parking lot Gen thought she saw the shadow of a bison.

Do they keep bison on this land? she asked.

No, Gabe said and he looked at her curiously. Why do you ask?

The single bison had become a herd, all of them walking through the trees. It couldn't be real, so Gen didn't say anything to Gabe. People could be weird when you saw something they didn't. Anyway Gen thought it could be that she was hallucinating and she didn't want him to call for the nurse, not tonight. Gen was wanting a drink that bad and right at that moment she wasn't sure she could do this thing and maybe she would just get in her car and drive on home but then she thought how last night and this morning when she'd laid out her tarot reading she got those Empress cards.

Gabe let the silence grow between them and then he gestured around the room, said, After the trains stopped coming they turned this into an institution for the mentally ill. Back then they called it a home for the retarded and insane. Doctors and staff used to stay in that building over there but this one was where the treatment happened. The things I could tell you. The things that happened here that people forgot.

Gabe clicked his tongue four times, then went on. The mental hospital got cleared out by a flood back in the 1960s. The river down the way, it overflowed its banks. Took a few lives but most everyone got out safe. The patients were sent on to other hospitals. The buildings were abandoned. That was the end of the mental hospital. Until somebody bought it cheap to start up a hotel and then a spa. They fixed a few things up around here but it didn't take too long to go bankrupt. A few years ago the center here bought it for next to nothing. And now you're here.

Gen was a bit cold so she left the window to look for her bathrobe. There it was, thick and warm. When she pulled it on over her nightgown and pushed her hands into the big fuzzy pockets, she felt like a big old bison. She was thinking if she should take anything to help her sleep and she turned around and there was Gabe, hovering in the doorway and about to leave. He said, Come on, I'll show you something downstairs.

Gen didn't want to leave those cards there alone, so she slid the Empresses into her pocket. She put on her slippers and closed the door and Gabe offered his arm again and they were walking slowly to the elevator and Gabe said, There's ghosts, you know, all kinds of ghosts here.

He shrugged then and pushed the button to call the elevator. Well, that's what they say anyway.

Afterlife, where Mamé knows herself

And so Maman is a tree in full fruit.

She says she has apples for me if I will come to her.

But I refuse. I can't pick them.

Soon the tree falls away and Maman is herself again, the wife and mother I've always known her to be.

I look into the heaven of her face for a long time.

My stomach twists and nausea overcomes me. I have to turn away. I lean forward and vomit up the last meal I ate down there on earth, but this being the place it is and myself being dead, nothing comes out of my stomach, nothing but light and air.

I steady myself and straighten my back.

Now I can see that those gates have thrown everything else into darkness.

The gates are so white and bright, like a bare bulb burning from the back porch in the middle of the night.

At that moment I know myself to be the moth.

I will not batter my wings against this electric light any longer, blinded to all else.

Solin begins a story

A blizzard moved in and we shifted the calves to the center. It was their first big snowstorm and they'd picked up on the thread of anxiety shared by us old ones. The young ones watched as we scanned the skies and sniffed the wind, listened as we talked of past snowstorms when someone was lost. They stared as the winged ones left our backs, preferring to wait out this onslaught from the safety of their roosts. The calves were restless. They pushed each other over, whispered in each other's ears, giggled. We all remembered our first snowstorm, and in our remembering we were patient with them. Those calves didn't know what was coming.

They thought because they'd seen a couple of snowfalls they knew what snow was, that snowing was fat flakes falling onto the curve of all our backs, onto the curve of the land, and then melting away. The first snows had left them skittish and jumpy and chasing each other around. The youngest of the lot twitched his nose, asked, This is what snow smells like? Their mothers and aunties and grandmothers left them to their fun and worried. Where was the best spot to wait out the cold? How far into the trees would they walk this year? Which auntie would they send ahead as a scout?

As the calves caught their first scent of a storm front, they knew it would be something new. They'd never seen how a storm sky hangs itself closer to the ground, how it can go dark as dusk in the middle of the day. As this storm moved in the aunties called the calves in close, enforced a ban on wandering. The aunties repeated, You can die if you get separated, until they were hoarse and the calves whispered about death among themselves, thrilled that it might come so close. Conserve your energy, the

MICHELLE PORTER

aunties said. Your job is to listen, the aunties said. The calves huddled together, saying to each other, What will it be like? We're packed here in the middle of everything, will we see any of this blizzard? Anything more than the shaggy beards and the shanks and the humps of the cows? The calves lowered their heads and peered between the cows' legs. Where is this blizzard?

The aunties arranged the herd. The calves in the center. Then the pregnant cows. There were only two in the group this year. Lor was carrying her third calf, birthed the first two easily. She was proud and calm. It was Dee who worried us. Her scent was desperate and unsatisfied. She couldn't focus on the teachings for any length of time. We pressed Dee toward the center but she resisted. Said she preferred to be on the outside, that she wanted an unobstructed view of the horizon. It's a blizzard, the aunties said. There'll be no horizon. I don't want to be shut in, she said. You'll need to be warm, we all said, and we pushed her in and that was that.

Dee's scent made the calves nervous and they started to whinny and bump against each other's hooves just to hear the click, clack, just to bother us old ones, who were listening to the storm. We listened for early warning of any shift so we could direct the herd to switch their positions or move on somewhere else for safety, and in which direction, and how quickly, not that anyone can move quickly in a blizzard.

Usually the center was a place of calm, surrounded by the warmth and the smell of aunties and grandmothers and sisters and brothers. I was an old grandmother and I could think of no better place to be. I'd missed being at the center since my pregnancies stopped coming, since they all began to look to me for what to do. I knew that the next time I was pressed to the center, that place would not feel the way it had before. The next time, it would be because I was too old and feeble to lead or to withstand the winds on my own. I didn't look forward to that time of life, to the coming of the end, to that return to the center. But I couldn't think about that anymore; there was too much to do. I listened to Dee's grunts and complaints and smelled the panic she threw into the air. Selfish cow, that one. The calves were going to get excited and bolt between the cows' legs and then we'd have to break up the circle. It was time for a story.

Different ways to tell a story. Some tellers make a noise to announce the coming of the story or get someone else to call everyone's attention. Some wait for people to gather around, for the quiet to settle. Others just begin. They don't wait for everyone to lean in—that'll happen soon enough. They don't speak loudly or even want everyone to hear. Those that hear are the ones the story was meant for. Me, I'm that last kind.

I got started in the middle of a story.

Perkins and Lottery hold auditions

In the backyard after lunch, beside the tree behind the play equipment, good dogs waited in lines that reached all the way to the large dog slide.

A little Yorkie belted out the first few lines of a song she'd learned from her littermate before she was adopted.

Perkins interrupted her. Stop, he said. I can see where this is going.

You can't see where anything's going, said Lottery.

The Yorkie snarled and ran at Perkins with the intention to bite but Lottery stepped in between the two dogs. The Yorkie stopped short and then shook herself and trotted off, headed for the doggie pool.

Perkins looked over the line of dogs waiting to audition. He said, I've changed my mind about the band. I'd rather leave.

I think we gotta let this thing play out.

Remember the day she left us?

Sure do.

Never smelled her like that before.

You didn't make it easy on her.

Perkins remembered how Gen had reached out a hand for him before she'd left the car. He'd stepped onto the driver's seat and licked her trembling old fingers. Good boy, Gen had said. What's going on? he'd asked in a single bark, tilting his head so she'd know what he was asking.

Gen left then and, as Lottery let herself be locked in a carrier, Perkins had shouted, Keep up the resistance. Lottery said things like, You're making it worse, and, I think we gotta do this, until the scent of Gen's guilt finally reached Perkins and his eyes went wide and he brought himself up short.

He knew what he had to do.

For Gen, he'd said.

And then he'd let himself be carried away from his old lady.

Inside, the man left Perkins's carrier beside Lottery's.

Lottery had sniffed and said, There are so many dogs here.

Perkins could feel that a change was coming and he'd said as much to Lottery. Now he was tired of waiting for it.

She left us, said Perkins. So why can't we leave?

Something's going to happen. I'm telling you.

Yeah, yeah.

And if we're going to wait, might as well do it with music, right?

Perkins, he looked over at the waiting dogs. Not much talent here, he said.

Who's next? Lottery called out.

Perkins watched a well-built white and gray husky step away from the line and jog over the grass toward him. Her eyes were this incredible shade of blue he'd never seen before. He sat up a little taller and straightened his tags.

When she raised her neck and opened her jaws and let her voice free, Perkins thought maybe, just maybe, his band was going to make a go of it.

Carter lives dangerously

There was a bird in Gramma. She buzzed me in to her apartment building, and by the time I got to her hallway her door was open and she'd poked her head out to see me walking toward her and then pulled it back in. When I stepped through her door I saw a little bird in a raspberry-red sweater with purple trim around the sleeves and the V neckline, in full makeup, lipstick matching her sweater. She hopped back so I could close the door and then forward to take my jacket, but I kept my shoulder bag with me, and then there was a quick little hug. She was such a small woman. Gramma was the same height as me. But where I was broad-shouldered, rounder, and strong for my size, Gramma was narrow and fragile. Her hair was pulled back and raven black, but that had to be dye because for sure she'd gone all gray or white by now. Her eyes were blue. The bird was so bright.

Gramma moved her head and the bird in her peered out again. She reached out to pull the waist of my jeans and I saw that we were wearing the same ones—same brand, same cut. Gramma tittered and said, Different size though? And I don't know what I expected from her but for sure I didn't think her first words to me in person would be about my pants, that she'd point out that I wore a bigger size than she did. She cocked her head and was I charmed by it or something? Because I couldn't help but laugh. I pulled my yellow sweatshirt down to cover my hips. It was on the tip of my tongue to say, And I got a bigger bra size, too, hey?

Sit down at the table, Gramma said. Tea? Pour. Milk or sugar? Just milk it is. Stir.

I watched her and tried to figure out which bird Gramma was. Some sort of grassland bird? I didn't know enough about birds. I pulled out my phone and googled prairie birds, but before

I could check out the results Gramma sat down and spoke so quiet I had to lean in to hear. And shit didn't Gramma go straight for it.

When will you do it?

I kept my face neutral. I lifted my shoulder bag from the floor to my lap and pulled out a little pile of forms. I said, I have a few demands. Stipulations, you could say. Addendums. For the contract.

Gramma leaned forward and both her hands were on the table. Contract? Gramma said.

Yes, for the killing. I have to protect myself. And I want a few things from you.

Me?

I want you to teach me a song.

Gramma leaned back and drew her elbows against her body as if they were feathers. She said, What do I have to do with that?

I heard you used to play. That you could fiddle.

Did Allan put you up to this?

Why would my mom do that?

It'd be just like her to put something like this in your head. Set you against me.

Mom said you played fiddle sometimes. She said you used to dance. Said you used to sew your own clothes and you used to cook big dinners. Like, thirty years ago, at least. She said that.

Gramma opened her mouth, but no sound came out. After a moment she pressed her lips closed, shifted her wings a bit. She looked so tiny in that chair, and I thought how Allie was so much bigger. Allie was sturdy. Allie had flesh and muscle and she was so strong except she wasted all her strength holding herself back, holding it all in, all the parts of herself she didn't want other people to see, didn't want to see herself. How could Allie have come from this fragile bird woman?

Gramma turned her head and as she looked away from me, said, I don't want to say it. I gave up on all that when I gave up on my mom—it all reminded me of her—Allan doesn't remember, she was too young and not exactly observant—

I said, I want to see a bit of that side of Gramma. Just so I have something after you're gone.

She didn't say anything, so I pushed the pile of papers across the table to her side. Gramma reached for her reading glasses and leaned over to peer at the forms. She took her time. I picked up my phone and looked at search results for prairie birds. I went right to images. No, not a prairie chicken. No, not the warbler or the pipit. A falcon? I looked at Gramma and realized there was more than one bird in her because I'd seen a glimpse of something like a falcon, and even when she was some other bird, the kind that ate worms and seeds, there was always the possibility of the predator about her, wasn't there. I shivered and then I saw it, the purple finch. I looked at her to be sure, and yes, this was the bird looking out at me right then. Okay, she sure wasn't the female one, the brown and white streaked bird. No, Gramma didn't blend into the background; she had all the cockiness of a tiny male bird that people said looked like it had been dipped in raspberry juice. And the purple finch wasn't really purple. They were a bright pink-red on the head and chest and back, so there was a lie built into the name and that fit this woman arranging her feathers across the table. I put my phone away.

Gramma was shaking her head over the killing contract I'd drawn up. I'd laughed my ass off putting it together.

Gramma pulled her glasses off, said, All I want to know is— are you going to get me the pills or not?

Are you going to dance?

I'll take you to one. That's it.

I thought how I'd never been to a dance. It wasn't Allie's thing. I said, Okay.

Gramma pushed the papers back at me. She said, You don't know what you're doing, child. Stubborn bitch.

I can tell I'm really going to enjoy killing you.

Gramma dropped her chin. Then she looked up at me with big eyes. Then do it, Gramma whispered.

I almost put a hand on Gramma's, almost promised her that I'd do anything to help her, anything. Whatever it was she did with her eyes and her voice, she was fucking good at it.

Forget the pills, I'll happily wring your neck now, I said.

Gramma's face shifted into contempt, then she said, Just the pills, please, that'll do, child.

Get me a copy of your birth certificate. Spend some time with me.

It's not going to work. Whatever it is you're trying to do.

Mom said it was dangerous to get to know you.

Allan said that?

Danger's exciting though, isn't it?

Geneviève plays a jig

Out of the elevator on the main floor there was a hallway to the right and one to the left. Gabe led Gen down the left one to the end where there was an open door. He let go of her arm and stepped back so she could walk through the narrow doorway.

A single lamp threw just enough light for her to see that the walls were painted blue. In the middle were sofas and chairs, and in the back, in front of a big bay window, was a piano. It was a baby grand and it looked eerily familiar. Did Gabe see it? She turned to ask, but he was gone. She could hear his footsteps fading down the hallway.

The piano had seen better days. It was old. She ran a hand over the keyboard and it felt just like one she used to know when she was a child in another part of the country. It couldn't be. And yet, when she sat down, her body remembered everything.

There was one way to check for sure.

It wasn't easy to get down on the floor but she did. Her knees ached something awful but there, scratched into the wood beneath the keys, was the infinity symbol, the one she'd carved with a pin when she was ten and left alone to wait for some reason she can't remember now.

How could *this* piano be here? The one from the performances she gave with her family at the children's hospital in Winnipeg when they'd been hired for some celebration she couldn't remember. It was the piano she played every afternoon and evening all week for the kids and the staff. Her whole family had been there, her sister, Velma, and her mother and father and her father's sister.

It took all of Gen's focus to get off her knees and heave herself back to her feet, so she didn't notice the Empresses slip from her pocket and slide under the piano. When Gen put a hand on the piano to lift herself up, she almost expected her hands to move through it because she couldn't understand why it would be here in this room after all these years. But the keyboard was solid and made a deep sound as she rose to her feet. How could they have found that piano and brought it all the way over here to the center? Her legs were shaking so she set herself carefully on the bench.

Her fingers fit the keys the way they used to; her fingers recognized the old instrument too. Yes, it was the one she played in Winnipeg, where her people were from, where she was from, where she'd like to return one day. She had played for the children who were sick and she remembered now how her father was so pleased with her for smiling big for the sick kids and for how well she could play, for her part in the family band.

The piano needed some work but maybe she could get some music in it that'd make everyone's feet jig.

She felt like she was falling from the earth of one life to the sky of another and she didn't know who was going to catch her or if she was going to drown. What good would come of an old woman's decision to quit drinking before she died? Her fingers moved slowly up and down the keys.

She thought how the ground of her old life was becoming the sky of this life, the life she had to make now. She didn't know that there was so much water beneath what she'd thought was the solid earth of her life. It was too late to clamber back up through that hole she'd fallen through. It was all her own doing. She'd made the calls and the arrangements and told them all the right things. She'd been digging up roots, searching for medicine.

Falling hadn't been part of her plan.

And now she was tumbling from the sky and the other side of the sky was here, in the blue room in an addictions center for First Nations and Métis.

A song rose from the piano now and sure enough there was an old jig in those keys still. The old contraption responded so much like that piano all those years ago that she looked up for her sister, expecting Velma to be standing there with her fiddle, moccasins on her feet, and her papa, too, with a sash around his waist and his old fiddle against his broad chest. Oh yes, she'd played this piano before. Who else could hear what her fingers were saying this night? Which was mostly that they'd like another drink and that she should walk back through that door, get in her car, and drive on back, sit with John and drink till she was sober again.

Mamé, where time unravels

And that is how I begin to look about myself properly and see what else is there.

At first I can't see much.

Only as far as the path I stand on, just the bit of earth beneath my feet.

But that is enough. I walk it.

I feel like I've been walking a long time. But I don't know how time is sewn into this place and I don't know how time can be unraveled.

A grandmother tells about the time before fences

Young ones were always asking where we come from. Best way to say it was, we come from the middle of things.

The wind whistled across our backs and the snow was already swirling so thick you couldn't see over the next hump so we hunched a little closer to the ground and I started by telling the calves that after everything that'd happened the middle had been thrown into everything, it was all over the place. But we were all here and we were all a people. The middle was the beginning of the story.

One of the calves said something about too many stories about the old ones.

This story isn't about the old ones, I told that calf. This is about the calves.

That got their attention.

Then they remembered how they were supposed to act when one of the grandmothers or grandfathers got to telling a story as a storm blew in.

I lifted each of my hooves one at a time. This storm was going to last for days, there was no rush. I rolled my shoulders back so my cape looked broader and I rocked back deeply onto my hind-quarters, searching for a bit more room in these old joints. They always got stiff when the wind blew like that. It was only when the calves were edging forward, pushing against each other in their impatience, that I started telling the story.

We come out of death.

We come out of the compassion that flows from an unexpected place.

We come out of making our voices heard in the darkness, a darkness deeper than this night of a blizzard, the one we've got coming.

We come out of the darkness of losing everything.

There are other stories. But they come before or after the middle.

The middle is the time death stalked us on the land we belonged to. They say death came in many forms then. With the pale-faced humans and their steel rifles. With the steel tracks they put into the ground and the trains that rode over them. They say the land was pregnant with the deaths of our ancestors.

They say we would have died completely if not for the calves.

The little ones couldn't help calling out, Calves?

The calves, I repeated. Yes.

Lots of times, the humans with their guns left the calves to wander instead of wasting a bullet. They knew the calves would die eventually. Any of us would die on our own, without our relations.

Think of it too. There were no fences then. Used to be herds of hundreds, thousands, stretching farther than you can see. So many of us on the land that you couldn't see the end, or the beginning. All you could ever see was the middle.

No way, the calves said to each other.

It would take them a long time to start to remember it enough to believe, even longer to figure out that I was telling them about the future.

I paused and looked at the calves, there at the center of us. Where should I take the story from there?

I said, It was the calves who made us what we are today.

One of the calves butted her head into the flank of another.

They say that after the killings, the calves would wander in the fields of their dead relatives. They were hungry and out of their senses with fear. All they wanted was to lie down and die. Wouldn't you?

The calves became perfectly still.

And some of them did. Lie down and die. But some of them, they did something else.

A calf shouted, What? What? What did they do? The rest of them giggled. A bit of tension was released.

I said, The calves called out to their dead relatives.

Gross, groaned one of the calves.

They kept calling for them. The ones who had just been killed by the humans.

A pause and then the same calf said, Aww, come on. That's it?

I waited until another calf said, Listen, will you? The story isn't over.

I said, This is the way we all began. The story of this herd begins with one calf who kept calling. We begin with the cry of the young.

It's the same after you are all born. We wait for you to call out, even before you stand.

The calls of our calves make a community from nothing.

That's why you're at the center of us now.

It's the calves who teach us what we need to know to sur-vive—to wait, to look for our chance to begin again. Always wait-ing for the moment to be moving on and beginning again.

Geneviève seeks refuge from the rain

Sometimes an old woman had to get out of her rehab center just so she can get away from the heaviness of everyone else's stories, maybe sit with her own. The rain was coming down hard, but after playing that piano Gen knew there'd be no sleep, not yet, so she went out the front door and stood looking through the rain at the trees and the parking lot a long while before she thought of going to her car. Back upstairs for keys, slow and lumbering as an old woman has to be, and then outside again.

It was still pouring when Gen opened the door to her Volvo and lowered herself in the seat that had long ago changed its shape to fit hers. She was wet by then and rain dripped from her hair and her arms and the car caught all the water it could for her. The drumming on the old roof was a steady rhythm that sang peace into her, kept her still.

She wanted to talk to someone, really talk to someone.

Bets, she said, I don't know if I can do this.

When she got to thinking again about the old days and the silence that came after her parents and her sister moved on to the spirit world, she started Bets's engine and turned on her radio. They were going on about that St. Mary's Canal and the water that would begin flowing into the Milk River any day, but Gen waited and sure enough the news poured into a song and she sighed and closed her eyes as the first notes came.

Can you feel it too, Bets?

And if the car could talk, Gen was sure it'd say, Oh yeah, I can feel it in my upholstery.

MICHELLE PORTER

Carter, dancing

Music filled every corner and crack of the hall.

The fiddles invited me in and shut me out, made me feel old and new all at once, offered me a new language to figure out and nagged at me, told me I should have known all this already and that I did know it in my bones if I could just figure out how to remember. I didn't like feeling that way and I didn't want to dance, not that Gramma was offering to teach me or anything. We stood at the edge of the dance floor, just watching.

The male dancers were taking their turn on the floor and I thought, Damn, I never knew there was something about the male body with a sash neat and tight around a slim waist, jigging to an old fiddle tune. Gramma was in a form-fitting red skirt, heels, and a top with a plunging neckline. A hairdo she must have spent hours on. I wore a pair of jeans I'd pulled from the dirty laundry pile and a white scoop-neck T-shirt that could've used an iron if I wasn't filling it out so well. I asked Gramma could she dance in those heels. She said, It's been too long. I didn't come here to dance.

All the fiddlers had gnarled fingers and swollen joints, except for one set of young hands, and still they kept their bows moving almost faster than the dancers could move their feet. Most of them wore vests that had been beaded in fine detail, probably by their wives, mothers, or girlfriends. Having sat in Allie's kitchen a few times, I had some idea of the hours of labor that went into each piece. The young fiddler didn't have a vest. His black hair was tied back and he wore beaded moccasins. I wondered who'd beaded the matching sets of red and pink flowers on his moccasins.

Gramma stood on one side of me. On the other side there was an older woman in a long ribbon skirt, a little girl hitched to her hip. The woman was dark skinned and the girl had light hair, pale skin. Our turn's coming up, the old woman said to the girl. Now watch, she said. Look how they move their feet. That's the dance I taught you. See? That's what we been doing in our kitchen. Okay now, see what they're doing next? That's the turn. So now here's where they can bring in their own thing. Always space for both. You see that? Look there, look what your brother is doing. He's good at those new parts, isn't he? He's doing the— oh what's it called? You both taught that to me when you came to stay the weekend that time. Used to be good at the new parts when I was a girl. Hmmm mmm. I dreamed all these new dances back then. Okay, yeah, I'll let you down.

The old woman let the girl slip off her hip. The girl took the old woman's hand and pulled her ahead, closer to the dancers. I felt like I recognized the song they were playing then, like maybe it was in my genes or maybe I was making that up because I wanted some stupid connection. I mean, why was I there? I leaned over to Gramma and I asked her why she didn't dance anymore, as if that was going to answer my question.

Allie had told me and my bio sisters the story when we were beading after one of my bio sisters had asked, Why doesn't she dance? But I wanted to hear it from Gramma.

Gramma didn't take her eyes off the dancers when she answered, I'm too old. Besides, I forget how.

That's all Gramma said. But Allie had said that Gramma Lucie used to tell stories about learning to fiddle and jig with her own mama, Geneviève, in the bush in B.C., that Gramma Lucie's family would go over to her auntie's, Aunt Velma's, when the men were away. All the Métis side of the family would get together and there'd be music and dancing. But in their early thirties,

Velma passed on and Lucie's mom got depressed and Lucie's dad put his foot down, said that's enough of that, nobody needs it anymore.

As she scooped two purple beads onto a needle, Allie said her mom started to go to dances when Allie was a little kid; she would get all dressed up and go out, but her dad didn't like it much and even after Gramma Lucie divorced him and got custody, Gramma Lucie said dancing made her think of her mom too much and she only wanted to move on with her life. Gramma Lucie said she couldn't stand to see her mom drinking, that the older she got the meaner she became when she was drunk. Gramma Lucie said it all made her feel like a little girl and most of the therapists she cycled through said tough love was the answer, to cut her mom off, to stop enabling her mom's addiction. They told her she was an adult child of alcoholics, to work on her codependency, to get rid of it. That's what Gramma Lucie did. After she left Allie's dad Gramma Lucie kept moving on, again and again, and she never went back to see her mom. I refuse to look back, she used to say. When Gramma Lucie looked ahead there was no time for dancing; there was only time for packing everything into black plastic bags and those cardboard boxes you could get free from the liquor store, only packing and unpacking. That's what Allie said that one time.

It seemed like it had all caught up to Gramma Lucie and now she was sick with all the looking back she hadn't done. It was funny that Allie didn't know she was a lot like Gramma Lucie. Or maybe she did know and that was what was wrong with her.

Gramma leaned over to me and yelled over the cheering. See that guy there, said Gramma. He's looking at you. She pointed into the crowd behind us. I saw the man she was pointing at, older than me by at least a decade, a big buckle over tight Wranglers, black hair slicked back, dark eyes hard, the kind of man you could cut yourself on. I didn't need Gramma's help. I'd already given my number out. I nodded at Gramma and turned back to watch the dancers and fiddlers. I couldn't believe how my fingers itched to play. It was curious to me because I'd never even had a lesson. Got the feeling that my fingers knew something my head didn't.

Gramma was good at flirting. Shit, I could have learned a thing or two from her. Hadn't been here half an hour and two guys had already sidled over to welcome her. Best I could tell there was a third trying to step in. The third guy was a snake and he slid easily ahead of the other two men to speak to Gramma.

Gramma did her thing, tipped her head and looked up at him in a way that got him fidgeting. Fuck, that look'd get me fidgeting. She glowed like she'd been shot full of estrogen, as if she had eggs begging for another shot. In the pause between one song and another, the first two guys sized up the third and kind of melted away and I knew it was up to me. I stepped in between them and said, Gramma, I gotta get you home now.

Gramma had to reach out and touch his arm before she followed me across the room. The fiddlers started playing another song and as she walked away from the music I felt my fingers move, remembering notes they'd never played. I shook it away. It was eerie.

Gramma said, He was such a good-looking man, don't you think?

I don't know, Gramma, I said. He's a bit old for me.

He gave me his number. Do you think I should text?

Gramma looked up at me. I swear to whatever fucking gods that are out there, swear to the ancestors and the spirits, that Gramma batted her eyes at me.

You're gorgeous as hell, Gramma, I said. Pretty sure he's gonna be waiting for your text.

MICHELLE PORTER

Gramma stuck her chin out and she flashed me a smile.

We had to stand at the doorway as a group of people came on in.

Maybe you could ask him to kill you, I said.

Gramma's face hardened that quick, all layers of sediments.

I shook my head in apology. Don't worry at all, I won't let no old guy do it, no matter how handsome he is. I'll kill you myself.

Gramma turned her face away to look around the room. Didn't you learn to respect your elders where you grew up?

Don't know why that stung more than anything had in a long while. Gramma made me nervous. Like she was toying with me before the final pounce. I felt like I could use a beer.

Outside we got a cab back to Gramma's place. I asked the cab driver to wait while I got Gramma inside to her apartment. She lived in a small one-bedroom in one of those new affordable rental units built for Métis seniors. I thought it was funny she lived here but didn't go to dances or things like that. But whatever. She lived on the ground floor and I walked with her down the hallway and waited while she unlocked the door and stepped in. She held the door open and turned back to me.

So, the pills now, she said.

I shook my head.

I got a bus to catch tomorrow, I said. I got to go get Tucker.

Who's Tucker?

He's my boy, Gramma.

You have a son?

Yeah. He's almost four.

You're only twenty-three.

Yep.

She shrugged, said, I was pretty young when I had mine, too. Better that way.

I don't know about that, I said.

Gramma waited in the doorway long enough for it to get awkward. She slipped off her shoes and put on the house slippers she'd left waiting by the front door. I could see her trying to figure out what would draw me in.

Who's the father?

My husband, I said. Better not to mention the separation, the coming divorce.

Does he have a name?

Slavko.

Where's that from?

Croatia.

Where?

Former Yugoslavia.

Oh, she said and she waved her hand. Fine, she said, go get your boy. Then get me them pills.

Don't you want to meet him before you die?

She narrowed her eyes, said, What'd I say about respecting your elders?

I gave up and started to turn away but then I stopped, thinking I might as well ask. I said, Why do you want to die anyway?

Gramma sagged against the door a little. Said, That your business?

I said, If I'm going to kill you, yes.

You're not going to kill me. I'm going to—

Kill yourself. Whatever. But why?

She dipped her chin and looked up at me in that way. How the fuck did she do that? I couldn't get over it.

She spoke so softly that I had to lean in, had to step closer to the door again to hear, ask her to repeat. It's my mom, Gramma said.

Oh, I said. I stepped back to create more space between us. Allie had never said anything about her grandmother.

She's getting so old, Gramma said, looking at the floor and fiddling with her keys so they jangled. Her face now was tired and so old. God, that woman had a thousand faces.

Gramma said, At her age my mom could pass any time. And I want to be there to meet her in heaven when she goes.

Did you ask her to kill you?

Gramma fiddled with her keys some more. No! I—

I'll go visit her with you. How about that?

No.

No?

I haven't seen her. Not in a long time. She drinks and—

You'd rather see her after you're dead than when you're alive. I get it.

Gramma's voice turned hard. No, it's not like that, she said and then she caught herself and made her voice soft and sad again. She said, It's just that I'm stuck here in the city and I hate cities. I want to be out on the land.

Where does she live? Your mom?

Gramma ignored that, said, My own grandma's on the other side. I miss her so much. I want to see her again, want to know if they finally got their land there. Said, My mooshum always said he was waiting for the land, that they'd been promised the land and he was still waiting for it. I was a little kid then and I used to tell him that I would wait for the land too, and that I'd build a nice warm log house on it.

Gramma stopped. She threw a laugh into the hallway behind me.

Look at me. No land. No log house, eh?

The cab driver honked. I jumped.

Gramma thought that was pretty funny.

Talk about the afterlife make you that nervous? Gramma asked. Maybe they're calling to you. You feel it too?

My phone buzzed just then. It was the cab driver asking if he should wait. Yes, I texted back. I dropped the phone back into my pocket and looked at Gramma to see her smiling in a way that seemed a little creepy to me somehow.

Gramma said, Child, I asked you to help me because you're outside it all. I know you don't want to hear that because you want to fit in and all that. But you aren't the way the rest are. You were raised outside us all.

I looked at her, blinking, stunned. My stomach lurched and I felt nauseous, thought I was going to throw up. This was what Mom was talking about. This was it.

And you should know I told your mom not to give you up, Gramma said. I told her it was a mistake. But she didn't want to keep you.

Gramma lifted one slippered foot and rubbed it against the other leg. She was deep in thought and her face had an expression I hadn't seen on anyone before. And I was thinking too, thinking that this was the reason Gramma had phoned me up. This was the switch after her bait, the bait I'd run after. But I wasn't Allie. I wouldn't roll over.

I said, The way I heard it, you kicked Allie out of the house when you married your last husband.

Gramma shook her head, said, I don't know who would say a thing like that.

I heard you were scared he might like your daughter more than you, that's what I heard.

Gramma tried to say something, but no words came out.

Look, I don't need anything from you. I only came here out of curiosity. That's it. I don't have to come back.

I turned and walked down the hallway. Gramma called out after me, actually said my name for the first time. Her voice was thick like she was trying not to cry.

Carter, I need those pills. Please.

I stopped, but I didn't look back at her. I said, After Tucker.

Please.

I promise.

My phone buzzed. I pulled it out and smiled. It was the fiddler I'd had my eye on.

I didn't look back. I turned the corner, crossed the rest of the hallway, pushed open the door, and got into the cab. My night had just filled up.

A grandmother finishes the story

By now the cold was punishing, the dark was thick as blood, and nothing but the stories to keep the calves warm. The snow was already too deep for them to move easily, and the storm had only just begun. Too early in the season for winds this strong but here we were. From my position near the center I gave the signal, it was time to move. The story would keep.

The edge of the circle opened to let me through. The calves were kicking in excitement because to them danger was a plaything. Everyone in the herd fell into line behind me and they followed the trail I made. I couldn't take them far because the calves couldn't cope. They don't have the dense coat or the thick layers of fat that we old ones have for protection. But I knew where to go. We were descendants of bison who walked themselves onto this land alongside winter over several generations. Our people had survived two million winters and I'd be damned if I was losing a single calf in that storm.

The wind blew clouds of snow that engulfed the herd. I couldn't see and I could barely smell, but I didn't need those senses. All I needed was instinct. Into the trees and down the knoll, ploughing the snow aside to make the path easier for the others. The snow at each side was taller than the youngest calf. I knew we'd been walking too long. The snow had changed the landscape so much that I couldn't tell how far away we were from the place I was leading us toward. Pounds of snow clung in balls to the fur on our backs and our capes. The wind shrieked. Very soon, the calves would need the herd's warmth again. They would need us all to circle around them again with our stories. A grandmother couldn't second-guess herself in a storm. Ever. So I didn't. I walked.

We are the ones who carry winter with us. With each step into the storm the calves were learning who we are, who they are. If they were afraid, they didn't say because the storm had made them silent followers. Then we were at the top of the knoll and then we went down and there was the small area of shelter, the break from the whipping wind. Almost immediately the circle was formed again and I was near the center with the calves. We could wait out the rest of the storm here.

Calves live their lives so quickly. They'd feel the cold and falter sooner than anybody else, but now at the center of us all they were knocking each other about again and already warmed up while the rest of us shuffled and stamped our feet, huffed and coughed. Already they were gathering near me and calling for the story.

Which story? I said, doing that same stretch onto my back haunches that I'd done earlier.

The little one shouted out, The one about the calves, the ones who save the world!

I grunted and chuckled. Holy bison, that stretch felt good. My neck was that tired after clearing all that snow, making way for the little ones. I took my time settling my body, letting the warmth reach my jaw, my tail, and my hooves. Then I picked up where I'd left off.

I said, Those calves were something else, you know? They wandered for days between life and death. They walked among the bodies of their dead relatives preparing to die, walked on land that still called on them to live.

As night set in, there were no elders to calm them, to tell the stories of their lives, to offer the safety that only comes with being with your people.

Instead of lying down and dying alongside their mothers and fathers and aunties and uncles, which they could have done, the calves kept on walking. As they walked they called out into the darkness.

In most of the places no one heard them. Not one living being. There had been so much death everywhere that everything alive was in shock or in hiding or had left. Except in one place.

In that place, there was a human woman who heard and who listened.

She must have been a mother herself.

I say she must have been a mother herself because she felt a swell of compassion for these babies who were wandering alone, unable to find a place to rest, stumbling over the dead.

A pale human in a dress to her ankles, they say.

They say she listened all night long. They say that the next morning she asked others to help her go out onto the prairie and find the calves she'd heard the night before, any who might still be alive. And because the calves' cries reached her, she would go on to gather two dozen of them together on a piece of land and use fences to protect them from the death that was everywhere. She would care for them and she would help them live. These are the calves who would create the next generation of people. They wouldn't live as their ancestors had, but they would find the new trails they had to walk, the ones we're walking now.

So you see how it was. Those calves were not afraid to call out in the darkness of night and death and to ask for what they wanted.

And it was a mother of another species who listened to their cries.

A mother who was moved by a compassion she hadn't felt before.

It only takes one.

We know what the old storytellers tell us. That one day the great-great-grandchildren of these calves will become strong enough to fill the land again.

When the prairie itself is dying out, the calves of the calves of the calves will return to heal the land and bring the grasslands back to life. It'll happen.

The calves weren't afraid to let their grief lead.

We've been following the cry of our young ones ever since.

Our creation story begins with the cry of the young and we follow that cry.

We'll follow those cries across the land and into the next world, too.

The blizzard was closing in. And now it was someone else's turn to tell a story. I was cold. I was old and cold.

Gramma, asking Carter

Way too early for my phone to be buzzing.

Why didn't I turn it off last night?

Fuck.

I reached out and groped the side table where I usually left it. That was when I realized why everything felt off.

I opened my eyes, blinking in the morning light. The guy beside me shifted onto his back, threw his right arm above his head. His chest rose and fell. It was a nice chest. Nice rest of him, too, best I could remember from last night. I wanted to reach under the sheets to touch him, start everything over again, but my phone buzzed again and I knew I should get dressed and get out of there before he woke.

Out of bed and on my feet.

I was wearing my underwear. I must have started to get dressed last night. I must have meant to leave.

I began to remember how he'd convinced me to stay, his arms and his stories.

He'd told me his grandmother's stories, rocked me in them until I'd fallen asleep.

The stories began to come back to me. A woman in the sky. A bison. A white calf.

The buzzing. Where was my phone?

It was under my shirt. I picked up the shirt and put it on. Then I picked up my phone.

It was Gramma.

I dropped the phone.

Where were my pants? I wanted to be wearing pants when I read those texts.

The phone kept buzzing and I started to panic. I think I was having a full-blown anxiety attack.

There were my pants. I stumbled into them, grabbed my phone, and headed to the front door for my shoes. Shoes on. My feet were in my shoes and I had my bag over my shoulder.

The phone, the texts.

The texts.

The guy from last night—what was his name?—he was somehow in front of me now. He was naked and everything was hanging out and he was asking what's wrong, asking was I okay. A hand on my arm.

Nothing, I said. It's nothing.

Who's texting?

My gramma.

He laughed. Course it is, he said. When he laughed his penis jiggled against his testicles. It made me smile and my guard slipped a little.

She wants to die.

Okay.

Actually she wants me to help her die.

He puckered his lips as if to point, except there was nowhere to point. Shiiiit, he said, drawing out the word like he was in agony.

My phone buzzed again. He stepped behind me so that he was between me and the door. He slid a hand beneath mine so his palm was cupping the back of the hand holding my phone. With his other hand he moved my thumb from the screen so he could read.

Shit, he said again. He leaned in against me then, hard, so I had something to push against. I could feel his penis and thigh against my ass and hip, his chest against my back. I pressed back against him, using all my angry strength, and together we fell back against the door that was behind him.

Leaning on the door, he hugged me against his chest and lowered his chin to the top of my head. Asked quietly, Who was it in your family? That went to one of those schools?

Velma looks down and there is Geneviève

Velma's in her dressing room pulling out curlers and yes she can hear Geneviève but she has a show to prepare for and she is not going to come running the minute her sister calls; there is so much to do in the spirit world. Geneviève will only want to talk and she doesn't have time for that. She doesn't know why the hell she keeps hearing her sister playing that bloody piano and she doesn't know why her sister is playing so badly. It hurt to listen to it. There is no such thing as playing badly where she is.

Velma's come a long way since she moved into the afterlife. She is backstage now, fixing her makeup and curling her dark hair. With her long forehead and straight hair, it isn't easy getting it to curl just right. In life, she'd had to get curlers in her hair the night before and wear them all day, even while practicing and on her way to the venue. A fashionable headscarf helped with that. The headscarf looked good on her and she looked good with hair that puffed up above her head a bit because of the high forehead and the way her eyes were set in her face, and that kind of a hairdo took time and didn't stand up a minute to rain, and it was always raining in Mission, B.C.

She could fill a room back then, men and women would crowd a place to hear her play, to watch her perform. It took her a while to figure the spirit world out, but now they know her name up here and they come in droves just to see the way she holds the violin on her collarbone and the way she teases a song out, the one they've been waiting to hear without really knowing it was what they needed. That is all she wants. She knows her papa, Bob, is in the spirit world somewhere and she could see him whenever she wants, but right now the audience is all she wants. Audiences don't want to talk about things that happened.

And she is aware, too, that Mamé Élise is still in between, is taking a while to arrive, that it's a whole journey for her to get here. She isn't in a rush to see her mama just yet, to be peppered with personal questions and be expected to listen to her stories.

She's done with her hair, and even though up here the makeup isn't needed—her skin has never been more glowing and her eyes don't look any better with it than without—it was part of her routine down there so she does it here too. It comforts her, makes her think of her sister who'd always teased her for fussing. Velma had never been beautiful enough, and when she lost weight she lost her bust, and when she gained a bust her hips strained against her best dresses, and her husband always wanted her to make her skin look paler and she always refused. She was dark eyed and dark skinned and those who didn't like it could look away. And up here nothing has changed, really, but she is beautiful just the way she is, turning heads like her sister had in their youth down in that place they called Canada in the province of British Columbia, in the little piece of woods they came out of. Oh, people loved to come see her play down there, but she wasn't the family beauty and her sister always let her know.

Well, her sister isn't much of a beauty now. Not down there on earth, an old woman who can't stop the drinking. Velma can't see why she wanted to stop anyway. Drinking had never been a problem for Velma. She could keep up with most of the men she knew. Until she met her husband. She stops herself right there. She isn't going to think about that. She hasn't thought about her husband since she passed on. Something told her to just get on with her playing and enjoy the good life, that there's nothing she wants to see down that path.

Her first day in the afterlife wasn't easy, but overall, she thinks it went well.

When she opened her eyes the first time in the spirit world, her fingers weren't crooked and the bandages were gone. She noticed that first thing. She was lying on the ground in some tall prairie grass. It was summer, even though it had been winter moments before, down where she'd come from, and it took her a while to learn that the seasons would come and go in the afterlife just like before but that she could learn to kind of shift the changes sometimes and anyway up here winter never made her uncomfortable. Still, she liked to shift the season to summer and liked to hold her hands out in front of her marveling at her straight fingers, without the memory of their having been broken. She remembered her papa's music and for this reason she could still make her songs because it seemed like so many of the songs she was making down on earth came from the stories told in the ache in her fingers, and now that the ache was gone, where would her songs come from? She could have left her songs on earth, with her body and her pain and her son and her daughter and everything else she'd left behind and never thought of anymore, not up here.

The ache was gone. That was important. After the absence of the ache in her fingers, she had to see: is there a piano in this place and can I get to it? I mean, what are the rules here? She didn't know if they'd let her play or if that was for angels.

All this and she was still lying there in that prairie grass. She sat up and suddenly there was a tree behind her, supporting her. This made her look around a bit. Was she in the place with angels? How would that work? If she was with the angels she might not be able to get a piano to play. On earth the nuns disapproved of her playing, with her father, with her mother, any of their family music. And the fiddle—wait, would there be a fiddle here?

Probably a fiddle wouldn't be part of her afterlife, not unless she was going to the bad place and she didn't really care which way she went, but she didn't think of the bad place as grass and trees, and that was part of the reason she wanted so much to hang on to life down below. Because she had to leave her fiddle behind and the fiddle, the nuns told her over and over again when they caught her trying to tap out her father's tunes on some violin she'd managed to get her hands on, was the devil's instrument. They wouldn't have minded so much if she'd only played the songs they wanted to teach, but, well, in the hands of a defiant Métis girl the songs all came out crooked anyway and that was the right way, the way her papa played and his papa and his uncle and his brothers. All the men in her family played like that. Even as a skin-and-bones child she'd played crooked and she wouldn't play any other way.

She was going to play hard and fast and so crooked they'd all come to see her and her papa and she'd never have to go to the school again and her parents would never have to go away to the logging camps to work. They could all stay together, a family. And it worked, sort of—the music kept them together, for a while. But it was better not to think about that. Better to see if there was a goddamn fiddle in this place, wherever it was.

Velma pulls the last curler out and winces. Gen's missed notes and sloppy playing are like burrs in the waist of Velma's dress. Okay, she says. You have my attention.

Gen's mistakes are the reason Velma leans away from her dressing room in the spirit world to get a look at what's going on, and when she sees Gen she rolls her eyes and gives in. She steps over the chasm and ends up standing by the piano, just behind her sister's shoulder.

The grassland witnesses the beginning of a snowstorm

It was the beginning of a winter snowstorm in the middle of the telling of a story and I could feel the nervous shift of Dee's hooves and I knew she was going to run from the herd. I knew, too, how the elders watched her closely—but not close enough. I knew what they would do when the time came. I was connected to each and every one of them. After all, their ancestors had made me, their bones and their blood. Still, I rushed ahead with Dee and I returned all the time to her because I was like her once. I saw myself in her. That was some time ago, but I remembered.

She hadn't come to talk with me in a while. I'd heard the rumor that had moved from one cow to another that Jay had left the herd to search for that land he believed in.

The grandmothers huddled for warmth, eyes closed against the swirling snow, spinning a story to match the moan of the wind. Their attention was offered to the calves at the center and Dee let herself slip closer to the outside of the circle with each shift of positions. It took some time but eventually she found herself on the edge. I reached up into her hooves to speak my bit. She kicked me off, or she thought she did. It didn't matter because I was with her wherever she went. I was with her when she left the circle and broke her own trail in the snow.

This isn't right, I said when she stumbled in a drift.

She lay there, panting. It's for my baby's future, she said.

The herd is your baby's future.

My baby deserves to know his father.

Dee got up and moved on.

Afterlife, where Mamé's feet still ache

It's still dark here so I have to trust the smell of a prairie summer to lead me farther from the gates, until I am surrounded by grass, until tendrils brush against my fingertips, until my feet begin to ache and I marvel that there is pain even here.

I find a place to sit beside the path to rest my heels and arches. As I am groping about, the long grass seems to lie flat to make room for me.

And right there on that soft earth seat I can't help myself, I start to think about going back to that other heaven and to Maman. Can such a thing as regret follow me even here?

I push those thoughts away and I lie back and listen to the wind in the grass all around me. That's something.

I hear a rustle behind me. I sit up, afraid. I look and see nothing.

I think, Is there fear in this place too? The teachings I'd heard didn't speak of it. Or maybe I had not understood how to listen in the proper way.

The rustle comes again. I shiver.

How fear takes hold is different for everyone. For me the habit of trembling hands returns.

I get to my feet. There are shades of gray creeping in from the horizon in the distance.

And above the waving ocean of grass, I see the silhouettes of nearly a dozen backs and humps.

I become still. I whisper, There are bison here.

My throat closes up. I cannot stop the tears then.

I think, How are there tears even here?

I hear the call of a bird, a whippoorwill, and the fear and pain I'd been carrying begin to drain away. The bird lands on my shoulder, still singing. How many times have I been told that the night belongs to the whippoorwill? I know that I no longer have to tie myself to those old feelings, that they are no longer necessary. When the crying packs itself up and goes away, I lie down again and the last thing I remember thinking is Even here there is sleep.

The grassland sees the weakness in the fence

I was there beneath Dee when she found the weakness in the fence and there when she entered the forest. She walked the whole night and the rest of the day without stopping to eat or drink, without a care for the wind or the storm.

And I was there that evening when she found Jay in a small clearing with a group of young bulls and two heifer calves. Dee's hooves cut so deep into the fungus of me that she couldn't end the connection between us, couldn't stop telling what she needed. Dee wanted to burn then and so did I. She told herself she could still turn around, still walk away. But she couldn't help herself; she called his name.

He looked up and when he saw her he laughed, and it was like snow falling from the branches of all the trees in the quiet after a snowfall. He walked right up close to her. She fell into his dark eyes, his musky scent. It's so good to see you, he said. He pressed his forehead to hers and her heart skittered and skipped. It was exactly what she'd imagined. In that moment, she returned to herself. She was happy again. She could breathe.

He took a step back and looked her over. Look at you, he said. You're so big. Then he grunted his approval of her, of everything he saw and smelled. It was a deep gravelly sound.

Then he asked, But what are you doing here?

Dee couldn't speak. She stepped close to him again and nuzzled his thick cape, breathing in that scent she'd been dreaming of. He laughed again.

He nudged her gently. Go back to the grandmothers, beautiful one. He turned back and said something to the two heifers that Dee didn't catch.

Go back home, Jay repeated.

He said, It's time for the grandmothers to care for you now. You'll need them soon, by the looks of you. Goodbye, Dee.

And then Jay said to the others, It's time to move on.

I caught her when she fell. Night turned to morning and morning to day and the cold crept into her bones and another night made her stiff and numb, as if she were already a corpse. I tried to warm her, but the snow started again and there was only so much I could do. Let the hunter come, let the rifle shoot from the helicopter, let the pack of wolves leap, there was nothing I could do. A layer of snow covered her like a shroud and in the early hours of the next morning her shivering stopped.

Geneviève asks about rehab in the spirit world

Geneviève switched on the standing lamp nearest the piano in the blue room. Shadows stretched across the floor and rose up the walls. The rain had kept on all day and now, deep into another night, it was only coming down harder.

Gen sat herself down on the bench. Her reflection floated in the bay window next to the piano. There was her tired face and there was her nightgown, but everything was faded at the edges. It was almost as if she and the baby grand were haunting the old building. Except she couldn't be a ghost because she was sweating so much her nightgown stuck to her back and stuck to her legs, stuck everywhere. That little nurse had talked with her about withdrawal and she'd told Gen how to calm her nervous system by slowing down her breathing, softening her eyes, and shifting her focus with a set of hand movements. It was all fine, but all Gen wanted was to come down to see the baby grand.

She was dying for a drink but instead she coaxed a slow tune out of the old girl. She hardly pushed on the keys, barely making any sound at all because she didn't want to wake anyone who was able to sleep. She missed notes and fumbled.

What the hell are you doing?

The song fell apart in her hands. She looked up and saw her big sister as a reflection in the window.

Velma, she whispered.

The dress her sister wore, oh God, it was something, long and deep red and beaded with Métis flowers and it swirled around her feet. A fiddle in one hand and right next to her was a burst of blinding light that Gen could barely look at. And then there was the smell of her sister's perfume and of hair burned in a curling iron and her face looked just like it had when they were young together.

Gen swallowed hard. She sniffed. She said, What, there's no rehab over there in the spirit world so you got to come here?

That's a welcome, said Velma.

How many decades you been gone? And this is the first time you come see me?

You need help with your playing.

With my playing? I need help with—

Can't let you ruin the family name, Velma said. She lifted the fiddle to her clavicle and said, Here's the note you need. She drew her bow across the strings.

The note unbent Gen's spine and helped her fingers find their way.

It was always my mistakes that caught your attention, Gen said.

She looked away from her sister's face and into her own reflection to find she was as young as she'd been when Velma was alive. Gen didn't breathe for a moment. She didn't want to stop seeing herself the way she'd been all those years ago, but she could feel Velma's glare, the one that said, Stop fooling around and play the bloody music. Gen didn't dare to turn and look behind her. She was afraid she might see nothing at all.

I could hear you butchering that song all the way into the spirit world, said Velma. And that was so much like the sister Gen knew that she played a few notes, let her fingers remember what they needed on their own and Velma nodded, said, That's right, that's right, and now this. Velma played a couple phrases of another song and Geneviève felt all the tension drain from her shoulders, and the part of her hip nearest the light that glowed near her sister stopped hurting.

Play those lines again, Gen said.

But Velma had turned to look back into the circle of light. Geneviève could hear chairs scraping across a plank floor in an old dance hall, the tuning of a fiddle, and the chatter of an audience before a performance. It was just like when they were kids, the smell of smoke and the slosh of the drink and the clink of the glasses and the murmur of a waiting crowd. Don't go, she said.

I've got a show in ten, Velma said, lifting the skirt of her dress to her knees so she could step easily. She turned and started to climb back into that circle of light. In the window Gen was a crooked old lady again.

Geneviève called out, You're still playing gigs? Why didn't you tell me that before?

I'd have told you if you asked.

Velma had almost disappeared into the light, but Gen kept on. Smells like a bar. Do they have the drink in the next world?

Velma looked back at her and laughed. They've got something better—I promise you.

Is Mama there?

No. She's taking her time coming over.

Is Papa there?

I haven't asked him to come so he doesn't come.

If I was there, I'd ask him.

Velma shrugged, said, Plenty of time for family reunions, no need to rush.

Gen swallowed hard, said, Can I come with you tonight?

A playful whistle rose from out of the light and the sound of laughter followed right after. Velma looked into the light, said, The way you are right now, you know you'd only waste the afterlife same way you did your life.

I don't want to do this thing anymore. It's too hard.

I got a show to do. Wait up for me, will you?

Velma moved fully into the light and then the light faded away.

Geneviève sat still for a long time. Her hip ached even worse than it did before. It took a long time to stand up and move from the piano to a red easy chair in the middle of the room. She sat on the thick cushions and watched the shadows play against the wall opposite the curve of the window and the piano. She could pick out the music in the rhythm of the heavy downpour. Her whole body was shaking now, and she thought she should go upstairs to her room for her medication, but she didn't get up, couldn't leave the piano and the window.

She finally fell asleep in the chair and dreamed of her sister and her papa, but then the shaking in her own limbs pulled her awake and she sat up suddenly, afraid and searching the room for light.

Mamé, where the bison roam

A good long sleep in that grass and I wake to find a calf napping, its head and shoulders draped over my body, almost crushing my ribs. Doesn't matter because here no one needs a rib anyway. The calf smells so much like a baby and so much like life that I just lie there taking in the scent for a bit.

The sky is gray now, and yellow and orange are just showing as streaks, leaking in from where I can't tell. I breathe in and am shocked that I can smell the colors as they come into the sky and each one has a different scent, a bit fruity maybe or floral. The grass above me waves in so many shades of green where before everything had been gray and black. The calf's back stretches across me, giving off the new smell of red-brown, and beside us both lies an awesome bison mother. I want to reach out to touch the texture of her beard or the cold wet of her nose, but all mothers need their sleep. I want to get back onto my feet to see and smell all the color as it fills in the spirit world. I push against the calf's back until the gangly baby begins to stir and stretch. I wait for the calf to wake and to stand. That doesn't take long, it being new to itself and curious.

The grandmothers go looking

Solin asked the others if Dee was alive.

The oldest of the three grandmothers who'd left the circle to search for Dee, Solin wasn't in the mood to pretty things up. She hadn't hesitated when the cry went up, Dee is gone, Dee is gone. Two others went out with her, and they'd walked into the storm together.

Hours of frigid bluster, thick snow, and tearing winds were still to come.

Dee's trail was nearly impossible to follow.

The air was crisp and crackling. The land spread out blinding white all the way to the horizon. They pressed on. Their search led to a nearly concealed rise in the snow that they would have passed on by without noticing had there not been a black-and-white magpie causing a ruckus, squawking and swooping low over their heads, crying, Follow me! The bird landed in the snow a ways off. Solin sighed and turned. Slowly, she broke a path in the snow toward the bird. The sleek little bundle of feathers hopped about impatiently and beneath its claws Solin saw bison fur. Could that be Dee?

Oh, and it was Dee—their search was over.

The magpie lifted up into the air and flew off.

Using their heads and beards, the grandmothers moved the snow off Dee's body. The young bison lay there unmoving and exposed. Solin stooped down and lay against Dee's chest and belly and—yes, yes!—there was a hint of warmth left. And then the other two lay over Dee as well, lending their body heat until Dee twitched and began to shiver.

Get her onto her feet now, the grandmothers said as one.

Leave me alone, Dee said.

The elders got into position.

He doesn't love me, Dee said, but she let herself be pushed to her feet.

He loved you when it was time to love you, the grandmothers said.

Solin said, It's time for you to love another into being.

They stepped back to give Dee room to move, but her legs collapsed beneath her and then she was down in the snow again.

My hooves hurt, she moaned.

The trio of grandmothers gathered around Dee again.

He's with another cow, Dee said.

The grandmothers nudged her up again, as if she were a calf.

Dee cursed and said, A calf actually, he's with a calf. No, two calves.

The three grandmothers made noises of disapproval but all they said was No bull is worth dying for. They said, You've got to use hope responsibly. They said, Have you been listening to our stories?

And they talked like this for a while, told her about the life she carried and the life she was going to bring into the world. You have work to do, the grandmothers said. For your calf, for yourself, and for your People.

Dee didn't have the strength to resist the grandmothers anymore. She let herself be persuaded to her feet. The grandmothers conferred. Solin stayed with Dee and walked her back to life.

And, as winter was leaving the land, it was Solin who walked Dee to a small stand of trees at the end of the pastures, and it was Solin who was there when Dee bellowed for her mother, when her body opened up so she could let life tumble through, when Tell fell to the half-frozen earth. Dee turned to look.

The bit of snow and grass and soil there was staggering under the weight of nearly fifty pounds of hope and for the first time since she'd been with Jay she thought that maybe it was all going to be okay. She reached over to lick her slimy boy and she thought that the end of this story might be beautiful after all. Dee didn't know that the story wasn't over. She couldn't tell where one story ended and another began, not when she was right there in the middle of it all.

Carter, saying yes

The texts, one after another: Carter this is your responsibility, Carter keep your promise.

Carter was back at her crow's nest by then, getting things ready for a trip, filling a backpack. Her hands were shaking, had been since she left the fiddler's place. She didn't know the answer to his last question, couldn't bring herself to think about it.

The texts kept coming in and Carter tossed the phone onto her bed.

Shut up, old lady.

But she couldn't help it; she walked around the bed and stood over the phone, reading the texts. Carter I can't wait. Carter I thought you could do this. Carter it's time now. Don't ignore me. Respect your elders.

What a mindfuck she was. Anyway, there was time for a quick shower. Carter stepped out of her pants. She pulled her shirt over her head.

Death is a natural stage of life, Carter thought. Birth, life, death. It's the order of things. All her time at the hospice showed her what fear of death could do.

Gramma wasn't afraid.

Or maybe Gramma was afraid. Was that what this was about?

Who was this old woman? What kind of person asks her granddaughter to kill her?

Carter turned around to look at her face in the little round magnifying mirror standing on the dresser. What kind of person thinks about killing her grandmother?

Carter picked up the phone. She stared at the words on the screen for a few seconds before walking out of her bedroom and into the bathroom across the hallway. The crow was in the window, looking at her. She pulled the blind between the two of them. She turned on the hot water and turned the handle to start the shower. She closed the toilet bowl lid and left her phone there. The texts kept coming in.

The shower stall was so small there was barely enough room to turn around. Steam began to rise and Carter stood under the water until her bra and underwear were wet and then she lathered her body with the thin remains of a bar of soap. She unhooked her bra and slid her underwear from her ankles and let them rinse out beneath the shower stream. She wrung them out and hung them on the towel rack just outside the stall. They dripped.

Her hair next. Lather, rinse. Her phone rang.

She didn't have to look to know who it was.

She leaned against the back of the stall, eyes closed. She wanted to ignore this call.

What tied her to this old woman?

After a few moments she opened the door, dried her hand on the sweaty T-shirt hanging on the rack, and reached for the phone on the toilet. She was half in the shower and half out when she tapped answer and said, Gramma, what do you want?

Respect, said Gramma.

You got it.

What's that I hear? Are you in the shower?

Yes, Gramma.

Get dressed. I don't talk to naked people on the phone.

Look, Gramma.

Are you going to get me the pills?

I been thinking. Why did you choose me?

Choose you for what?

To kill you.

You're mixed up, girl. You're not killing me.

As good as.

You're just a supplier. Nothing more.

Why me?

Gramma let out an impatient sigh.

God, Carter. Really? Is this all you think about? This is all about you, now?

It kind of is, isn't it?

No, Carter. It's about me. You don't matter.

I can hang up if you—

You really want to know why? Because you're not part of the family. You don't really care, do you?

Carter wanted to sit down, but she was wet and naked and still in the shower. She said, Is that what you think?

Your stories aren't part of ours. If you do this for me, your story will be part of ours.

This is revenge, isn't it?

You can be part of us if you want.

Revenge on my mother.

I don't know the woman who adopted you, Carter.

My birth mom. Your daughter. For giving me up.

Why would I care—

Making you look like a fool. Because whose daughter gives a baby up, right?

So self-centered. This isn't about you.

I see you. I know you.

I'm done with life. That's it. Don't think this makes you special.

You know what—I'll make a call. My husband will get it to you. Tomorrow. That quick enough?

No. He's white. He's not one of us.

So what? Anyway, where he's from they don't think he's white enough.

Doesn't matter. I'm not taking this off of the hands of a guy from Europe.

You want me to get brown hands to deliver this to you?

I want it from your hands.

What the fuck?

Respect for your elders.

Why me? You never even met me before all this kill-me shit.

I did.

Fuck off.

In my dreams. I've seen you every night since Allan sent you away. Every night.

Sent me away? She wanted to give me a home.

Your hands.

Did you hear what I said?

I want those pills from your hands.

You know what? I'm on my way.

That's my girl.

You're fucked up, that's what you are.

I took you to a dance. Now we're good.

Why are you in such a rush to die?

Look, Carter. Listen. I have cancer, okay. Didn't want to tell you because I didn't want to be a burden. But if you're going to be so difficult about everything—

Carter turned the water off, closed her eyes. What kind?

Don't know where it started; it's all over now.

Carter pushed the stall door further open. She hadn't brought a towel into the bathroom. Her grandmother was saying something, but she cut her off and ended the call. She left the bathroom. Where had she put the towel?

Geneviève looks into the fire

The rain kept on, steady as a train, and Gen held on until the night began to think about morning, until Velma clambered back through that light.

She said, I knew you'd wait up, you always did.

The nurse's advice about withdrawal had been haunting Gen as much as her damned body's need for a drink. Don't be afraid if you experience hallucinations, the nurse had said to Gen. They're temporary.

Gen brought herself to her feet again and found herself swaying between belief and doubt, but she said, Let me close the doors so we don't wake them up with our playing.

Velma put her fiddle on her clavicle, lifted her bow, and waited. Velma's hair was falling over her shoulders. At her armpits the dress had turned a darker red because she'd just been playing and she always played with her whole self, every muscle in her body making the music. Gen sat at the bench.

I've been waiting to play with you since you left for the spirit world, you bloody no-good bastard, Gen said.

Velma held the bow over the strings. It's only intermission and I'll have to get back on stage over there pretty quick so don't mess up my entrance by talking shit to me.

Gen pointed at the fiddle with her chin. Looks like grandpa's, the one his own papa gave him, the one with all the stories.

Velma nodded. The very one.

But Papa's sister burned it. That's what they said.

Yes, and how nice of her to send it up here in smoke. It was waiting for me. You want to know how it was when I got my hands on it?

She tried to burn anything that told who we were.

As if anybody could do that. But listen to you—you've got to go on and on about a thing even after it's dead, don't you? I forgot that about you. Oh wait—hold on a second, the audience over there needs me a bit.

Velma went back into the light, but she left it open somehow and this time Geneviève could see in just a little bit, like she was watching from backstage. There was Velma's back and there was an audience in a room packed with people at tables, all their faces turned to Velma. The microphone amplified Velma's deep voice so Gen could hear it well from where she was, sitting at a piano in a rehab center in Southern Alberta.

Velma began with a story. Gen remembered how Velma had started telling stories to her audience when she was first working on her solo performances, after they'd moved to British Columbia. She used to say it was hard to tell if they came more for her stories or her music. Every spirit in that audience on the other side of the light leaned forward just a bit and at the end of the story Velma stepped back and let out a laugh. This one is for my sister, Velma said then, and she lifted the fiddle to her shoulder. Geneviève recognized the tune and her fingers found their place on the piano. She knew nobody in that audience could hear her playing, but she accompanied her sister anyway and for that one song it was like it used to be. Felt like the song went on for as many hours and days as it needed but it couldn't have been that long on earth, where she was, because the first light was only just coming on. That little hint of day was enough to wash out Velma's reflection so that when one of the staff opened the door Velma had vanished and Gen was alone.

Have you been here all night?

Gen pushed the bench back and stood up with ease. But as she walked away from the piano, she turned back into a slow-moving arthritic old woman suffering from withdrawal. Let's get you to your bed, the woman said. You're shaking something awful.

Afterlife, where Mamé moves along

Bright colors smell the strongest in this place.

My skirt sends off such a scent that when I sit up I bring the hem to my nose. Four silky ribbons have been sewn into the bottom panel.

One day I'll tell a story that tries to describe the way those colors smell.

But not today.

Anyway, I'm not smelling my skirt for long because the calf is up and bothering her mom, nudging her awake.

I stand up and there I am surrounded by bison as far as I can see.

During my life, I'd never been close to even one buffalo.

Some lie in the grass, asleep. Some stand and watch, and some reach for something to eat.

That old habit of fear returns to me when I find I can understand what the bison are saying. It's hard to let the things of the earth stay with the earth.

Mama, mama, the calf is saying, nudging the big bison. The big cow stirs and groans and says, Go play, daughter.

I can't tell if these bison are alive. They don't feel dead, like I know I am.

The calf looks at me and kicks in excitement, says, Mama, she's awake, the human.

The old mother bison finally lifts her great head and turns to look at me. Good, she says. Her voice is deep as the darkness that is receding, silty as the soil that holds the grass, and calming as the smell of the blue ribbon on my skirt. She says, Now we can move along.

Dee answers questions

Dee's calf jumped up from the snow right quick after she birthed him, and oh yes, the sight of him, the smell of him, filled her up.

You're a root, she said to Tell on his first night.

What kind of root?
Why am I a root?
Aren't I a bison?
Where's my father?

Tell was the root holding Dee in place. Somehow he carried her mother with him and Dee didn't know how this could be, his back was so small and the past was so large. With him, she was flooded with memories of Roam, of her warm beard and fuzzy cape, a firm tongue, of those first months of milk, and the rise and fall of the canyons her mother loved so much.

Dee said to Tell, You bring my mother back to me—except my mother didn't like to talk, not like you.

Is your mother my grandmother?
Why was she named Roam?
Why isn't she here? Was she big like you?
Can we go live in the canyons with her?
Why not?
I think I smell Father.
Is he here now?
Where was he before? Can I go see him?
Don't you like canyons?

Dee said, My baby, you are a root holding Roam in place. Dee told Tell all the stories her mother had told her and all the stories the grandmothers said she needed to pass on because she wanted her son to remember her voice even after she was gone. It was good—it was good until the day Jay walked back to the herd, full of wild stories.

Mama, have you heard what Father says?
There's a land beyond the fences.
He says there are bison who roam free.
He says bulls there live different than we do.
Is it true? Mama?
Can I go see Father?

Dee said, You carry your father's scent to me. Tell was a root but the soil was rocky, and though he was big and strong already, he didn't weigh enough to hold Dee together.

Mama, the rutting started.
Can I go watch?
Mama, why aren't you rutting?
Why did the aunties tell you to wait?
Father's not waiting.
Father's fighting another bull!
Mama, can I go watch him?

Dee said, Because you need so much milk right now.
Dee said, My baby, I'll join the rut next year—there's lots of time.
She didn't say, The aunties tell me I crave him too much.
Dee nursed Tell as the other cows gossiped about Jay's stories of the land beyond their fences. Jay said there was land that went

on and on over the horizon, the land their ancestors had walked. He said there were bison who roamed free; he said they needed to go there.

Dee only needed Jay to love her the way he had before.

Her craving for him cleared the soil of her, made her ready. And still the aunties said she had to wait for the next mating season. They said to wait, take your time, take care of yourself, take care of your calf.

Mama, why don't you eat?
Mama, they're saying you're sick.
Mama, can I bring you some grass?
Do you know what Father showed me?
How to spot a fence's weakness.
And how to knock them down.
Mama, eat some grass.

Jay came to see Dee once after a spring storm. Snow was melting on his hump and clinging to his beard. He pressed his forehead to hers. He said, You are. Then he said the same two words again. That was it.

She was going to ask what the hell he meant, but she couldn't say a word. His closeness took her words from her. He left then. Stupid me, she thought.

His scent lingered on her fur. She could go anywhere in the pasture and there was the smell of him, on the breeze, in the wallow, on the fence post where he'd rubbed an itch. She waited for him to come back to her. She was sure he would.

Mama, guess what?
Father lets me charge him.
And he says I'm just like a big bull.

He says I'll grow bigger than him.

Bigger than you, even.

The elder cows wouldn't let Jay near the two heifer calves he'd been with out in the woods. They'd matured, but both hovered close to the grandmothers and their stories. You haven't had the teachings, the grandmothers said to Jay. Look what's happened to Dee, they said. When he tried to charge his way past the grandmothers to get at the young cows, the aunties created a circle, blocking him. Dee isn't my fault, he said. No, Dee isn't your fault but it shows you haven't had the teachings, they said. There's a bull who offers the teachings—go find him, the grandmothers said.

Jay found other willing partners for the rut but he resented the two young cows, how canny and selective they'd become. They said they wanted bulls who understood their place in the herd. Not Jay.

Anyway, Jay wasn't planning to stick around. He wanted to change everything. He'd been on his own since his mother had been taken away from the place he'd been born. And then a number of winters ago he'd been corralled, put in a truck, and dumped off here, where he knew no one.

Jay had heard stories about other herds, about a People without fences. He was planning to go in search of them. One day soon he would go.

Mama, Father sent me on an errand.

Asked me to get two cows to come to him.

They wouldn't.

But Father said I'm a big help.

Mama, let me get you some grass.

Mama, you aren't as big as you used to be.

Mama, are you sick? Are you?

Carter seals a baggie

The pills were in a sealed baggie. There were enough for Gramma to take one a day for a few months, at least. They were small, thick, and round. They were white.

Gramma opened the door. Carter handed her the bag with her left hand. Gramma covered Carter's offering hand with both her own and then took the bag. She said, Come in for tea. Carter said, No, I got a bus to catch.

Gramma stepped forward and pulled Carter close by her arm. She leaned in for a hug and Carter didn't know what to do with her hands and her arms. Gramma was so small that Carter was afraid she'd break a bone, hurt her in some way, and she thought how stupid that was considering the bag of pills she'd just handed over.

You're a good girl, Gramma said.

Carter was already backing away, down the hallway.

How many do I need to take? she asked. There's so many.

It's not how many, Gramma, Carter said, stopping about ten feet away. It's which ones.

Gramma looked at Carter, sharp and frowning.

I know you like to play games, Gramma. How about Russian roulette?

Gramma was a knowing old bird of prey and Carter was a young rodent. Gramma's beak was fierce and Carter's flesh was wobbly.

There's some of what you want in that bag, Carter said. She hated herself for the squeak in her voice. She added, Maybe it's enough . . .

What do you mean?

The rest of them are aspirin and sugar candy.

Child.

I used a nail file. Rubbed them all clean of markings and shit.

Don't swear around me, child. Did you keep your word to me?

Sure did, Gramma.

What's in this bag?

But you gotta do some of your own work for it too. Traditional, isn't it?

Respect, Gramma almost hissed. I told you—

You'll figure it out. If you really want to.

I know what I want. Unlike you. You can't figure out a damn thing, can you? Look at you, only thing you're good at is running.

I have confidence in you.

Carter turned and slipped around the corner and down the hallway toward the exit. Gramma let loose with a string of obscenities and then slammed the door so hard the walls shook. Carter heard the call of a bird on the hunt and everything went still. For a moment she was sure talons were coming to rip her apart. Once she got outside, Carter had to sit on the steps because she was laughing so much. She laughed until there were tears running down her cheeks.

Geneviève makes a sign

Gen taped a sign on her door.

In black marker, the sign read *Tarot Readings: Drop In Anytime.* She wrote it in quick loops on the back of a list of rules for living at the center, rules that told how early to turn out lights, how often they had to go to group, things that Gen doesn't pay more attention to than she has to.

That sign was an item of discussion at the next staff meeting.

At the meeting, the program director said, This is unusual. There was a long silence until the case manager said that some of the other patients were enjoying it. What he didn't say was that Gen had put the cards in his hand and told him to think about his partner, that he'd let her do a reading because his relationship was falling apart and he didn't know what to do. He'd ended up with his head in her lap, wiping his tears on her skirt, and when he got home that night he thought maybe there was a way forward.

The admissions coordinator said she never heard of a patient offering tarot readings, but she didn't see any harm in it. She didn't say that Gen had handed her a deck of tarot cards in the half hour before the meeting and that she'd dropped them on the floor, every single one of them, and had just been on her hands and knees picking them up and laying them on Gen's lap. Gen said the same thing had happened to her, too, when her auntie let her hold her old tarot deck. From my child's hands to the plank floor, Gen had said, and she'd said it in the old French Michif that her aunties spoke with her those years in Winnipeg.

One of the counselors said that the cards seemed to help Gen connect with other clients. He didn't say that he had asked Gen as a joke whether the cards might tell him how to overcome his phobia and Gen had turned three cards for him and said, I don't think it's dogs you're really afraid of, and he'd said he had to run to a meeting, couldn't stay with her a minute longer.

The cleaning staff weren't at the meeting but the man who regularly did the floors in the blue room found two tarot cards underneath the piano. He reached out to grab them, but something stopped his hand before he picked them up. The women on the cards were facing each other and one looked so regal and the other so proud he didn't want to touch them. He left them where they were, cleaned the floor around them.

The case manager said that the real issue was that Gen wasn't opening up as much as they wanted to see at this point. Pamela, the nurse, agreed. The case manager said, She takes care of everyone else. It's a problem, said the other counselor. It could be her age, someone offered. She's older than everyone else here. She hasn't reached out to an elder yet, has she? No, she hasn't, they agreed. I think perhaps she needs a visit with Elaine. Everyone needs someone to talk to.

Let's move on to all that water in the basement, the program director said. There were damp areas in the lower level and the rain hadn't stopped and it had been almost three weeks. There were staff offices and physical therapy rooms down there: could they be moved up to the main level?

Gen didn't care to lay the cards for herself anymore.

She wanted fresh cards to read.

Might as well do some good while I'm here, she'd thought when she taped up her sign.

Mamé's first journey with the buffalo

At the beginning I am just as I always was, on two feet, my arms swinging with the rhythm of my legs.

As we travel it begins to feel strange to walk on two legs. It makes sense to be using all four limbs to wander across this great land.

The first I feel of the change is when I begin to play with a stoop, bending forward and melting a little into a bison shape, like hot plastic pours into a mold in the place I had just come from.

That little calf, she kicks up a fuss when she sees me do that, races ahead to her mama and back again to me. I lag behind. It's slow going to learn how to change. The calf is so loud, I can hear her say, Mama, mama, it's happening. She's bisoning!

I heard her mama laugh and she sounds like thunder rolling across the earth. She says, It always happens, child. Let's see if it stays with this one.

The calf races back to me. She circles, prancing. You got this, she says. It helps if you close your eyes, she says. Lean into your nose, she says. Smell your way ahead. That's it. That's it!

My arms reach for the earth and my hands grow into sturdy, comfortable hooves. Over my body I grow a thin layer of soft fine hair and an outer layer of coarse thick hair that sometimes appears in the colors of my skirt ribbons. My body becomes heavier than it has ever been but I feel lighter. I develop great muscles that shift and tense over the frame of a new skeleton. I am and I am not bison.

There is another thing. When I inhale in a certain way I can smell the map of the landscape flickering on and off.

I am flickering, too, a bison one moment and a woman the next. One moment I might be walking on two feet and the next moment I move along on four hooves, stirring up the earth that even up there needed me, needed all of us.

The longer I travel, the more like them I become.

I grow a long thick beard and a beautiful hump and walk with a rambling gait. I wallow. I graze. I give off a scent like theirs when I want, which is almost all the time. How permeable are the boundaries between my body and the ways theirs inhabit this world? At times I can slip back and forth with ease. And yet I am never in control of the changing, or the bisoning, as the calf said. It is the bisoning that is in control and sometimes it will yield to my tinkering, my leaning in, my stooping and my desires, and sometimes it refuses. Sometimes I can live inside the body of a bison and sometimes I am on my two legs.

Sometimes the horizon gives off a strong smell that calls to me and at these times I want to walk directly into it. But the old mother stays close and she reminds me that I am walking with a purpose and that the horizon will be waiting for me if there is need of it in the future.

We come to a river and we drink. After I've had my fill, I ask, What is the horizon for?

It's the next birth, she says.

I don't want to be born back on earth, I say in the voice that moves between human and bison. And I don't—not as a buffalo for sure, nor a human woman. Neither have it easy in that world, I remember that much.

This whole herd will be there one day, the old mother says as she watches her calf splash in the water. The next birth will come to the trail we are walking.

The horizon still hums in my belly and teases my nostrils, but after that I can make myself turn away.

MICHELLE PORTER

The grassland and a thunderstorm

Oh but I love a thunderstorm, the drama of it, you know?

The buildup to it, all that tension and expectation, the steel in the air. Everyone feels it. Jay felt it.

In the days before this storm unleashed itself, Jay couldn't take any more of the tautness that anticipates streaks of lightning. Under the weight of it he told everyone he was making a run for it. He left. If he thought he could outrun the rain, well, he couldn't do it. It was pouring where he was walking now.

Dee hadn't eaten since he left. I tried to offer my most healing grasses to her, but she was mired in the mud of indecision. When the rain came, she was hungry and got to shivering and I was so caught up with the feeling of water soaking in, the pooling and the trickling and the joy of roots expanding, that I didn't attend to her.

Dark clouds rolled across that big old sky and I inhaled beneath all the hooves that walked upon me. I was so heady with the hint of a lightning strike and the possibility of fire that I could barely pay attention to anything else. The rain poured off all their backs onto the land and I tried to drink it all up, as much as I could.

Dee stood all day in the rain by a fence. Tell kept coming to her, chatting, nudging, and prodding. And then in the gray of early evening, he came to find her and there was only the gap in the fence. Dee was gone.

I flooded a little for Tell in my streams and rivers. The elders and aunties organized a search, went after Dee. The rain in torrents, streaks of electricity across the sky, and that calf just standing in the space he'd last seen his mother. I held him up best I could. That was a long night.

Next morning the rain was heavy and still Tell hadn't given up his watch. He'd been joined by others, who stood silent and expectant. When he saw his mother emerge from the curtains of rain, when he watched his mother walk back to him between Solin and an auntie, Tell bleated like a newborn.

Dee was skinny and ragged and milk leaked from her teats. She was silent. Lightning struck the ground a few kilometres away and a tree split in half, and I worried because there was no fire, but then Tell drew my attention back. He ran up to his mother. Solin and the auntie moved a bit to give him room to get close, to press his face against her cape, to smell her.

Leave me alone, she snapped. She pushed him away and walked on. Solin and the auntie moved with her, leaving Tell behind.

Take care of him, Solin called to the cows standing with Tell.

I will, I told her, though she didn't hear me, not really. She was focused on Dee. They stopped not too far away, coaxing her, talking to her.

Tell took a few wobbly steps backward, splashing into a puddle. He lay himself down, wheezing in a calf panic. He was sunk near to his belly in mud, so it was hard for me to feel what was going to happen.

I became angry with Dee then. Oh, I wanted to shock some sense into her. I knew there was little I could do. Still, that anger made me reach through the water with the mud and find the little hooves. It's okay, I said. It's okay. I'm here to hold you up.

Tell said nothing, but he felt my speaking in his legs and his body and even his hump. I was mad and with my temper flaring I might have come on a little strong.

The aunties explained to him about the sickness of some kinds of love, about how you had to be careful and not ask for too much or you could lose yourself, about how Dee needed care. Stepping out of the mud of me, Tell walked away from his mother.

MICHELLE PORTER

A grandmother overtook him and blocked his way, said, Your mother needs you now.

Be brave, an auntie said.

Another auntie stepped close to Tell and said, I've been there myself and your mother needs her child close to her right now. Go on.

Tell let himself be led across the soft half-drowned grass to his mother. I could feel all his muscles tense and his jaw set hard and grim. He reached his hooves down into me and I pressed back, holding him up just a little. He bellowed low and quiet that he would never trust his mother again. But he did what had been asked of him. He offered himself as medicine to his mother; he let that happen. Oh yes, he went to her even though he didn't want to.

Allie texts again

You're not answering the
phone so
I'm texting

    . . .

I don't know what to say
Write

    . . .

Could you help me out here

    . . .

Don't know the right
thing to do now

    . . .

    Stop trying to be so fucking
    good

. . .
Okay

    . . .

    Not doing anyone any good
    Just sucking up

Okay

    . . .

I'm just concerned about
you and my mom

    Been concerned your whole
    life
    Never did any good

Yeah
True

MICHELLE PORTER

Why don't you go talk to ur
mom?
Maybe she wouldn't have
come to me if you were talking

I can't
It's not safe, not for
my mental health

Fuck your mental health you
think you have mental
health?

. . .

Better for your mental health
if you GIVE HER HELL

?

So clueless sometimes

What can I do for my mom?
I haven't seen her in years

STOP TRYING TO BE
GOOD
It's humble bragging
I mean you think you can be
better than everyone

I don't

Lying to yourself

. . .

Give Gramma HELL
She deserves it

What happened?
I warned you

It's the only honest thing you
can do
She deserves a taking down

I can't do that

You have to. No one else can

I have no power with her that's
the point

Do it for her I mean

. . .

She needs to be angry at
someone
so she doesn't have room
for self-pity
Let her be angry at YOU

She'll try to hurt me

So what
You're a big girl now right?
Just let it make you more
angry
She'll live for the fight, trust
me
And you can let all your anger
out

I'm not angry

You fucking should be
Give her shit tell her what's
what and then take her out
to meet all the jig dancers at
the socials to get into a bad
relationship again so do all
the things she wants you to
with her
and then just give her hell
when she's out of line

Which will be all the time

MICHELLE PORTER

Sure, so pick your fights
But give her a fight to live for
And give her a daughter to
piss off
You'll both enjoy it
Maybe learn something too

Where this advice coming
from?
is

I get it'll be messy as hell and
you like neat
That's what I was right?
A mess.
And you wanted to smooth
everything out
Well GUESS WHAT?
Nothing's smooth is it

No.

. . .

Don't make this about you
again

. . .

that's not true and it's not a
good way
to think about it

Shit on GOOD
Okay?

. . .

I got a bus to catch

Geneviève and the trouble with remembering

Gabe knocked on her door and said, Let me bring you down. She said, Let me get my coat, and she pulled it on and took his arm and they walked to the elevator. Going down, the elevator whined and winced and Gen welcomed Gabe's quiet presence. And then she was at the piano and Gabe had vanished and she was left in the arms of the rain and the dark and her wait for Velma.

Gen began this night with a newer tune, one she'd never played with Velma.

And then she looked into the window and Velma's face looked out of that circle of light. Gen wondered about that light. Was it a bridge or a passage between this world and the spirit world?

Velma frowned, said, Why are you always alone? Why don't you play for anybody?

I'm not looking for an audience. Not like you.

You're the same. I see you loving your group therapy audience.

Gen shook her head, said, I don't play music for anybody else but myself. Not anymore.

Gen's hands were trembling. Her fingers tripped over the keys here and there as if they were drunk even though she was stone cold sober, so sober she could hardly stand herself. She kept stopping and starting the song over again.

Stop that, said Velma. She stepped out of the light and into the reflection in the window. Watching Velma, Geneviève wished she'd brought a different wardrobe. Velma was beautiful again, wearing a knee-length dancing dress and heels. Her hair was pulled into thick braids and she wore a beaded hair clip. Gen watched Velma walk across the old wooden frames and into the adjoining set of windows.

Never could stay in one place, Gen muttered to herself.

You call this playing? What happened to your fingers, Velma said.

I'm doing fine, said Gen. She pressed the keys with more strength than usual. Takes time to remember, Gen said.

You stopped performing after pregnancy number three. Remember? And you kept getting pregnant.

Geneviève stopped playing to glare at her sister and said, You stopped performing too, I remember. For a while. Your husband made sure of that.

Maybe. I don't remember. Anyway, Mama told you that many miscarriages was too hard on your body.

This flattened out Gen's sharpness. All at once she wanted a beer and she wanted to hear her mother's voice. In a quieter voice she said, Why hasn't Mom come to see me?

Oh sweetie. It's not personal. How long in your years have I been here? Not as long as Mom right?

Mom passed on first. So, yeah.

But I moved on quicker.

And Mom?

She's been taking her time crossing. I mean your time. For her it's nothing. Time's more random than that over here. You'll see.

She's crossing over?

Yeah, something's holding her up. She's trying to let go.

And you aren't?

No.

Why didn't you come to see me until now?

How can I explain?

You didn't want to see me.

I've been performing. I mean I could see and everything but it's the way it is with gigs up here. I don't book them. They come whenever and last for as long as they last. It's been one after another.

You could've seen me. You're seeing me now.

I didn't make that happen. Or maybe I did. You were playing so badly. I don't know. Best way I can say it is: it was time.

I'll play with you up there after I die.

Practice a bit first, hey?

I'm doing fine. The music's coming back to me a little more every day.

Velma was in the far window, slow-stepping a jig dance. She said, Anyway, you'd get bored of the music in the afterlife. You'll want to get yourself a piece of land and fill the house with kids like you wanted on earth, babies you can love the way you need.

Fuck, said Gen. What do you know about me? You left so long ago.

Velma stopped jigging and pointed her lips at her sister. Oh get yourself a drink, why don't you.

Geneviève banged on the piano keys once with both hands. She pushed the bench back and as she stood up it scraped against the floor.

I'm dying.

Velma was climbing between windows again, coming back toward the piano and the circle of light. She said, Everyone's dying.

You're not, you fucker. You already died.

Technically, sure.

You know what I'm doing here? In this place? I'm killing a part of myself right now.

You were always trying to kill yourself.

Geneviève bent over and banged on the piano again, then dragged her hands across the keys. The noise made Velma shiver and she said, Can you not do that?

Listen to me. I'm trying to tell you something important. Right now I'm trying to kill the part of myself that was always trying to kill myself.

Sounds exciting, said Velma. Looking into the circle of light, she said, I don't get what's the problem with drinking. I haven't been keeping tabs on things down there, but why come to this place? Why rehab? It's kind of dramatic of you.

Gen wanted to raise her voice, but she kept it low and spoke slowly. You'd have gone this road too. You know it.

I could always hold my alcohol.

So could I.

Velma paused, said, Oh that's right. I remember that now.

What else do you remember?

Velma shrugged. Only what I want to remember.

Not enough though, is it?

Velma smiled and tucked her fiddle beneath her chin, said, I know: I remember that you are going to be the best old woman at rehab. I remember that you died on the boring old wagon and that you were proud of it, for some curious reason.

Oh shut the fuck up, said Geneviève. She sat back down and pulled a few notes from between the keys and her aching old fingers. She said, We've got things to talk about, things we have to talk about.

Velma waved at someone beyond the light, said, I don't have time for talking.

For tonight it's enough if you come stand behind me so the pain goes away for just a bit. I just want to play.

Velma looked back at her sister and her dark eyes softened. Velma stepped behind Gen, all close like, and the pain slipped away from Geneviève and all the songs remembered her fingers.

Mamé and tomorrow

With each step my hooves dig into the grass and I feel all my old ways of knowing fall away. The map of the land flickers in and out of my nose. I can't understand its possibilities because I only want to *know*, don't I? And knowing is a fair distance from understanding.

Is there a map inside all bison? I ask this in my stilted buffalo voice.

What's a map? asks the old mother who stays close to me.

That doesn't satisfy me, so I ask again, this time in my human voice and form, and she repeats her answer. The calf moves in close to me then and speaks to me the way I might have spoken to a toddler before my passing. It's okay, she says, nudging me with her forehead in a way meant to be gentle but that almost knocks me off my human feet. I stoop into a bison again and she continues, We don't talk much when we're wandering. I ask why and the calf, she snorts in annoyance. You're worse than a newborn, she says and runs off to join a group of other calves who'd been watching us.

The herd splits off into little gatherings and spreads out over the prairie to graze and wallow.

The dirt feels gritty and clean on my back as I sprawl and roll and sigh in it. Never felt anything like that in my human form. We are lolling there and I explain what a map is and ask again, Do you all have maps inside?

The old mother has her hooves in the air and the back of her head against the ground. She shifts from side to side, snorting and huffing. She says, I've never seen a map.

I'm not going to be put off. I flicker back to my human form and have to use my squeaky human voice, but I ask again, How do you know where you are going?

She lies on one side and laughs. We always go where we're going, naked child—and there's always the horizon.

I'm not naked. I am in my skirt and black T-shirt, but all that thick bison hair is gone and I have to admit I do feel unclothed there with my legs and bare arms in the dirt. I leave the wallow.

You must navigate somehow, I say.

Old mother replies, All of us are going somewhere, whether we intend to or not.

But how do you know where to go?

If I tell you again that one day we will all be going over the horizon, will that calm your anxiety?

I'm not anxious, I say, standing in the grass and shaking the dirt from my hair. But I'm not sure about the horizon.

It's a home, says the mother. We're taking you home.

I say, I feel at home now. I say this even as I look over at the pond I want to swim in to clean the dust from my face. I say, I'm at home on this trail just walking, at home in this in-between body, at home with all you bison.

Nothing stays the same, the old mother says. We're always moving on.

Where to?

Over the horizon.

When.

When it's time.

I stoop back into my bison form and I drink from the pool. I don't ask again about the horizon, because by then I know, or I think I do.

We walk under the sky. We walk through the grass. We walk in the rain. Standing tight together we wait out blizzards. We walk in the wind and change our course for fire. There are births and there are calves asking questions and there are afternoons of sun, when all we do is wallow until we get back up again and walk some more.

It's something, too, that the skies are always clear at night. I don't know the constellations here but sometimes the elders tell star stories as darkness falls, telling the shape of the night in the stories until we all drift into sleep.

One of these nights after the others fall asleep and the stories have ended, the old mother says to me, Tomorrow, you are waking.

I tell her I have never felt more awake, just as I do right then.

Old mother huffs softly. She says, Tomorrow is the day you leave us.

Are you sending me away?

It's where you have to go.

I snort. Does tomorrow have to come?

Tomorrow will come, the old mother says. Even here, tomorrow is always on its way.

Dee, after the thunderstorm

Tell watched his mother throw herself against posts, rails, and wires until she was bruised and panting, until the aunties muttered about her—until she attracted the attention of humans.

Tell leaned against Solin the day they took Dee away in the back of a big truck. His mother and no one else. The aunties whispered, offered milk. Tell worried. Solin stayed close until another truck brought Dee back days and days later. She walked from the truck ramp and through the gate with a new tag in her ear. No one else had a tag like that. And her milk was gone, dried up. Everyone asked what had happened. Tell the story, the aunties said. Dee refused to speak about any of it.

Tell wandered from auntie to auntie for the milk he still wanted. He heard one of the grandmothers say to Solin that what had happened to Dee could happen to any of the cows. But they didn't say what had happened, at least not when he was within earshot. Maybe it's time to move on, one of them said. But to where? Some of the aunties said they felt in their bones and in their flesh that they should leave, but they had to remember how to live without fences and that took time. A couple of bulls who'd joined the herd for the coming winter brought stories that had reached them about Jay. The grandmothers said it felt like the old stories they used to live by were moving on and some of them should follow. Soon, they said to each other, but not yet.

Tell watched the new calves play at freedom hunting. They bickered over who would pretend to be Jay. One said, Jay is a boy so I should be Jay, and another said, So what? It's the aunties who remember how to get anywhere.

Tell gave his mother all the stories he collected during the day so she'd have something to hold on to. Tell told her about the grass turning different shades, how strong he was when he challenged the other bull calves to fighting games, why the aunties bickered over something, how the grassland spoke to him about the past, how fast he was running with his strong legs, the different sounds the birds were making as they flew overhead, and the stories the groundhogs shared about their homes under the ground. He told the stories Solin had shared about the first bison in the sky who had leapt to earth and how her first steps had grown the grass and healed the land. Dee didn't seem to hear any of it. There wasn't enough medicine inside Tell to help his mother.

Carter at the bus station

Almost nine in the morning and the heat was already big. Carter stood outside the bus station in a spring sun that was hard as it was bright. She wanted to get out of Calgary. She was supposed to buy a ticket to Winnipeg. Tucker was in Winnipeg. So was Slavko. They had gone to stay with Slavko's parents.

She'd been to his parents' place once before, just after she and Slavko married. She'd been impatient to meet them. She'd thought she was going to feel like she belonged in his family. Slavko had told stories about his parents and the war back in Croatia, how their ground-floor apartment there had become a check-in center for everyone in their building and how they'd made sure everyone made it down to the shelter during shelling attacks. She hadn't even met them yet, but she'd married them as much as Slavko the day they went to city hall in the middle of a January cold spell.

They'd gone to stay with his parents right after signing the papers. A thirteen-hour drive and they stopped only to get snacks and gas up. What about a hotel? she'd asked. That'd be an insult to my parents, he said, and she didn't want to insult her new family, so she thanked his younger brother for giving up the bunkbed he and Slavko had shared growing up and taking the pullout couch in the living room. Everyone said she had to excuse Slavko's little brother because even though Petar was in his mid-twenties he was still too shy to speak to new people. In all the years she knew him after that, she never made it past new and he'd never once talked directly to her.

Nobody had spoken much English when they were all together. She'd been learning the language: Ja sam Carter, kako si? Učim Hrvatski. Govorim samo malo. But it wasn't enough.

His parents weren't fluent, even after so many years in the country; English was such a slow language for them. They were all of them brown eyed like her, with skin that was a shade or two darker and reminded her of her bio mom's, and for that reason she thought she could almost fit in. Did they open their family to her? Sometimes she thought yes, they'd tried, but most times she thought no, they didn't. She figured she was rough around the edges and there was something about her that didn't know how to step into someone else's circle, even when she wanted to join. If someone had taken her in hand, pulled her in, insisted. And then the language shut her out. They didn't know how to make room in their talk for her. They spoke over one another, one syllable tripping over the next, and Slavko became so caught up in the politics, the teasing, the banter, and the stories that most of the time he forgot to translate. His family absorbed his entire attention. That boisterous laughter of Slavko's—the reason she'd fallen for him—belonged to his parents and his brother. She never heard the words she'd longed to hear, *sestra* and *kćer*. Instead they called her Slavkova žena. She learned that the words for *woman* and *wife* were the same.

Inside the station, she had her ticket to Winnipeg in hand and was queasy with memories. There were snarls of people gathering here and there. Her gut clenched and she thought maybe she could use a smoke. She hadn't had one in forever, had been trying to quit. But maybe going to see your ex warranted just one?

Back in front of the building she squinted against the light. She was shielding her face from the glare of the sky when she saw a guy sitting on the ground with his back against the wall of the station. There were a couple of flags sewn onto his backpack. He was sucking on a joint with his head tilted back and his eyes closed. His hair was too short and his face too sharp. He was skinny. She could beat him up easy, she thought. He probably has a skinny dick, too, she thought, and she laughed. He looked like he'd seen better days, like everything had been going sideways for a while, which was exactly how she felt about herself.

The man must have heard her laugh because he opened his eyes. He cocked his head to the side. His gaze found her tits and he grinned. He said, Angel of death fucking kill me now and I'll be happy.

His accent was British. He held out his hand, offered her his joint. She took it from him, sucked it in.

Yeah, just like that, he said, taking his eyes off her breasts to watch her inhale.

Where are you going? she asked.

To a beach. You?

She passed his joint back to him. She had a choice. She looked down at the ticket in her hand.

Same, she said.

He looked her over again, made his own decision.

Well, come with me, why don't you?

Her phone buzzed. She ignored it.

Sure, she said.

He grinned.

My ticket's for Vancouver, he said.

I'll have to get one of those, she said.

She turned and opened the door back into the station.

What Geneviève doesn't say (to Pam)

That little nurse made me want to talk. She'd come on in with her blood pressure cuff and ask me how I was feeling and I didn't want to hold anything back. Something about her. She was like one of my own. So I didn't tell her anything real.

I didn't tell her that I'd lived in the bush in British Columbia with my first husband and lost all those pregnancies by myself out there, that I wished I could go back and do it all differently but what's the use of even wishing. I wanted to tell her about darkness. I wanted to tell her that I got to drinking one night after the doctor told me how much time I had and after a couple of bottles I phoned Lucie. She didn't pick up, of course, but I left a message after the beep, told her I had the cancer and would she come see me. She never called back. I wanted to tell her that I'd stopped seeing Lucie because I couldn't stand the way she looked at me, that I had too much pride. But no, no, I'm lying to myself about pride being the reason. I couldn't tell Pam anything or I'd have told her about that night Lucie came over with little Allie in tow, found me passed out in my basement. Lucie set Allie in front of the TV, cleaned me up and got me into bed, and took Allie home. But later she let herself back into my place, gave me her key, and told me she couldn't stand wondering if she'd found her mother's corpse every other month and she couldn't do it anymore; she wasn't going to see me until I was sober. Oh God, I couldn't tell Pam that.

I couldn't tell her the easier things either, that I was born in the back of an old dance hall on the outskirts of Winnipeg in the middle of a fiddle competition. My father won and later he said that song was the best reel he ever played, and my mama, who never drank a drop of anything, had to take a shot of whiskey

MICHELLE PORTER

that night to help bring me into the world as quietly as she did, in a back corner with only my older sister for help. Velma was four years old. I couldn't tell Pam how my mama said there was no way she was going to miss our father's performance that night and that anyway the best way to give birth was in the company of the very best fiddlers in Red River territory. Velma said she remembered how our dad filled up the whole room with his music and how she didn't remember even seeing Mama or me because she couldn't take her eyes off the stage and the fiddle and all the men playing. But she must have looked, right? She must have seen our mother's bloody thighs that night and me a scrawny baby gasping for my first breath and taking my first milk while the men moved their bows over the instruments they held over their hearts. Velma said all she remembered about my birth was being furious that Mama kept her in the back of the room when she wanted to be up there with the spoons and jigging with Papa. She remembered our mother's hand squeezing her little one so hard she yanked it away and told Mama to stop. The only other thing she said she remembered is how Mama was too weak to carry the new baby, all wrapped up in one of Mama's own scarves, all the way home, so Dad passed his special fiddle—his uncle's fiddle—to Velma. Mama said she didn't want to ride in a cab and her legs were strong and not to waste his competition winnings on that, she could sit down when they got home. She could have said all this in French, her mother tongue, or she could have said it all in Michif, the language she had picked up in the years since she'd run away to marry Papa. It was probably like it was when we lived in those little Métis communities around Winnipeg, when the words of both languages flowed easily between them. Velma was not much bigger than the fiddle herself and her arms ached with the weight of it, but she never said anything for fear she'd be relieved of this awesome burden. Papa gave her his fiddle that night so he could carry me in his arms in the dark of the night all that long walk home.

Well, I didn't say all that to Pamela. And I was never going to either.

What Pam doesn't say (to Geneviève)

Gen scared me. She held so much back she had to be ready to burst. Gen looked at me like my kokum used to when she was alive, as if she wanted to see inside my skin. Only my kokum was comfortable with silence. Mama said I got the same way about me. Except that way of looking, that way of seeing inside a person to their thoughts that my kokum had and Gen had, that wasn't my gift. I'm just a nurse.

Gen scared me so I didn't say even simple things. Like how much I loved the long dry summers of Southern Alberta, how the rain was getting inside my head. I missed the dust. Always liked the way Mama's horses kicked up dust when I took them out. I liked hauling buckets of water from the creek to my mama's patch of beans, squash, and corn and I liked the shock of jumping into a lake nobody else knew about early in the morning and I liked even more how fast I dried out and how quick the water was a memory on my skin. I liked driving down into the reserves nearby to make house calls and see how everybody was doing, drinking tea, sharing cookies, and eating bannock. I didn't tell her that none of us had heard from my brother in months now, that I couldn't sleep nights anymore for worrying about him, that I used to give him piggybacks when we were goofing around as kids, that he sucked his thumb until he was, I don't know, fifteen at least.

The rain didn't make sense to me, it was like another language, but I couldn't say that. I only talked with Gen about withdrawal and the medication. I didn't tell her how every time I looked out a window there was a world I didn't recognize, all heavy and swollen with clouds, hardly any light getting through, and I was thinking about the horses and the dogs at my mama's place and all the stuff I had to do after work to keep the flood away.

Mamé follows the herd to the river

I wait for tomorrow.

There is a river flowing deep and slow. We drink there together.

When my thirst is sated I ask, Which way now?

Old bison mother, she says, Us buffalo will go the way the river runs.

I look and the river's path stretches as far out as I can see.

Right over the horizon? I ask.

Old mother lifts her head. She says, Death and rebirth are waiting for all of us.

But do you know if there's room for you on earth?

We lived like rivers when we last lived on earth. We moved like water and when we travel over the horizon we'll live that way again.

There's hardly any land for you there. You know that, right? The prairies are dying. It's all farms and suburbs now.

The earth will give what we need.

I don't think I want to be alive again, I say.

MICHELLE PORTER

Dee brings hope along

The tag didn't stop Dee from escaping again, from finding Jay's path and making it her own. She didn't run after his dreams of land or his talk of freedom. She wanted the heat of him against her body. It was just the bull she hoped for, nothing more.

She'd left Tell with an auntie. Her body ached for her son even as her hope took her closer to Jay and her udder produced a little milk again. Her teats leaked as she walked, dripping onto the dry prairie earth.

She didn't turn back. She needed Jay more than she needed her son, more than her mother had needed the canyons, and more than she'd ever needed her mother. She hadn't even been able to cross a broken fence for her mother, but she hadn't lasted two days without Jay before the panic set in and she knew she'd have to follow again. She'd lost track of how it all got to be this way. She would never have been able to say to another cow, It began when this happened.

The forest was still green, but the nights cooled quickly.

At first her hope was light and sweet there in her broad chest and she focused on the trail. This thing called hope led her on, gave her strength. She believed if she could say the right things she could have Jay the way she'd had him two summers ago. He would whisper into her cape again, he would pant to mount her, he would stand so close that the boundaries between their bodies blurred.

As the days passed hope began to turn against her and her teats swelled, became distended with pain that she could rely on, pain that kept her moving. The forest turned to grass and hills. She knew Jay was a steady traveler so she stopped grazing much and started walking late into the nights. She needed to get to Jay.

Carter in the bathroom

Goddamn curiosity, Carter thought. She was pressed up against the toilet in a cubicle-sized washroom, trying not to laugh as this guy she'd just met on the bus unzipped his pants. The door was latched and the occupied light was on. He was muttering so low she couldn't understand anything except the word *blowjob*.

Fifteen minutes ago, she'd been asleep in her seat.

She'd been dreaming.

In her dream she'd been back in her childhood home. There was the kitchen island with the marble countertop. There, the dark wood oval dining table with the curved detailing, and there, the window looking out on a swing set. In the middle of the kitchen stood R, her adopted mother. She could see R's back and the shoulder-length gray hair held in a ponytail with an elastic.

There was a child there too. Carter could see the child press her forehead against the window and cover her ears with her hands. R was yelling at the child. It was as if she had always been shouting and always would be. In the brief pauses between words and insults, Carter could hear the child sob.

The woman with gray hair whose name began with R reached out for the child. Carter tensed and wanted to throw up. This isn't a dream, she thought. This is a memory. R grabbed a shank of the child's brown hair and pulled the child to the floor, pinning her there.

Carter set her own child's hand on the island and she saw that her hand was trembling.

R yanked the child's head back and small clumps of hair came out in her hand.

The child, she howled.

R slapped the girl until she held back her noise.

Carter had to look away. She couldn't move.

Then the hand, her hand, on the island changed and it was no longer like a child's. The hand on the island was an adult hand. It was all she needed. She rushed at R and pushed her off the child.

The woman with gray hair fell back and Carter crouched down, took the child's body into her lap and her arms. Carter was no longer scared. It was her job to comfort now. R turned into water and poured through a drain that appeared on the floor. Carter rested the small child's head against her chest. She stroked the child's hair, picking out the clumps that were pulled away. She whispered over and over again, You're safe, you're safe, you're safe.

The girl's trembling calmed. She shifted in Carter's arms. She wriggled until she could move her left arm and slip her thumb into her mouth.

That was the dream she'd been having when a man's voice pulled her out of the dream. Hey, he said and he shook her arm.

She shook away the dream, the need to stay with it. She was on a bus seat and her head was on the shoulder of the guy next to her. It took her a minute to remember that the man next to her was the British guy she met at the station and they were going to Vancouver together.

The man leaning over her was tall and fair and he wore a light beard. His hand was gently shaking her arm. She shifted in her seat toward this new man and found herself looking into a pair of blue eyes.

He your boyfriend? the pale man asked, nodding to the British guy.

Groggy and confused, she shook her head no.

Your brother?

She rubbed her eyes and shook her head again, no. I don't even know his name. Why are you asking?

The pale man smirked. He moved his hand off her arm and

turned it so that the back of his hand slid hard against the rise of her breasts. It was so sudden that her first instinct was to freeze in confusion. What was happening? He turned his hand and cupped her left breast with his palm and squeezed gently. Sexy, he said with such significance that she almost burst out laughing and that released her from her confusion.

Her second instinct was to hit him. Her hand itched to form a fist and to strike his straight-ass jaw. Something held her back. She could smell his cologne. Close up she could see he was no young pup; he was in his forties. Like it? he asked and squeezed again. She thought how he was still a spoiled baby who thought he could reach for what he wanted whenever he wanted. The flash in her eyes and the slap hanging in the air between them seemed to interest him. Come with me, he said.

Her phone rang. She brushed the strange man's hand away and picked up her phone to see who was calling. Slavko. Ha, of course he'd be phoning while some random dude was groping her. Lovemaking hadn't been a strong point in their marriage. Tucker was a bit of a miracle baby because after they were married Slavko just lost all interest in sex. For a while she thought if she approached things right or if she could get him to relax it'd work out, because shit, if any of the gods above were watching down below for just five minutes, they'd know how much she liked to fuck. Nothing worked. By the time she got to thinking about leaving him, he'd get so angry if she brought up sex that he'd just leave their apartment and slam the door on his way out. That's when things really fell apart.

She declined the call and turned off her phone.

What the hell, she thought as she stood to follow this tall thin man. Her curiosity led her down the aisle to the back of the bus and her curiosity pressed her, smiling, into the bathroom. He pushed her against the sink and he groped at her breasts.

Whoa there, she said, laughing.

He pressed his face to hers. Is this a kiss? she wondered.

His tongue was thick. She pulled his hand off her breast.

Maybe take off your wedding ring, she said.

He slapped her.

Shock made everything go completely still. Her lungs burned and her body screamed for oxygen and she realized she'd stopped breathing. She told herself to inhale.

The man pulled out his dick and the shock wore off. Carter gulped back a breath of air and then she started to laugh.

No, no, she said. This isn't my scene. Let me out.

His eyes became hard.

You fucking aren't going to hit me again, she said, pressing a hand against his chest. She reached for his dick, yanked and twisted. He screamed.

She reached behind him and lifted the latch to the unoccupied position.

Get out, Carter said in a loud voice. I want you out of here now.

He stepped back.

The door opened. A man waited there and he spoke quick and loud. He grabbed the back of the bearded man's shirt and pulled him backward a step. Frantically, the bearded man folded his flaccid dick back into his pants, backed out, and then he was gone. The other man stayed to talk to her, but Carter held up her hand. Give me a minute, she said. She closed the door again and latched it.

Carter grabbed a handful of paper towels from the dispenser and ran them under the tap at the sink. Fucking curiosity, she said out loud. Then she looked up and saw R's face in the small circular mirror. She screamed and jumped back, dropping the wet paper towels onto the grimy black floor. She pulled out another bunch of paper towels and approached the sink to run these under the water. She braced herself for the reflection. There was R's face again.

No, she said to the mirror.

The pale face, sunburnt and freckled.

She said, You can't stay here, R.

The gray hair. Those pale blue eyes.

She said, It's time for you to go.

R put up a fight. Carter stared her down. She gripped the sides of the sink and R slid out of her face and fell through the washroom floor. Carter looked up again and found her own face looking back at her from the mirror.

Her own face felt raw.

The wet paper towels were cool on her skin. She pulled another to wipe her face dry.

She opened the door. The man who'd helped her before was there and he began talking.

She said, I'm okay, I'm okay.

She backed away from him and turned and almost knocked over an old woman who was standing there. The woman was frail and bent. She wore a red kerchief over her white hair. She was wearing a peasant dress and big white running shoes. Her skin was dark and her eyes were light. I'm so sorry, said Carter. She turned and reached down to pick up something that had fallen from the woman's bag and by the time she had it in hand the woman was gone. Carter looked up and down the aisle, sure she'd see the old woman, but there was no trace of her. Carter looked at the object in her hand.

It was a beaded flower on a piece of black felt, done in pink and purple. She'd seen this style of flower before, in Allie's book on beading. Carter looked around again, but the woman was definitely gone. There was nothing to do but go back to her seat and take the flower with her.

Geneviève gets a ride in an ambulance

Gabe met her at her door and noticed the cane right away.

Pamela brought it to me, Gen said, gripping it tight in her right hand.

Gen wasn't shaking as much as she had been, but she'd been having trouble with walking, as if the earth she was walking on now was different from the one she'd walked when she was drinking.

It suits you, said Gabe.

What happened is I fell over after group, said Gen. It took me a while to get up so someone called the nurse and Pamela said she didn't want me roaming wild anymore without something to lean on.

She said that?

Well, something like that, said Gen.

Gabe said she could lean on him whenever. The elevator door opened and let them out on the main floor.

Geneviève patted his arm and said, I don't tell her about you and anyway you aren't always around, are you?

He walked her to the door and she went in on her own. The windows were wet with rain and the shadows were dripping. She sat at the piano. Her fingers were steadier on the keys now and the songs came to her easier.

Velma peered out and then stepped down into the blue room with her sister, said, That's a good tune.

Velma danced a few steps, toe-heel, toe-heel, then said, Wait for me while I get my fiddle. And then the fiddle appeared in her hands. Oh never mind, said Velma, laughing. I forget sometimes how the things I need just appear.

Gen didn't bother to look up at her sister or at her own reflection. She said, Been there long enough to get used to it, haven't you?

Velma held the fiddle up for Geneviève to see. She said, Tell me you recognize this fiddle.

Geneviève glanced up at it, said, It's not the fiddle that was burned, right? No, I know it. It's the one Papa gave you when you were twelve. The one he got from his uncle.

That's the one.

I remember. Papa said he played that old thing all over the prairies. He said the old songs would sing in your hands. He always talked like that.

Listen to you. Sometimes I think it's all the remembering you're doing that makes you sick.

There's things that need remembering.

The fiddle in Velma's hands vanished. She let her arms drop to her sides and looked behind her into the warm glow of light.

No one needs to remember, said Velma.

Gen thought Velma was about to walk back into the light, so she stood up suddenly, knocking both the bench and her cane onto the floor. She turned around and there was Velma, right behind her. She leaned a little on the piano for support.

I remember everything, Geneviève said.

And look at you.

At least I lived.

Barely.

You left me.

Gen stepped away from the piano. She was so close to Velma and yet there she was, fading. I remember the day you died, Gen said.

Velma became so transparent then that Gen could barely see her at all.

Gen tried to stop herself from saying it, but the words tumbled out. I never got to tell you I'm sorry, she said, and she held her breath.

MICHELLE PORTER

Shut your mouth.

It was my fault.

I don't even know what you're talking about. And I don't want to.

It's what started me drinking heavy.

No, it didn't.

You and Mama and Papa. You all left. All three of you dead in one year.

Play a song for Christ's sake.

Geneviève started one of their dad's favorites, "The Red River Jig."

Velma reappeared with her fiddle and at first she played along with the piano but then she ran ahead, leading the piano into the song. They finished the song and then began a slower one together.

Velma said, No time to think about all that while I'm up here.

Remember playing with Mama and Papa and the band in Winnipeg?

That I do remember.

Remember how Mama used to tuck us in under all the coats.

The smell.

Yeah. The perfume and the wool.

Just the smell of them.

And the fiddle lulling us to sleep.

Remember the streets of Vancouver back in the day?

That night we got tired of walking.

To the dance.

You swooned as if you were injured and I flagged an ambulance.

They were going to take us to the hospital, we were that convincing. But when we got near the street where the dance was.

We jumped out.

Shit, we laughed.

We ran.

Gen said, That was a good dance that night.

We agree on that.

Gen stopped playing then. She put her hands on the ledge of the piano, said, You met Reggie that night.

Velma dropped her arm to her side, said, Play, would you?

Why can't we talk?

Look, I don't do much talking here. Not in that my-life-was-so-hard way that you love.

You'd think all your time up there in the afterlife would've made you wise or something.

I never got old, did I—that wise enough for you? Velma brought the bow back to the strings of the fiddle, said, You're the old woman, not me. Now, play me another song and shut it.

I want to talk.

Look, I'm only here to play.

You've got to face up to things.

Shut up, shithead. Make your pretty little fingers dance.

Mamé, where a rib is broken

And so tomorrow comes and the river invites us to join her. We stay near her banks, moving in the direction she flows.

The old mother seeks me out, speaks to me as we walk in a way she'd never done before. The things she says to me.

She steps strong and sure beside my bison self, saying, I left a calf down there when I was shot.

She says, You know what happened. The mothers and fathers fallen. The few calves wandering among the dead, trying to suck milk from the leaking teats of the dead. My daughter wouldn't leave my dead body for two days and two nights.

It was a terrible responsibility to leave it to them, to live and to tell the stories and to build again. We waited for them here. And we waited for their children and grandchildren. We needed them to teach us about the changes that had come to the earth since we lived there, to help us prepare for our return.

I reach out with a human hand, though the rest of me is basically bison, and press it into her fur. I hold on.

I turn my eyes toward the horizon that has been calling out to me. We walk on until the sky fills with stars that are so thick and so low I think I can reach up and touch them from where I am, walking there on my human feet beside the old mother. Mother bison nudges my side with her great forehead. She means tenderness but her small movement knocks me to the ground. When I get back to my feet I pass a hand over the left side of my ribcage and find that I have a broken rib.

The old mother lets me lean against her.

Tomorrow, she says. You see that faint light over there and the smoke rising in it?

But isn't today the tomorrow you spoke of yesterday?

The old mother laughs and the thunder of it rolls over me.

She says, There is another river in that direction that will take you where you are going.

Dee catches up to anger

As her teats hardened, she felt a stab of pain with each step, an awful searing hope that bullied her to the top of a knoll, where, in a shallow depression in the land just below, she found Jay. He was grazing there as if he belonged. He had rejected her the winter she was pregnant but she told herself he wouldn't reject her again, not now. She couldn't hold herself back, didn't even try. Down the hill she went, picking up speed and calling his name. He raised his head.

He isn't surprised to see me, Dee thought.

She lengthened her stride and increased her pace, ignoring the jolt and throb of her udder.

Jay didn't greet her. He pawed the ground and snorted. He raised his tail. Dee slowed and then she stopped, leaving the length of ten bison between them. Her front end was heaving. Her udder tortured her. She was confused. What was he doing?

Dee bellowed low and stepped toward him, head bowed. When she looked up he'd frozen in place and there seemed to be a softness in his eyes. Dee was sure he was regretting his aggression. She launched herself at him, her joy as big as the sky.

Then his eyes flashed. He backed up and tossed his head to show his horns. Dee brought herself up short, dust rising around her. He charged at her with a bellow but stopped a calf's length from her. It looked like a warning. But why? He'd loved her, hadn't he? He snorted and shook his head again and his horns looked broader, longer, deadlier.

She stumbled out of his path. He backed up, recalibrated, and charged her again.

She turned and scrambled halfway up the knoll. Panting heavily, she dug her hooves into the grassy soil and turned around to get a look at him. What was going on?

At the bottom of the hill, he swaggered and tossed his head from side to side. He snorted and bellowed, watched for her next move. And what was it that Dee saw in his eyes? The answer hit her—it was contempt. She was no more to him now than just another tiresome cow.

The rest of the hill was nothing to tear up now. She galloped across the flat land as far from that repulsive female she'd glimpsed in his eyes as she could get. She came to a stop only when her udder screamed so loud she couldn't hear or see anything else. Heaving, she collapsed to the grass. The land held her for a long time, until she could stand again, until she could set her shoulders square and strong and until a flickering sort of hope returned to her chest, brought her back to the path that led to Jay. She'd chosen this way and she would see it to the end. That pain in her teats was familiar now and it led her on, whispered that everything would turn out somehow.

But Dee knew she couldn't go on the way she had. She forced herself to eat properly again, to sleep again, to keep a trembling safe distance between herself and the bull she loved, and on she went, following Jay.

Carter texts her mom from the bus

On the bus

                                    Didn't know you were going
                                    somewhere

To Vancouver
Before I go I want a real answer

                                    Vacation?

No, something else
Why'd you give me up?

                                    . . .

A real answer

                                    . . .

Gramma said she told you to
keep me

                                    I wanted you to have a better
                                    life

Couldn't have a good life with
you?

                                    . . .

Read about all these 1st Nation
and Métis kids taken away
from
their parents who try for yrs to
get them back
You do it voluntarily
That's shit

                                    You're right

THAT'S IT?

That's what they do in the
end. They get us to do it all
to ourselves so they don't
have to bother doing it

Colonization

What the fuck?

That's about land
Not your own kid

. . .

You know what just go fuck
yourself
A better life without my mom
what were you thinking

It's about my mom too . . .
and her mom
And her mom.

Gramma would have helped u
She told me

Gramma was getting beat up
by her new husband

That's shit
U cd have found help

you're stronger now
than I was then
Didn't know how to ask
for help
my mom had snuffed that
out in me
I know it's hard to
understand

Blaming Gramma?
Fuck that

MICHELLE PORTER

Look I can call you we can
talk

You didn't want me, fucker

I wanted you back every
single day
I still do
Maybe I didn't feel I had
a right to you

YOU DIDN'T WANT ME

Let me call

On the fucking bus
Abt to turn this off

Ok
Well I'm glad Gramma didn't
get to you

Fuck Gramma

All I can say is I was broken
back then

Rlly?
So am I
I can thank you for that

Is that all you have to say?

Ok . . . true

Hard by text . . . please don't
pretend it would have
been roses with me
No guarantees
Don't believe you wouldn't
have been hurt if you were
with me
Would have had a hundred
mean boyfriends

That's where I was going to
take you

I don't care
I would have chosen that

Did you get that?
I didn't get to choose

I'm crying . . . I don't can't
know

Why the fuck are you crying

Nobody chose me

You don't know

I thought I was only.
Hurting myself

You aren't your mother
You know that right?
You're not her
Not even a little bit

Okay. You're angry.

No shit
Maybe it would have been
better if you were like her
Want to know what it was like
growing up in that fucking
family

I've been thinking it was
self harm

You were taken in by their
white lives

I don't know. They weren't
me.

That's what I thought you
needed

You could have trusted yourself
With me

No.
Maybe
No.

It's okay to say you didn't want
me

I did want you

I didn't want Tucker when

I did. So much.

I first got pregnant

Wanting was dangerous

Say it
That you didn't want me

Other kids I knew back then
cut themselves
Drank bleach, overdosed
drugs, whatever
I cut myself with. Adoption

You don't make any fucking
sense
What's the use of talking to
you?

I know

You used your baby me to hurt
yourself
You used ME to hurt yourself
Because your mother didn't
love you?

It was selfish

Fucking fight with me
will you?
I fucking hate martyrs
Stop agreeing with every
shitty thing I say about you

I said worse to myself every
damn year since I let you go
You can't really hurt me any
more than I've hurt myself.
You have free rein . . .
Have a go at me I think you
need to

Got to turn this off
Buddy next to me waking up

Geneviève's elder

Geneviève saw the elder in the doorway, leaning on Pamela's arm. She's older than me, Geneviève thought. Older than I'll ever be.

She wore a black dress and orthopaedic shoes with soles that scuffled along the floor as she entered. Her great head was held high as she looked around the room. She wore her long gray hair loose and there was a pronounced hump in her back. Pamela helped the elder get seated in the chair next to Geneviève. Gen smelled something musty that reminded her of her childhood, or maybe of her dogs, or the breeze that blew into the car along the river on the drive up—she couldn't quite place it. It was gone in a flash and the elder craned her neck to smile at Pamela and thank her for her help and Pamela left her bag at her feet and said, Call if you need anything, Elaine.

Elaine turned her ancient head toward Geneviève and her long hair shifted over her shoulders. Elaine just looked at Gen for a few minutes, until the restlessness returned to Gen's hands and she leaned forward and picked up a teapot and held it over a mug. Do you want a tea? she said.

I'm an alcoholic, said Elaine.

Gen didn't know whether to put the teapot down or not. So am I? said Gen.

Elaine ducked her head and laughed to herself. Well, are you or aren't you? You aren't sure? I've been saying I'm an alcoholic since I was thirty years old. Never had to ask anyone if I was an alcoholic. You don't know?

No. Yes, I do.

Then say it like that then.

Like what?

Like you know.

I'm an alcoholic?

Are you?

I'm an alcoholic.

Okay then, you have the answer.

I'm sorry. The answer to what?

The elder laughed again, shaking all over with life, and she said, To tea.

You want tea? I can pour you some tea.

It's only the caffeine that keeps any of us going these days. I quit the cigarettes, too, a few years back. I sure didn't want to. My great-grandchildren nagged me to quit. They teach them how to do that in schools these days, how to nag. What are you doing with that pot? Of course I want a tea.

Geneviève poured. She didn't know if she should ask about milk and sugar.

Some people like their tea black, Gen said as she poured tea into her own mug.

I'm not some people, Elaine said.

Geneviève made Elaine's tea with milk and sugar. Elaine watched and then lifted her hands up for Gen to see briefly, saying, My hands aren't what they used to be. Her hands were curled up and stiff. Geneviève moved closer to Elaine and lifted the tea to her lips. Elaine slurped and closed her eyes for a moment. When she opened her eyes again she gestured for Gen to put the tea down and then Elaine said, My ancestors are all from this land here, way back when. They had to move on because they didn't own the land, you know, according to some document some lawyer had. Never mind who really owns what. You know the river here?

Gen said she'd met the river on her way up.

Elaine laughed quietly. Then you don't know her, she said.

She was almost dry.

We all ran dry, almost.

But now with all this rain, she's running high, said Gen. They're saying she's near running over the banks now in some places. They're happy about it, after the drought.

It's not normal, said Elaine.

The rain.

Yes, the rain. And the river so high. This time of year? No.

They let the silence spread out between them, each of them thinking of their rivers, until Gen said, My people are from the Red River.

Elaine looked down at Gen's hands and reached out one of her arthritic claws to touch Gen's fingers. Born with the music, by the looks of you?

Gen nodded. I was playing before I was walking, she said. Gen paused a moment and then added, But we moved to B.C. Left all that behind.

Is that your story?

What do you mean?

Are you telling me your story or someone else's version of your story?

It's just what happened.

No, it's your story. So what is it you're trying to forget?

I don't forget anything.

Really? Elaine said and brought her hand back into her lap, on top of her right. She smiled. Now that's unusual, isn't it?

Remembering things? Gen asked.

Elaine gestured down to her bag with her hand. Get the hair-brush out of my bag, she said.

It wasn't easy for Gen to get up and bend over to reach into Elaine's bag, but she did and she held it up and asked, Would you like me to brush your hair?

No, said Elaine.

Okay then, said Gen.

No, child. I'm going to brush your hair.

I'm wearing a wig. You don't need—

Take it off. Yes. Good. There you go. Unpin your hair. Let it down. Okay. Now sit.

I don't know if I can—

Sit.

A minute, Gen said and she went over to the piano to half push and half pull the piano bench over to where Elaine was sitting. Breathing heavily, she pushed it into place and sat her rump down.

Good girl, said Elaine.

Elaine wrapped one hand around the brush handle and settled the side of her other hand on Gen's hair at the nape of her neck. Gen shivered. She felt goosebumps up and down her arms and her back. Elaine gently pressed the brush into Gen's hair and against her scalp and pulled it through the full length of her hair to just below her shoulders. Geneviève closed her eyes, stopped breathing for a moment. Elaine's curled hands worked that brush through Gen's hair and settled it around her neck.

Elaine said, This happened after the droughts began to eat up this land many years ago. The men went up into the hills. The women strapped their babies to bison and let them be carried away. They took their older children into valleys in search of hidden springs. Those were hard times.

After the sky restored the rain to the land, the bison returned with babies on their backs and the women and children returned from the valleys. The men came back but they left their stories behind, having dropped them in the hills. This loss burned hotter every day until the men stole a woman's life—and her child's too. Oh, yes. That's when the bison came to walk with the women. Together they decided that the men had to remember the first water stories.

So they told the men, You have to walk into the deepest, fastest bend of the river where the current is the most dangerous. Let it cover you and pull you down to its rocky bottom until you wake with the stories in the other world. This is what you must do, if you have the courage.

The brush fell from Elaine's hand and clattered to the floor.

I'm tired now, Elaine said. Where's Pamela?

I'll brush your hair now, Gen said.

I'm tired, Elaine said again. Where's Pamela?

Gen stood up. I can go get her, she said.

Do you bead?

Gen looked at Elaine. Do I what?

With those lovely long fingers of yours. Do you bead?

I never learned, no. Not that.

That's too bad.

It's too late.

Elaine laughed. No, it's not, she said. You'll see.

Gen hesitated. Should I get Pamela? she asked.

There's something in my bag for you, said Elaine.

Okay, said Gen and she leaned on the piano bench so she could reach into the bag. It was a small square of black cloth with a single beautifully beaded flower. The stems reached off the edge of the square. Gen ran her fingers over the beads.

Pamela stepped into the room then, asked, Was Elaine ready to go? Elaine said she was, and as Pamela was helping Elaine get up, she looked over at Gen, smiled, and said, Your hair.

What?

It's beautiful.

Gen put a hand to her hair and felt how soft the brush had made it. Then she pushed the square of beading into her pocket with her cigarettes. She picked up her wig and didn't know what to do with it, so she just put it on her head, over her unpinned hair.

Mamé and the magpies in the sky

The next morning I see in the distance a congregation of magpies, wheeling in the air and calling, and so I step into my full human form, broken rib and all, and let my feet carry me away from the herd. At first the smells of the black of the birds' wings and the flash of white that shows when they twist are sharp, but the longer I walk on my two feet the milder they become until I can't smell colors at all. And I am glad of it because when I reach the birds I see they are circling a pair of coyotes feeding on the pink and red carcass of a young deer. The magpies dive down and peck out pieces of flesh with black beaks, then rise in the air to gulp it down while turning into the wind. Just beyond them is the river the bison mother had told me about, the other river, and beyond that there is smoke rising into the air from campfires. I walk in the direction the river runs. That whippoorwill who sang to me the first night appears again, rushing ahead as I walk and then speeding back to swoop around my face. I do not turn around to watch the herd meander in the other direction. I do not know if any calf or cow or elder pauses in their journey to watch me leave.

Tell, the stars, and a grandmother

The stars were loud the night Tell followed his mother's trail.

He let the noise of the stars draw him through the dark. Hunger hooked him and dragged him through the next day alone. His mother's trail was fresh so he knew he was close. The wind brought the smell of a grandmother from behind and he knew that if the wind carried news of Solin's pursuit ahead to him then his scent would also be carried ahead to his mother. Dee would know he was following.

Dusk was coming on when he stopped at a stream for a drink. A magpie swooped over him and scared two starlings off his back before taking the space they'd just vacated and then the bird walked to Tell's head. Tell shook his head to dislodge the bird but the magpie fluttered his wings to keep his balance and said in a sudden squawk, My mother knows your mother. What? Tell said. The magpie flew off Tell's head and landed near the water's edge. The bird cocked its head, croaked, and then hopped between the rocks in search of an evening snack.

Tell ignored the bird. The last time he'd had milk was early the day before. More than anything he wanted his mother to come back for him. When a bison stepped out of a stand of trees a ways off, he imagined it was her.

But it was Solin who crossed the distance toward him, one worn-out step at a time. She greeted him and sniffed him to make sure he was okay. She trampled a bit of grass and earth to make a bed for him, said, Sleep.

Tell lay down so that his back was against Solin's belly. The little bird who'd come to him earlier returned and scratched out a place to rest nearby. Tell wanted to sleep but he was worried. He asked, Are you here to take us back?

Solin shook her head, said, I've come to see the open land once more before I die.

Are you dying?

We're all dying. Even you.

Me?

Yes, even you, though a little bit less than I am.

How can I be dying less than you?

Tell, my child, a grandmother is cold even on easy nights like this and my hips ache at the end of the day so sleep can get away from me pretty easily. Will you tell me a story?

You know all of them. What story can I tell?

Tell me the stories of the land we're going to, she said, so I'll know if that land is anything like the land I was born on or like the land my grandmother told stories about.

Solin waited for Tell to begin. She hadn't been this far from the fences since she'd been a heifer. Her grandmother had taught her about hiding out on the land and that had been their lives for some time, just the two of them. But then her grandmother became ill and she started to lose weight and her fur fell out in patches. One day she didn't get up. Didn't take long for Solin to be found after that. She'd been brought to another kind of hiding, the inside of the fences. She thought maybe the time for hiding was over. She had a lot of old stories, but now it was time for new stories.

Tell began.

Carter with the guys

It was so easy not to know someone, Carter thought. She had never asked the Englishman for his name. She always called him Englishman and from the start he'd answered to it without a comment. If she ever came to know his name somehow, she thought she'd have to leave or make a decision or share her name. It was better to have everything a bit hazy, a bit uncertain, as if she wasn't really there. It was better if she numbed everything from the boobs up, both her heart and her mind. Everything below did the loving and the thinking, and that morning her lower body was thinking about the ocean.

She left the Englishman sleeping in bed and walked out into a shared apartment that was littered with ashtrays, empty bottles, and half-naked snoring men. In a small kitchenette she filled a glass with water and opened the shutters to let the sun pour in. Over there was the swimsuit she'd bought when they arrived in Vancouver—that was what, the day before? She was losing track of time—and over there was the door to the balcony and the stairs to the stone path below. She saw an old woman in a long housedress and a scarf over her head instead of a hat, and she asked, Which way to the beach? The woman pointed and said, Follow that path to the end, stay near the water.

She did what the old woman said. Private beaches and blue water spread out on her left and on her right were trees that provided shade. Sometimes she caught a glimpse of other early risers, people who were stripping off T-shirts or shorts and jumping into the water. Where the path ended was a closed kiosk and scattered tables. She walked by all that and then, all of a sudden, between the rise of rocks and cliffs, there was the beach, tucked in a small bay.

Garbage littered the sand, but she was taken by the blue of the ocean and the scatter of breathing mountains that rose up out of it. Nobody else was there so she left her swimsuit top, towel, and flip-flops on the beach. The ocean rocked her and on impulse she slipped out of her bikini bottom and floated with it in her hand. After a while she swam back to shore and lay in the shallows of the waves for a while longer, letting the salt water wash over her body as it wanted. She felt new. For a moment she left even her lower body and she floated above, seeing herself there in the water, naked and unafraid. It was good.

Back at the apartment the Englishman had rented with his buddies, she found the Englishman awake in their room, passing a joint back to a guy on the next bed. The Englishman was in his underwear and the second guy pulled a sheet over his dick. The Englishman smiled when she came in and said, Come on sit down here, sweetie, and then to his buddy, Mate, we're going to need some time here.

Carter sat and squeezed the Englishman's erection through his underwear. The Englishman pulled her top down and stroked her breasts. His buddy leaned in, his breath coming harder. The Englishman grinned and put his hands on her hips, said, These are handles, hips that'll take you where you want to go. Carter said, I've gotta piss. The Englishman's friend reached out and squeezed her right breast and the Englishman said, Nice, hey? Carter left them both in bed, peed, and then decided to shower the salt water off. When she returned to the room, the Englishman had passed out again and his buddy was gone. She laughed and lay beside him feeling the heat in her groin and the throb in her clit. Unfamiliar sounds rose and fell, voices calling and cars passing, and then she fell into a light sleep too.

He was on top of her when she woke again. He nuzzled her breasts and licked her nipples as she groaned. He said, Let me

MICHELLE PORTER

in—I'm wearing a condom. She opened her thighs. He rolled over onto his back and gestured for her to get on. She straddled him and he let his hands wander from her hips to her breasts and back.

The door to the room opened wide. One of the Englishman's buddies leaned in. Carter laughed, said, Come on in!

Fuck off, the Englishman said, but three of his buddies came in. They gathered around and their hands were all over her as she moved on top of the Englishman. Assholes, the Englishman said, but he was laughing now. I'm almost there, guys, let me come. One of the Englishman's buddies leaned in to kiss her and another reached down to her vulva, fumbling around a bit to find her clit. Someone else had her breasts in his hands and was kissing her nipple; another said to the Englishman, I'll stroke your sac while you come, and then the Englishman reared up and said, No way, and she fell off the Englishman and into the arms of one of his buddies. The guy who'd been kissing her, the one with the French accent, said, My turn. The Englishman and his other buddies shouted and wrestled while she followed this man's irresistible scent to the couch in the front room where he stroked her thighs until she was near climax and then she was out of her body again, the second time that day. She saw herself from above, saw herself opening her thighs so he could kiss and touch and suck her swollen clit, saw herself moan with an orgasm that rocked and swayed her body like the ocean she'd just been in. He reached for a condom from a bowl on the side table and he unrolled it down the shaft of his penis with a practiced motion. He put one knee on the couch and held himself with one hand until he found the right position to press himself inside her. He stroked her hair and whispered in her ear about how nice her cunt smelled, how good it felt inside her, how soft her skin was, and how beautiful she'd looked coming. She was no longer looking at herself from above but had slipped back into her body as she lifted her pelvis to meet his. After he came they both lay still, her stroking the small of his back and this man, whose name she would never know, offering small shivery kisses to her neck and her breasts.

A reading with Norah

Seemed to Gen that this child was too young to be able to say, I've been an alcoholic for five years.

Oh, baby girl, Gen said to her when Norah came to Gen's room and asked for a reading. The girl had just moved to a room down the hall because there was a leak in the ceiling in her old room on the top floor. Sit on my bed, hold the cards, think about what you want to learn, shuffle them, and lay them out like this.

She did just what Gen told her to do.

And what's on the bed? Three cards: the Moon reversed, Ace of Wands, and Three of Wands.

I see your story, said Gen.

Is it like your story? asked the girl.

Same root. Everyone's stories come from the same earth.

Why did you start drinking?

The same reason you did, child. There was a hole inside of me.

Where did the hole come from?

I'm reading your cards now but, honest, they're mine as well as yours. That's the way I read the cards anyway.

Yeah, sure.

Okay, now look. The big loneliness that wouldn't go away, all that stuff you talked about in group, all that about being in foster care? It's all here in your past card. Emotions out of control, right?

The girl nodded, pushed her hair behind an ear, revealed a bit more of her face, looked down at the cards, and back up at Gen.

There's emotions you aren't able to forget, said Gen and she added, You're not like my sister at all. Now, this next card is about where you are now. Some sort of breakthrough?

The girl nodded. Yeah, that's why I came here. You too?

Nah. Too old for a breakthrough, aren't I? I'm just here for the piano.

No, really. We all think you're so brave.

Gen shot a dark look at the girl. Norah rushed to fill in the silence, said, Where'd you learn tarot?

My auntie. The one who did whatever the hell she wanted. She gave me my first deck. Mama didn't like the cards. Didn't like that I took after my auntie either. Anyway, said Gen, pointing to the next card. Life is branching out for you. It's like your life is still a blank canvas.

I'm gonna go back to school, Norah said, looking down and letting her hair fall in front of her face again.

Gen reached out and lifted the girl's chin up with her hand. Gen said, We're tough, us Métis. You'll make yourself proud. And you said your father's Cree, do I remember right?

Yeah.

His parents are alive? Yes? You think they'll want to know you?

The girl shook her head, said, I don't know. Nobody would even guess that my mom's Métis, the way I look. Never mind my father's family.

It probably matters more to you than to them.

Do you know your grandchildren?

Geneviève picked up the cards and shuffled.

And you, pressed the girl, what is opening up for you?

What are you talking about now?

The cards. They're yours too. What's opening up in your life?

I'm dying, child. Death is opening up. The spirit world is calling. That's it for me.

What's it like to quit drinking after all this time? My adopted father died before he could quit.

My girl, you're not wearing a bra under that big old T-shirt are you? I can't tell because you're sitting there with your arms like little wings you wrap around yourself.

Her eyes went wide and she looked right up at Gen, forgetting to cover her face. No, she said. It's my pajama T-shirt.

You should wear your bra all the time, even to bed you know.

I don't like to wear it all the time. It's not—

It's to keep them firm and high. You're young, sure, but protect what you got. Put one of mine on. Second drawer. Go on. One of the new ones, still wrapped up. Not the one with the beading, I'm saving that one. Cost me a lot to get that one made. There's a powder-blue one, a pink one, and a black one.

The young woman giggled but she opened the drawer and fished out the blue bra. She held it out in front of her chest and laughed. It's way too big, she said.

Wouldn't do anything for you, would it?

No, she said, but she draped the bra around her shoulders like a shawl and sat back down on the bed with Gen.

I've got good boobs, right?

Um . . . yeah.

I do. It's okay to say it. They're good.

Yes.

You want yours to be good. Don't let them flop around at night. Okay, yours are little and light and mine were always heavy, but if you want to keep them high, wear a bra to bed. You got a lot to be proud of.

Okay?

You sound unsure. Gen stood up and opened the top of her muumuu a bit to show the top of her still-impressive cleavage and shimmied.

The girl covered her mouth.

Gen laughed out loud. Never cover a good laugh, child! Now

look at me. I can't hardly walk but I can still shake 'em, right? Now you shake yours.

The young woman doubled over laughing. She was trying to say something but couldn't. Gen sat down on the bed and laughed until she was weak.

All right, child. I'm tired and I still got to talk to my sister.

The phone room is closing soon, the girl said. You won't have much time.

Gen put the deck on the side table. The girl got up, returned the bra to the drawer, and went to the door. She looked back at Gen.

So you think I should see my father's parents? My dad's family?

What do you think? I'm just an old woman. Sure, I've got good boobs but that doesn't help. The next part of this story is all yours.

Afterlife, where Mamé finds the camp

A fiddle calls me farther down the river, away from the coyotes and the magpies.

I don't see any people at first. I see teepees and log houses and Red River carts and houses made from stone and wood and materials I don't recognize that behave in strange ways, growing or moving around like living beings.

I walk from log house to stone building to teepee, aware of the other houses that move and breathe around me.

As I near the end of the row, an old woman appears on the path ahead. She is tall and round and her face has seen a lot of sun. She wears blue jeans, a red T-shirt, and a long gray braid over one shoulder.

She touches my shoulder and when she turns away I follow.

She leads me into a sighing house. Sleep here, the old woman says. Light the smudge, she says. Eat, she says. And I do and it brings me pleasure even without the hunger that is part of earth. Drink tea, she says. And I do. Don't ask questions yet, she says. And I don't. When she tells me to follow her out the back door to a sweat lodge that is almost hidden among the trees behind the house, I do.

The sweat lodge is built out of long thin trunks and covered in canvas. A charm of magpies has gathered on its roof and they fly away as we push aside the flap.

She crawls in.

Come in, she calls.

I've never been in a sweat lodge like this before.

Sometimes my husband and his family picked a day to visit their relations outside the city to get a sweat going. I had always meant to go. There was always so much to do—tend to the garden, book the next gigs, get our performance clothes ready. I sent my girls sometimes, but I never took the time. So now it is something to get on my hands and knees and enter that hot still space. I can hear rain. Sweat, the old woman says. The lodge has been made ready for us and in all that heat and steam I begin the process of arriving.

Solin remembers

Solin kept walking the path like a grandmother.

They fell into a routine.

Tell liked to wake early and leave before Solin woke, with the magpie cartwheeling around him. She let herself doze until he'd gone ahead, his quick steps taking him over the grass and into the trees. She took her time. She was an old cow and her shoulders and hips ached something awful most of the time. Early mornings were the worst. She lifted each limb in circles, stretching to open each hip and ease her old joints. She sniffed to get a sense of the morning, a sense of the new stories that might be made during the day. She stood and gave thanks to the water, to the land, to the sky, and to her ancestors. She grazed a bit before she followed in the trail of the mother and the calf. As she walked she told herself the stories her grandmother had told her all those years ago. It'd been a long time since she'd walked on land she hadn't walked on before. Sometimes she crossed over bits of struggling grassland and sometimes she found herself in the trees where she stepped lightly and thanked the shade for its coolness and honored the leaves for turning color. Tell didn't have time for all that. He traveled ahead during the day, keeping within range of his mother.

Each evening Tell circled back with that magpie to bed down next to Solin and tell her of the day's events. Tell's stories. The deer he'd seen, the wolves he'd crept close to. The streams he'd crossed by himself. The fish he would catch one day. The groundhogs he'd counted. His mother letting him get closer. His mother forgetting about the need to rest. Tell had traveled on ahead of his mother and seen his father in the distance. Didn't Solin think his father moved like a mighty river? The changing rhythms of the land, the movement of the clouds. My mother stopped to drink there and when she was done I stopped there too. My mother doesn't eat very often but she ate this here and so I knew I could eat it too. I think she left some for me. My mother walks very fast and I almost lost her.

After he ran out of stories and he was feeling how young he really was, Solin told a story, began planting the old stories in him. She said, There are some stories I wanted the grandfathers to teach you one day and I don't know if I should tell what I know. Solin had been watching Tell's belly swell up with too much grass and not enough milk. She wondered how much he was able to carry on his young back and his little hump. Too much too early was worse than too little, she thought. He would have to come asking when he was ready for more. The way the world was for this youngest generation, she wasn't sure what the right time for anything was.

In the old world, in the one her grandmother told stories about, the females would let the bulls know when the calves were ready for their teaching. She knew she hadn't heard most of the stories and she knew how much she didn't know. She still didn't feel she knew enough to be called grandmother or elder. Tell's father hadn't had the teachings and that was what made him so willing to sprint ahead of everyone else. She wondered how it felt to rush ahead.

Carter enters a garden

Carter opened her eyes and saw an old woman crouching on her chest. The woman was so heavy Carter couldn't breathe, even though she was also so skinny that Carter could break her in two. The smell of the old hag, her hard flinty eyes, the creep of bony hands around Carter's neck.

And Carter, she couldn't move. She was trapped beneath this silent old woman, breathing in her stinking breath. The weight of the woman, it was like she was made of iron and Carter couldn't get a breath in—she gasped and choked. She struggled without moving. She couldn't lift an arm. She couldn't turn over. This is the end, she thought.

And then, across the room, her phone buzzed. Carter turned toward the noise and it was a moment before she realized that the old woman was gone. Her chest was light again.

She took a moment to breathe, to think about what just happened. A dream? She'd never had a dream like that.

Carter rolled out of bed and opened a window as if that would prevent the old woman's return. The smell of her was still in Carter's nose. The Englishman slept on, snoring lightly. Her phone buzzed again, but she turned away from it. Her phone had been buzzing the whole time she'd been on the island.

She wouldn't answer it yet. Instead, she put on her clothes and stepped outside.

It was so early in the morning only the locals were beginning to stir. A mishmash of fences and stone walls lined the path she was walking. Ahead of her a gate opened and an old woman with a thin white braid stepped out and picked up a bucket that had been left by the wall. She wore a faded ankle-length dress that gave her room to move and a pale blue kerchief on her head.

Carter recognized her as the woman who'd offered directions to the sea the other morning. She saw Carter and beckoned to her, said, Come, come.

Carter paused, thinking about the old woman who'd been on her chest that morning. But the smell here was so different: it was the smell of life. And Carter was curious, so she followed the woman through the gate. There was a garden on the other side.

She'd never seen a garden like this. Fruit trees in rows, with glorious crowns that offered shade to all that grew at their roots. There were limes and lemons, tomatoes and olives, pears and apples and another fruit Carter didn't recognize.

It's a quince, the old woman said in an accent Carter couldn't quite place. The stories said a man once traveled for nine months to get one of those for the woman he loved. The old woman looked up at Carter with warm brown eyes. Would you like one?

Carter couldn't speak so she nodded and the old woman conjured a couple of grocery bags from somewhere and moved about picking from her garden to fill the bags. Carter gawked, forgot how to use her legs. She wondered if she would have come here earlier if she knew this place existed.

The old woman pulled a tomato from the vine and she picked greens for Carter to eat with dinner and there was spinach and there were peas, everything right out of the earth or pulled from its branch. There were pears, so many pears it made Carter's chest ache. Carter wanted to ask the old woman's name but she was afraid of knowing too much. The bags were getting full. The old woman took Carter to a water barrel to wash the dirt away.

As they were washing each fruit and vegetable, the old woman spoke in a language Carter didn't know and then switched back to English to tell Carter that her husband had been injured soon after their children were born and, from that time on, wasn't able to come to the garden. He couldn't work after that, she said. So the garden became only hers and with it she fed her family.

She led Carter back to the gate. Carter walked slowly. Outside the garden, Carter turned to tell the old woman thank you. She was closing the gate and locking it. The tourists, she said, they get drunk and then they feel they can just come in and take what they want.

Can I come back? Carter asked. The old woman nodded and said, I am here every morning starting at four and then again at seven in the evening. Carter was about to leave but had one more question. Who helps you? The old woman waved away the question. It's just me, she said, just me. Who else?

Carter returned to the apartment. She brought the food up the stairs, set the bags on the floor near the sink, and left again for the beach, this time with the Englishman at her side and his arm draped around her shoulder.

Carter laughed at the Englishman in the same way she laughed at herself. She didn't take him seriously and didn't want to. He seemed to stumble through the days, never thinking about the next minute or the previous one, and she wanted that for herself so badly she could kill for it. He was red as a lobster and wore a hat that he pulled down low over his forehead. He sat on his towel and watched the girls. This was why he came to the beach, he said, to watch girls' tits. He was amused by Carter, who kept her top on if there were other people around.

All that water called Carter back for a swim and as she entered the water this time she got a new kind of feeling and the only words she knew for this feeling were *sacred* or maybe *blessing*, but she hated both those words. She swam as far out as she dared and pretended she was completely alone until eventually she floated back toward the beach. Her legs were weak as she stood up out of the water and walked the last bit to shore. Her

Englishman had settled back down onto his towel. Carter walked to her towel and stood over him with a smirk on her face. You're hard, she said. He smirked and said that the sun always gave him an erection. Then he looked Carter up and down and told her that she had the best tits on the beach. That got her laughing and she shimmied her boobs and raised her eyebrows invitingly until he got laughing, too, and he laughed his erection away. Soon after he suggested they walk back.

That evening the Englishman said he had a headache and could they stay in? Carter unpacked the bags of food from the garden. She roasted some peppers, onions, and zucchini. She tossed a green salad and sliced up some of the fruit. She thought how her son would like the pears, his favorite fruit, but just as quickly as the thought appeared she pushed it away. Not now, she said out loud. She brought all the food to their bed and they ate together. He liked the fruit. He popped a piece of pear in his mouth and reached out to squeeze a boob. She swatted his hand away with an impatience that surprised them both. She hadn't objected at all to his play before. She thought of the woman who'd given her all this food and told the Englishman about her. Not so he'd react in any way but just to hear herself tell the story. He was incredulous. An old woman in a long dress? Her phone buzzed and she looked over at it, but she didn't answer.

Geneviève has a smoke

In all her years on the prairies, Gen didn't think she'd seen so much rain. She was at the piano in the dark again, looking for a song in the black and white keys.

Velma stepped into the window, said, You got a smoke?

Are you kidding?

What, you quit smoking too?

Gen stopped playing, turned to look at Velma. She had a show the next day, whatever that meant in the spirit world, and half her hair was still up in curlers.

You smoke still? Gen asked.

We got cigarettes here. They're different though. They're not like yours.

God almighty, you really want a cigarette. Okay, yeah, I been carrying a few in my pocket all the time these days. And a lighter. It helps. I'm always wanting to find a place to light up but it's always raining and—oh there, how's that?

Gen put the cigarette to her lips and blew smoke at her sister. Velma inhaled deeply and smiled. That brought back memories, Velma said.

Gen held out the cigarette to Velma. Can you take a puff?

Don't know, said Velma.

She reached over and took the cigarette from her sister, holding it triumphantly. Looks like I can, she said.

Velma sucked in some smoke. Mama always said they were pretty.

You can have that smoke. I've got more.

Thanks.

You mean my hands?

What?

You said Mama always said they were pretty.

Yes, your hands. You just wanted me to say that again.

Geneviève pulled another cigarette from her pocket. Still jealous? she asked.

Velma shrugged, said, They're kind of knobbly and witchy looking now.

They can still play.

Mama taught me to play too. Christ, why would I still want those fingers?

Because Mama loved them.

So what? Papa thought my hands were good for the fiddle.

Gen held the cigarette between two fingers and tapped it against the corner of her mouth. Gen said, You were his favorite.

No, I wasn't. Christ, why do I still want those fingers?

Can't you get anything you want up there?

No. Sort of, but no. It doesn't work that way.

I bet it does. Make your fingers long and elegant. Go on.

No.

See? You don't really want them.

You were the pretty one.

You were the one with the fiddle.

You got what you wanted.

Gen put the cigarette between her lips, held the lighter at the end, and sucked in a breath of air. Didn't you?

Well, it feels good to smoke again.

Makes me want a drink.

Why don't you get one?

I can't. Not here.

Then leave. Get a drink. Play your piano for an audience. Be happy.

Like you?

I'm not joking around. I always said you got to live your life. If drinking makes you happy, what's the problem?

I'm not sure it ever made me happy.

Happiest I saw you was with a drink in the years before.

Before what?

Before I left.

The ash on the end of Gen's cigarette was getting long. She flicked it into the piano. She said, Those years were the worst you ever saw me.

How many times did you try to kill yourself?

All the pills I took.

What it did to your kid.

Oh, don't get started.

That one time, Christmas Eve?

Oh shut the fuck up.

Hey, you wanted to talk.

Not about this.

Velma flicked the ash from her cigarette back into the light that always came with her. Well, your girl's first memory is that Christmas Eve you took all them pills. That night she found you and watched you get carried out of the house, unconscious and limp.

I thought you didn't watch what goes on here.

I don't. But sometimes images sort of come to me whether I want them or not. Mostly I don't. That one came to me.

Leave it alone.

Your little Lucie creeping into your room and finding you still as stone on your bed. The calling for help, the crying. Lucie following behind your body like a lost little bird as they carried you out.

I didn't know that.

She's still not over it, by the way. And you can thank me for that information later.

Like mother, like daughter, I guess, because I never got over those nuns.

Your daughter wants to die. You know, right?

What?

She asked your great-granddaughter to get her some pills.

Which one? Which great-granddaughter.

The one you've never met. The one who needs you. The one you're going to call.

Lord. You mean the one who . . . You mean Kat or Kate?

Carter.

Right. And what does this Carter need with a dying old woman?

You're all dying down there. It's why you need each other.

And this thing Lucie's asked. Is Carter going to kill her?

I don't know. She doesn't know.

You have to know. You're up there. You know.

You're wrong too. Worst I saw of you wasn't after the pills. It was when you came back from the shock stuff. Electroshock. That scared the shit out of me.

Tell me. Is Carter going to kill my daughter?

It was the empty eyes that got me.

Stop.

Your memory was just shot. You had huge blank spaces.

I know. I remember. Stop telling me about it.

Do you remember how much you forgot?

A hill the shape of a bison's hump

Solin passed the tree line. For a moment, she couldn't breathe. The splendor of the wide-open plains.

This is what the afterlife will look like, she thought.

The land called to her. Her hooves were so eager to press into the earth ahead that she took quicker steps than she had in years. The land spread out in an unbroken sweep. The grass was tall and moved with the breeze.

Why not stay right here, on this land? she thought.

She didn't have to follow anyone anymore.

The subtle greens, the flickering yellows, and the glorious smell of it all. Oh, this land was something else. It was a song and she'd stepped into the middle of it, become a note.

Birds flitted and called. Grasshoppers played their fiddles.

The land spoke to Solin about recovering, and though the land said plenty, Solin couldn't understand what it was that had happened, only that it had something to do with humans and farming. There were signs. There were only a few different species of grass and no sweetgrass at all. She could remember grazing on a stretch of land with hundreds of different grasses, but that was when she was a calf.

The sun was still climbing into the sky, and she could almost believe she'd passed to the spirit world overnight and that her mama was waiting for her.

She kept moving on.

At the end of the day, she saw dark shapes in the distance. She picked up her pace a little and walked over a slight rise in the landscape. From there, she could see Tell walking with that tiny bird on his back. He was trailing some way behind Dee. Ahead of them both was a bison-shaped shadow Solin recognized as Jay.

He was walking at a steady pace alongside a small group of bison, all unknown to Solin. They all seemed to be heading toward the peak of a hill, one the shape of a bison's hump. Oh, Solin had a bad feeling about that.

Light was beginning to fade so Solin stayed where she was to graze a little and watch them all walk over the hump and disappear from view. She bedded down for the night beneath the stars. Tell didn't come back to her that night and she wondered what stories he would have told. She thought maybe she should let the young ones alone and go her own way. In the morning, she'd decide what to do.

Dawn's first light found her on her way to the hill the shape of a bison's hump and midmorning found her at the peak, looking out over a very human landscape. A spread of short grass and beyond that concrete and cars and houses. There was the magpie flying ahead of Tell, who was following after Dee, who was still heading for Jay. They were wary, she could see it in how they moved. Frightened even.

Ahead, the hill under Solin's hooves dropped away at a steep angle. The grass below was crisscrossed with the curving black asphalt walkways that humans traveled, breaking apart the open space. On the other side was even more asphalt and concrete, and on top of that were rows of buildings surrounded by fences and cars. One car was driving away while two blue vans were driving toward the houses and fences, the asphalt and the bison.

It all made her dizzy.

Solin wanted to turn right around, to get away from this unnatural place as quickly as possible. It wasn't a place for bison, she could smell that.

The vans stopped. A group of humans got out. Some were holding signs. They started calling and shouting and they were

MICHELLE PORTER

pointing at the bison. More cars arrived, more people got out. They pointed at Tell and Dee and Jay and the others.

It was never good to draw the attention of the humans, Solin knew that.

A murder of magpies wheeled out of the sky and dropped down to perch along the fences, on the wires, and in the tops of the few trees.

Nausea overcame the old cow. She turned from the scene below, heaving and retching. Her bellow was a low moan and she vomited up all the grass she'd eaten that morning.

Every muscle began to shake, and she knew that her body had decided for her. She was not going down that slope.

Solin turned and looked out over everything she'd just walked across. The prairie behind was a comfort to Solin. Her grand-mother's stories still lived in the grassland, altered and damaged as it was. She could go back there, tell her own stories to the grass and the land, make wallows with the earth, and die happily. Yes, that was what she would do.

She walked away from it all, from the confused bison, from the humans who brought destruction everywhere, from the warning of concrete. She walked back the way she came.

Allan tears a strip off Carter

WHAT DRUGS DID
YOU GIVE HER?

. . .

For God's sake what drugs did
you give her?

. . .

We NEED to know
what you gave mom
PLEASE tell me what she took

. . .

She said you gave her a bunch
of pills
She's in hospital right now
Doctors trying to figure out
what she took
They're pumping her stomach
now

. . .

How shitty and selfish can you
be?
Always judging everyone
like you're so great. FUCK
YOU!

. . .

I took a minute to breathe . . .
really sorry.
Shouldn't swear won't help . . .
sorry

. . .

Look she took the pills you
gave her
and then she called me
She said you gave her the pills
to help her die
but she changed her mind
could I call her an ambulance

· · ·

We need to know what you
gave her
I don't want my mom to die
Doctors need to know.
PLEASE

· · ·

God WHY WON'T YOU
ANSWER?
My mom wants to live she
wants
to live again

· · ·

Did you know her mother tried
to commit suicide
lots of times when she was a
kid
that her mom kept overdosing
on sleeping pills
did she tell you that?
She doesn't want to die she just
doesn't
want to remember

· · ·

I don't think I can bear this

Why didn't you tell me what
she asked you to do?
I would have helped you
I know what she's like . . . oh
God
ANSWER ME
ANSWER ME

. . .

Velma curls her hair

Velma was finishing her fifth cigarette in ten minutes. She dropped a butt into the light and lifted her skirt a little so she could crush the butt with one foot. Gen fished in the pocket of her bathrobe for another cigarette but came up empty. She held out the end of the cigarette she'd been puffing on. Here, you can finish this, she said.

Velma took it and flicked the ash into the light.

That's all the cigarettes I've got right now, said Gen. I'd have more, only the road here is flooded, they can't get stuff in.

I forget what it can be like on earth, Velma said and put the cigarette to her lips, inhaled.

Coming on a month of rain, said Gen.

Gen's fingers needed something to do so she started to play the piano. Her fingers decided on a reel. She thought how sometimes it was like their conversations never really finished, that there was no time between one midnight encounter and the next.

This is the reel that was playing the night you met Reg. You remember that dance?

I don't dwell, Gen.

I never saw you like you were that night.

Quit it.

You were nineteen.

Velma laughed, said, All those men couldn't get enough of dancing with you, all fifteen years of you.

But then the band gave you a fiddle and you got up there.

God, I loved performing back then.

Nobody could keep their eyes off you.

When I was on the stage I felt like I was flying.

And there was Reginald pushing his way to the front, ahead of all the men wanting a piece of you.

Here I always feel like I'm flying. The spirit world's like that.

He was hard.

My Reggie was all passion.

Like a moth.

What?

He was like a moth to your flame.

Reg wasn't any kind of moth, said Velma, shaking her head.

What was he then?

He was the flame.

No. You were the goddamn bonfire.

I was the moth. Just one of the common moths that he liked to have circling around him.

The brightest flame. Never saw anything like what you were on the stage.

I loved the fire in his eyes.

He wanted to own you. Pin your wings to a display.

He loved me, said Velma.

He's the kind that thinks hate is love. His family hated Métis.

He hated his parents.

And then he finds you. Marries you.

Don't regret anything.

That's what I don't get. You never wished for another life.

No, that's what you do. Sit on your ass and wish things had turned out differently.

How many times did he break your fingers so you couldn't play?

Velma threw the cigarette butt back into the light and stepped back in to crush it underfoot. I'm getting bored of this conversation, she said.

How many times did you call me for help?

From the light rose sounds of people calling and cheering, like there was a party of some kind. Velma looked back into the light. She put on her stage smile and waved. More cheers rose. Someone called her name and she stepped farther into the light.

I'm getting ready, she called out. Won't be long at all.

Velma was making spirit world small talk and there was Gen with the feeling that something was missing. She groped in her pockets. Nothing. But there had been something and that was what was bothering her. The two Empresses. When had she last had them? She was more upset than she thought she should be. They were just cards after all.

Someone from the spirit world whistled and Velma was laughing when she said goodbye, but when she turned back to her sister her brow was furrowed.

Velma asked, You sure you don't have any more cigarettes?

Not even the sorry end of a cigarette.

I'm going to bring another piano out here, said Velma and the moment she said it there was an upright piano, the sturdy kind found in church basements. She sat down at the bench and held her fingers over the keys, hesitating.

It's been so long since I played the piano, Velma said.

Gen dropped her hands onto the keys to make an angry sound.

Velma played a soft chord and looked at Geneviève.

And you had it any better? Your Englishman?

He didn't hit me.

No?

Only the once.

And when was that, Gen? Do you remember the reason? Or did all that electroshock make you forget? For all your talk, you were just like me after you married. You weren't allowed to speak Michif, were you? Or French. What was that like for you? Holding in all those words he wanted to control, holding all that self and all that knowledge in, for a marriage. I only had a few years of it, but you—you must have been nearly bursting.

Gen balled her hands into fists and banged them against the keys, making her sister wince with the noise.

There was more to our story than that, she said.

Velma switched to another song, a faster one. Go on then, tell it.

We were stupid, you and me.

Me, I blazed a trail right to Reggie and learned what I needed to learn and then I left. It was the work of my life. It's still the work of your life.

What happened to it all?

To what?

To our music. Our family out in Manitoba. All those Goulets. We hardly ever saw them again after we moved away.

Just a typical Métis story.

I hated the English language after I got married. Each word was heavy like a rock.

You and me, we talked to each other in Michif every day. We had that.

What if we could have had love in Michif?

Oh, shut up and listen, said Velma and she let her fingers move along the keys. Do you remember this song?

Do you remember how you died?

Velma dove into a rambunctious show tune. The music opened Gen's fingers and settled them on the keys. She followed Velma's lead. The song unraveled in that old familiar way. Their notes rushed ahead over the rocks and then hung back in a trembling eddy by the bank.

After a while Velma said over their playing, It didn't occur to them that we'd resist, did it?

Geneviève was out of breath, trying to keep up with Velma.

Velma said, Me with my fire and anger and cast-iron pans flung across the room.

And Gen said, Me with pills and alcohol.

No, Velma said right away, shaking her head. That's not your story. Don't sell your performance short. No, you resisted with ice and waiting and lasting longer than anybody else.

Geneviève played until her arms ached, until she couldn't play anymore. When she couldn't keep up, she stood and reached for her cane. She walked to one of the windows and turned the handle until it opened enough to let in the sound of the rain and the distant roar of rising water. There was no screen, so Gen stuck her hand outside the window. The rain pooled in her palm. She said, The work of my life was to leave my husband, that's what you said.

Uh-huh, said Velma. She stopped playing and the piano vanished. A vanity table appeared in its place and then she was sitting before a large mirror.

But it's fucking alcohol I have to leave.

Velma lifted a twist of hair with a hot curling iron, said, It's the same thing, isn't it?

A silence eased itself down between them and Gen stood looking out into the darkness, leaning on her cane. She couldn't see it, but she knew there was so much silt heading down the river now, caught in the speed of the current. All the rain had churned up debris from the bottom and the river would run brown.

The smell of the rain had changed after the first few days and the air that entered the open window was filled with mud and told of disturbed riverbanks. It reached Velma and traveled all the way into the spirit world. It was the promise of something coming, Velma thought. When she was a child, alive and on earth, she'd have waited impatiently for the rains to end so she could swim in the rushing waters.

You got another cigarette? Velma asked.

No, no. Tomorrow though. They're supposed to get stuff in tomorrow by some other road.

Oh right, I forgot. When is tomorrow down there?

Velma, I think there's something I have to tell you.

I keep telling myself just one more smoke. But as soon as I'm done, I want another.

Gen walked from the window back to the piano. She sat down, said, It's about your Reginald.

The cigarettes here in the spirit world aren't like that. They're just right every time you have one.

And how you died.

Shit, stop talking would you? Get me another cigarette.

Don't want to wait anymore. I've been waiting most of my life to have this conversation.

I got away from him, didn't I? Just tell me that I got away.

Velma.

I need to know I got away from that man in the end.

Sis.

Then I can really let this audience have it. A real wallop. They're waiting.

Velma stood up from the mirror and it vanished. Velma's hair was shining black. Her dress was so beautiful it took Gen's breath away, made her feel so small beside her, just a little old lady in the blue room.

I don't know. Okay, sure. You got away.

Another piano appeared, a concert piano. Velma sat down and stretched her fingers, said, I don't want to hear anything else.

You got away from him, Velma. Like nobody else.

Gen started with another old tune and then Velma dropped her hands onto the piano and crashed into Gen's song, tearing up Gen's harmony and racing on ahead, pouring fuel onto her own notes, burning the song higher, burning away all the rules she'd ever learned, playing so loud she drowned out the sound of Geneviève's thoughts.

Gen tried to play with her, but she couldn't. Even at the piano, Velma was her better. The music careened around the room and Geneviève trembled at her bench, her old fingers useless. She couldn't stop reliving that day. Hearing the phone ring. Her sister's panic, a man's voice roaring in the background. Velma's begging, He's here and he's breaking the door down—come get me now! Gen saying they would come, saying they'd be right there. A short drive over rough land through the trees between their two houses, but Gen's husband, the strong, quiet, hardworking Englishman, said no. He would not drive that truck—no one would drive that truck—not until he'd had a proper dinner. Gen served him his dinner. He said nothing about her trembling hands.

Felt like Velma's music could bring the house down, could bring the world down.

Gen wanted to say, You died because I didn't save you.

Gen wanted to ask, Why won't you let me tell you?

Gen straightened her shoulders and clenched her jaw. She could not confess so she put her fingers on the piano keys and accompanied Velma's fury note for note, phrase by phrase. Gen pounded at the keys with a bitterness she'd never let loose before. There was so much of it. She thought the river of her fury would kill her before it left her body and let her be.

It was only when that song was over, after Velma had stepped back into her light, with a look on her face that Geneviève knew meant she was gone for good, it was only then, after Gen had caught her breath and was sitting alone in the darkness hearing nothing but the unending rain, it was only then she said for the first time, You died because he killed you.

Mamé, looking back

There I am covered in sweat, slick as a newborn.

My skirt sticks to my legs. My shirt clings to my back.

The air is thick with the scent of burning wood. Sparks rise from the firepit, lighting the old woman's face.

She does not seem to sweat. I marvel how she can stay dry in this place. She sits cross-legged near the wall of the lodge and passes water to me when I need it.

The journey I've just taken—I don't know, it kind of softened me up, made me relax about not having control over this next part, over what's going to happen. Am I even eager now? I am ready to let the sweat lodge and the old woman take me through this next leg, carry me closer to arrival and whatever it is that will happen after.

I reach out for the old woman's hand and she nods at me. It's quiet then, except for the fire and drip of sweat from my back.

Letting go is part of arriving, the old woman says and I feel my body begin the transition. I am being pressed on all sides and the dark inside me is becoming light, pure and brilliant.

And then this happens. Then I am pulled up short, as if I'm attached to a rope or a leash and my handler wants me to heel. Extinguished.

I'm pulled back into the sweat lodge and I fall back clawing at the invisible tether that has kept me from moving on. But I can't get rid of it.

So I put my palms on the ground. I push myself back to sitting.

I look at the old woman, say, The arrival's jammed, isn't it?

Happens like this sometimes, she tells me. You pass on and you make your choices and then you come on here for the transition and—surprise, surprise—something holds you up. For you it's someone down there who's holding up your arrival. I'm telling you. It's different for everyone but I could tell stories. You got to relax, that's all. That's all.

Now I'm like a fetus in breech, twisting this way and that just so I can maybe get a peek at what I've left down on earth, trying to see the people I left behind. It's my girls I try to see first, the one already here and the one down below, but I can't, just plain can't. I am raw. All the others float out of my reach, cousins and nieces and nephews and grandchildren, all the generations after, all of them so far away from where I am beneath those tarps.

I can't help it, I'm looking back, I say to the old woman.

She shifts her legs and smiles big. She says, One thing we've got here is time. So take it. If there's a thing I love, little one, it's a good long sweat. I'll be here.

Carter, unwritten

Tucker was beside me in bed in the early hours of the morning. He curled up against me and groped and nuzzled to find my nipple. If I fed him he'd sleep for another twenty minutes and I could wake up slowly. I changed position a bit to make it easier for him to suckle. I was filled with a simple peace. It had been a while since he breastfed and I couldn't quite think why that should be. My head was fuzzy with all the wine from last night. I inhaled deeply to get a bit of beautiful baby smell but instead I breathed in sour morning breath and I remembered that my boy was across the country and anyway he was too old to breastfeed anymore. I opened my eyes and it was the Englishman at my tit. I groaned, pushed him away, and turned over. I curled into a ball, overcome with the sudden need to hold my boy close, to smell his childhood.

Hey, said the Englishman.

I said, Can you make me a coffee?

Sure, he said and he left the room and there I was with the ghost of my boy, the boy I was meant to get and the one I was running away from.

Could I do this? Could I leave him with my husband's parents so he'd grow up with a real family? Could I keep myself to the edges of his life? They had everything to give him and here I was, nothing but a mess. It'd be selfish to go get him. I knew that. My phone buzzed across the room. I knew I'd have to answer soon.

I pulled on a pair of shorts and a clean T-shirt. I put my phone in my back pocket and went to the kitchen. The Englishman was working on the coffee. He grinned at me. On the table was a bowl with the last of the pears. I didn't know how we still had any pears left. It seemed to me we should have finished them days ago, but here they were still filling the bowl. I picked two and went out to the balcony where I could see the ocean on the horizon. They were so ripe the juice dribbled down my chin when I took a bite, dripped onto my shirt until it looked like I was leaking milk. I'd never tasted such sweet pears. I sucked as much juice from the core as I could. My phone buzzed and I lay the cores on the balcony ledge and wiped my hands on my shirt before I pulled it out of my pocket. I knew I had to make a decision before I answered. If I didn't, I'd make the wrong decision, blurt out the wrong thing to my ex. I'd say his parents could keep my boy or I'd say I was coming to get him, fuck what's best for Tucker. And I didn't know which one I would do.

I unlocked the phone. There were texts. Lots of texts. From Allie. I tapped hers first. She was in the hospital with her mother, with Lucie. She was pissed at me. Lucie can't have swallowed all those pills, I thought. But I was crying, I couldn't help it. And I knew then that I couldn't be a mother. What kind of mother gave drugs to her grandmother, one she'd just met? I knew what I had to do. I just had to get my strength together and do it.

I shoved my phone in my back pocket again and went down the stairs to the stone path and I walked. Down by the water I watched people with their boats and small cruise ships at the docks and thought, What would it be like to just sail out, to cut my ties to land entirely? I didn't want to know what happened back home or what it meant that the pills Gramma took came from my hands. Not yet.

I'd come down here to tell myself once and for all that my boy didn't need me. Not when he had so much there with his dad and his dad's family, Baka and Deda and Teta and all of them treating Tucker like some crown prince. I'd been trying to avoid this thought that had been bouncing around in my head but then it was finally clear: maybe I was just like Allie.

My thoughts were so loud I hadn't really heard the sloshing of the waves and the calling of the gulls but when over all of that came the sound of a kid sobbing I snapped to attention, the mother in me all alert and ready for action.

I couldn't see the kid, so I followed the sound to the other side of the beach around a rocky cliff where there was this cove with a little bit of sand that not many tourists ever found. Fuck, the phone wouldn't quit. It was buzzing and beeping. The child was screaming now, but I couldn't see him. There was the buzzing again—leave me alone.

To my right the ocean was blue, blue, blue. To my left were the rocky outcrops rising above me and the boy was still crying. I knew what sobbing like that looked like. When I found him, he'd have lost himself in his own fear and he'd be standing rigid, mouth open, eyes clenched shut, wailing. Dark hair, dark eyes, in a blue swim shirt and blue swim trunks. Just over three years old. Why couldn't I find him?

The phone buzzed. Could be Allie or maybe Slavko. I climbed up into the outcrop. Maybe he'd fallen between the rocks and couldn't climb out. The rocks were slippery. I lost my footing and cut my knee open on a sharp edge. The crying was so urgent I was on the move again right away. I thought how when I reached him I'd know what to do. I'd crouch down to his level and speak gently to him. I'd pull him into a hug to comfort him. He'd try to be brave and he'd heave and gulp back his tears. But I couldn't find him—and now his cries were changing, becoming more like an animal.

Just like that his cries stopped and there were only these birds wheeling in the sky, calling out to each other. Why had he stopped? Was he conscious? My knee stung. My phone kept on buzzing.

I stood on the highest rock and squinted into the distance. I saw movement between the rocks. But it wasn't a boy: it was a

MICHELLE PORTER

young coyote, barely more than a puppy, raising its snout to cry out. The pup was afraid, I could hear that, and I moved without thinking in its direction. And then another sound raised the hairs on the back of my neck—this time it was a snarl, and I turned to see a coyote coming over the rocks behind me and I knew I'd come between a mother and her pup.

She slinked along the rocks, ears down. I backed off slowly to the side so I was no longer in between, gave her as much room as possible to get to her pup. I stepped off the rocks and waded knee deep into the water, let the waves splash up on my body. She considered her next move, watched me closely for a few seconds, but another cry from her baby and she rushed ahead to him.

Oh God, what relief. I waded back to shore, still scanning the area in case the boy I heard wasn't the pup I just saw. But there was no boy anywhere.

I walked along the beach away from the coyote mother and called out to a woman I saw walking in my direction. Had she seen a little boy? Had she heard him?

No, she hadn't.

She'd seen nothing. She'd heard nothing.

Had she seen a coyote?

No.

There's a mom and her pup out there—be careful.

My phone was buzzing. My arms were empty. My phone was buzzing. My arms were too light. I pulled my phone out. I didn't recognize the number. I approached the entrance to the cove where there was a little hut and tables where drinks flowed in the evening. I wanted to distract myself from the boy who would have been on my hip, head on my shoulder. Fuck it. I answered the phone.

Hello?

It was an old woman. Carter, she said.

Who was this? I didn't recognize the voice but my legs were suddenly weak. I moved to the short set of stairs near the hut and I sat.

The voice repeated my name. Carter? Carter?

A slight breeze rattled the leaves on the trees around the hut and tables. I shivered in the heat. The old woman harrumphed impatiently. Carter! she said. You there? Is this a bad connection? Can you hear me?

I knew that voice because it was my own, but old somehow.

She was impatient, said, Carter, you there?

The sun was pounding down on my uncovered head. I needed some shade, but I didn't get up. I couldn't. The old woman I was going to become was somehow reaching back in time. My hands started to shake.

Yes, I said, yes.

I knew how to listen to death in the voices of the sick and the lingering, but this was different. This was the voice that I was going to have, that I did have. This was the voice I would become.

You got to come get me. You hear me, Carter?

Yes, I said again.

I'm dying, Carter, she said.

I know, I said.

And I did know then. I could hear myself dying. I couldn't tell if I was doing it well or if I was thrashing in search of I don't know what. As hard as I listened to the voice on the phone I couldn't know all that. I was going to vomit.

I leaned over the side of the stairs and I spewed all that pear onto the ground. I was wiping my chin with my shirt when I looked up to see an old man on the other side of the tables. His face twisted in disgust and he shouted something about junkies and whores, but most of his words fell away. He turned his back to me and stalked off. A part of me wanted to shout back at him but I was shaking. I felt as if I might suffocate right there in the crushing heat of the sun beside an ocean that felt worlds away from where I was born.

The old woman spoke again, my own voice from the future said, You have to come help me.

I was slick with sweat. I got off those stairs and started to walk. The shirt I was wearing clung to my back. I felt as if I'd crossed over.

How many people have asked me to help them die and how little did I know about dying really? I wanted to hear everything this voice wanted to tell me.

I don't know what to do, I said and then I realized there was only silence. Fuck, the call had been cut off. Was it when I stood up?

Shit. Only I would get a call from myself in trouble in the future and accidentally cut myself off. Was there a number, could you call a future version of yourself? I looked at my recent calls. There were none recorded.

I closed recent calls and opened them again. Same thing. No call recorded. I turned my phone off and turned it on again. No call had been recorded. How could I reconnect with my dying self? Not by phone, I thought.

I buried my head in my hands and the phone was kind of resting against my head when it buzzed. I started and dropped the phone. I hesitated before picking it up. No caller ID. I took a deep breath and I answered.

Hello? It was the old lady's voice. She was cranky. Do you hear me? she said. I'm dying, she said. You have to come help me, she said. My sister said that you would help me. Well, my sister didn't say it like that; she kind of insulted me until I came to the idea that it would help you out to help me die. So when can you come get me?

I took another deep breath. Who are you?

Does that matter? she asked.

And I laughed because she was right. It didn't matter who she was. Somehow I knew I was going to say yes to whatever she asked. I would do whatever this old dying woman wanted.

You understand? she said. So you have to come pick me up. I can't drive any distance anymore. Not since I quit drinking. The shaking.

Okay, I said. It'll take some time, I'm—

I don't have time for long explanations or stupid talk. Go get your son from his dad. Then come get me. I'm at the damned rehab place near Milk River. You know it?

I'll find it.

Good girl. I can't remember the fucking name. Everything in my head works different now that I quit drinking. But the heart's working better, so that's a thing. I'm ready to die. Okay? I'll pay you to help me die. Just come get me as soon as you can. I'll be waiting.

She hung up.

Two more readings and an insult

What happened after the women asked the men to throw themselves in the river?

Gen thought about the elder's story most nights as she tried to go to sleep. It distracted her from the way everything was falling apart around her. The leaking on the top floor had become so bad they'd evacuated everyone to the second floor, to old storage rooms and offices and even some shared rooms.

No risk of another dry spell here, she thought.

Gen was in her room watching the rain. She could hear the sounds of upheaval in the hallways, staff and patients helping to move bags, bed frames, and mattresses. Her lamp glowed and the radio was on to old country music. She kept looking out over the parking lot and trees for signs of that bison herd she saw sometimes, and she was trying to remember the way Elaine had started the story about the bison, the exact words she'd used.

Gen needed to know the end of Elaine's story. She'd asked the staff to invite Elaine again. They said Elaine had many demands on her time, but they could book her again for the last week of Gen's rehab program. Until then, Gen was left alone with the beginning of the story. The bison had carried the babies on their backs to keep them safe from the drought, Gen remembered that. But what about the mothers?

There was a knock on her door then and Gen called out, Come in. It was one of the other patients, a man whose name she couldn't remember but she remembered the awkward way he held his skinny shoulders and the way he pulled at his long black hair when he was nervous. He said he was waiting for his next room to be ready and he thought maybe a tarot reading would pass the time?

Gen sat down and shuffled her Rider-Waite-Smith cards, laid them out for a simple three-card reading. She invited him to sit.

The cards say you're in limbo, she said.

Between rooms? He laughed.

Could be that. I'm also getting that there's a choice here, with the Two of Swords.

His hands began to shake just like that, and Gen reached out to steady his hands without thinking. He took a deep breath.

Not giving them the chance to reject me again, he said. I'll never be enough for them.

Gen said for him to look in her top drawer and get himself a wig. He frowned but opened the top drawer and picked out a wig at random. He moved over to the mirror and stood in front of it, adjusting the long curly blonde wig. He said, I'd have looked amazing in the red one too.

Gen looked at his other cards, the Star and the King of Swords, both reversed.

It's like you've never been enough for yourself, she said. Or like you're rejecting yourself.

He sat on the bed again. He took off the wig and held it in his lap, playing with the curls. He said, Yeah, it's weird.

The song on the radio changed and someone knocked on the door to ask was he in there and his room was ready. Gen gathered the cards together and put the deck back on her bedside table, beside the Mary statue. Go on, just leave the wig, Gen said.

All that night she dreamed of fire and floods and bison walking to watered ground. She'd wake and between dreams think about what Elaine meant to tell her with that story. Was it about rebirth? Like after a drought? Or was it a crossing over to the spirit world? What would the women do without the men? Eventually she gave up sleep and turned on her lamp as if the light could burn away the fog of her thoughts.

MICHELLE PORTER

When a knock came at her door Gen called out, I'm awake. She watched the door curiously, half expecting some ghost of a bison to walk in. The door opened and Pamela leaned in.

Is it too early for a reading? Pam asked.

Gen shook her head. Come on in, she said. She reached for her cards and as Pam sat down in the chair near her bed, said, What are you doing here?

Pamela said, The roads home are flooded. I've got a bed in the supply closet.

You couldn't get a better room? You're a nurse.

I been up most the night walking the hallways. Then I saw a light shine from the crack under your door.

Gen asked Pamela to cut the deck. Gen laid out three cards.

I don't really need a reading, to be honest, but everyone's been wondering who is this old woman who decides to get clean just to die . . .

Everyone or just you?

I mean if I were dying I'd have a real big party, the kind everyone would remember. I'd get trashed and even get a line of something, who cares what.

Didn't know you were in recovery.

Oh, I'm not. It's not that. I've never even smoked weed. And I don't drink. I've seen too much of what it does to people. But if I was going to die, why not try it out without any fucking consequences?

That got a smile out of Gen. She scooped up all the cards and handed them to Pamela. She said, I think you should lay your own cards. Shuffle.

Pamela shuffled and at Gen's urging she pulled three cards from the deck, one from the top, one from the middle, and one from the bottom. She laid them on her lap: the Ten of Wands, the Nine of Swords reversed, and the Six of Pentacles.

Gen said, The first's your past, the second your present, the third your future.

That guy carrying a handful of staffs, that's my past?

The Ten of Wands, yeah. It's a card of burden. This man is carrying ten long wands. It means you've already struggled and won. You're just walking the last leg to the resting place.

That's a laugh.

Yeah?

Fuck, where should I start? My brother finally answered my texts last night and . . . No, I can't talk about this with you. You're a client.

Ha—you're going to be one wise elder.

My kokum taught me to be careful with my words. And she taught me the language. Those two things.

Gen hadn't spoken the language her grandmother had taught her in so long, but all of a sudden there the words were, ready to spill out.

Anyway, Pam said, tapping the second card. What's this one mean? This man giving away money?

Could mean you'll get the help you need in the future. That there will be angels in your life, but you won't recognize them for what they are right away.

Pam's phone buzzed. She glanced at the text that'd come in and stood up. I got to go, she said. But thanks for all this.

You don't want to read your third card?

Don't need to. My present is blowing up my phone right now.

Gen gathered the cards in one pile and put them on the bedside table. Her back ached and she felt tired to her bones. She said, Next time we do a real reading or don't bother.

What? Pam said and stopped texting.

Look, you knocked on my door. You think I'm your angel? Not a chance.

Pam's face went red. She grabbed the deck of tarot cards and tossed them onto Gen's lap. She said, You're a bitch.

Not the first time someone noticed, said Gen.

A real first-class bitch, said Pam.

Say hi to your brother for me, said Gen.

I don't need this, Pam muttered. But at the door she stopped and said, Lucky for me I like bitches.

Mamé speaks to Lucie

I drink more water. I let the earth take my sweat. Sparks rise.

When I look back I can't see anybody but you, Lucie.

That gets me thinking about being a grandma, how your life began with me.

Maybe your desire to die began with me.

My Gen always struggled with that desire too.

I wish I had been there the night you'd found Gen nearly dead next to an empty bottle of pills.

The times I should have been more than I was, should have done more than I did.

I have to confess to you now that I was not always happy either.

You were too little to understand what life was like for me, how I stumbled as I carried my life about as a woman carries buckets of water from the river in winter.

Can you hear me from where you are? Yes? No?

And then I see you. You're down there in a hospital bed with Allie by your side and I know you've wanted her by your side for a long time.

I see a doctor come in and I see you asking your daughter to leave.

And I know the doctor is about to tell you what you don't want your girl, your Allie, to hear.

My daughter's daughter, what have you done? What did our Carter do to you to deserve this?

My temper flares so high and hot I have to pull away. I don't want to witness it.

Lucie, this thing you've done—please don't hurt anyone anymore.

I know you're unhappy. But what's the purpose of happy? I lived a lot of years without it down there and I still got on.

The old woman in this lodge with me offers more water, says, Drink.

Right there in that lodge, I think how something else is more important than this happiness you are chasing, and if you'd stop holding me back then I'd get to go find it.

Might be that once I arrive I'll understand enough to share with you, even while you're down there on earth.

If you let me go maybe I can give more to you than you ever thought possible.

Solin hears a roar

How many steps had Solin taken toward her other life when that roar filled the sky? At first it was just a buzz and she shook it off like she would an insect, kept walking. Then the noise grew and it was like thunder except she'd never heard a thunder like this one. Solin turned and saw a screaming red helicopter drop from the sky. It threw itself over Jay and his scrabble of followers and they scattered. They ran, charging in different directions, bellowing with terror.

Now she ran too. No, she was falling more than running, down that steep embankment and yes she fell. She rolled back onto her hooves and, panting, she saw the helicopter single Jay out and follow him, saw Jay turn and run for the man-made hill she'd just tumbled down. She couldn't see where Tell had gone.

She ran in the direction of the houses, where the magpies jostled and cackled, where the other bison were.

Where is Tell? she screamed out at Jay as he galloped past her. The helicopter swooped down. The fences, Jay shouted back.

The helicopter followed him as he ran, dipping even closer to the ground than before. A panel opened in the side of the helicopter and a human head appeared, and then a rifle.

Solin could see Dee now, panicked by the noise. She careened down a street, grunting and bellowing for Tell. Shots exploded from the helicopter behind Solin. She did not look back. She moved as fast as her old joints would allow, on a path to Tell. As she ran she keened, mournful and steady. More staccato shots.

She heard Jay's booming voice as she ran. Don't move, Tell, he screamed, your grandmother is coming. Your—

More staccato shots.

Carter crosses over

The light was bending Carter in impossible directions. There was no curtain to block the sun and she sat in a soft seat, looking over the heads of the other passengers, feeling the pulse of the engine and the rocking and the swaying of the ferry on its way to the mainland. She felt as though something important was happening, though what that was she didn't know. She almost fell asleep, but the jolting of the ferry picked up and pushed her this way and that way. She was being carried along and all she had to do was let it happen, if she could just let it happen.

At first she didn't know she was in darkness, because the sun was high and the ferry was hot, so hot, stretched out under the sun. The light refracted her memories. She was being pressed on all sides. It almost hurt. The light was too bright and she was in darkness. For Carter, the darkness was fucking awesome but it was also so terrible that she tried to turn this way and that, tried to wriggle away from it. Never could learn not to fight, only to fight a little less, to let the scream and the rage move it all along.

The ferry became a pulsating canal. The muscle walls contracted to encourage the way through the transition. Carter was being pressed on, into what she didn't know.

Geneviève, her cane, and a cigarette

The rain finally stopped in the middle of the night. The sudden silence woke Geneviève. No rain on the window. This was something. She pulled on a sweater as quick as she could. Put her shoes on. She took her cane and she slipped into the elevator, down to the ground floor, past the blue room, and out the front door. The sky had put out a half moon and all her stars were there and everything above impossibly close to the earth. Gen stood for a moment, tapping a rhythm with her fingers on the crook of her cane, before she made her way to the bench near the entrance. She looked for Gabe but he wasn't around. She leaned the cane against her knees and lit a cigarette. She rested one hand on the curve of the handle. The nurse had called the cane a *temporary aide* when she gave it to Gen, but Gen knew that wasn't true.

Gen inhaled and felt the nicotine do its thing. She thought how her mother had been angry when she and Velma began smoking.

Geneviève tapped her pack against the bench. Want a smoke? Velma didn't answer.

Geneviève stared into the parking lot. The cars were sleeping shadows. She tried to pick out Bets but right then she couldn't remember where she'd left her. The trees rose up on the other side of the parking lot, inviting her. If not for the cane and the trembling, she'd have accepted.

I want a drink right now, Geneviève said. Then, after a few minutes, Geneviève asked, Where are you?

She sighed. I fucking don't want to leave alcohol, she said, tapping her thumb against the end of the cigarette so the ash fell. The ember glowed red in the dark.

I thought someone would save me, you know?

A long drag. Exhale. Smoke streaming from mouth and nostrils.

The fucking nuns, you know?

Another drag. Not much of the cigarette left. The sky, big and silent. And there were the ruins of the third building, half covered by pools of water.

Yeah. But Papa did come get us in the end.

She pressed the butt against the bench, put it in her pocket. Fumbling with the lighter.

Really? That afraid of talking to me?

A second cigarette in silence. Then a third.

Okay. Have it your way.

She gripped the handle of the cane and leaned her weight onto it as she stood.

Fuck you, Velma.

She knew she should return to the leaky old building, to her second-floor room. But she didn't. She walked into the parking lot, cane tapping the asphalt.

Afterlife, where Mamé begins

I'm back in the hospital with you, Lucie, in the doorway, looking in your room.

The lights are low. The doctor is gone. Is it night here? Yes, it is. And you're sleeping.

At first, I'm not sure what to do, but when I reach out to touch your hair I know that I want to lie in bed next to you.

I wrap my arms around you and I hold you. I tell you, I'm doing now what I should have done for the child you were all those years ago.

The connection between us shimmers.

What if someone walks in?

I keep talking to you. I say, When I was alive I'd walk to get you from your mother's wooden house across the trees, bring you over to mine and Bob's and make you bannock, speak to you in my husband's Michif so you could hear its sound. Your first fiddle I set against your shoulder; I let you hold my best guitar on your lap and strum; your first jig you learned watching my feet. I sat you down and told you how the piano keys worked. Think on those things, Lucie.

I hold you now in the hospital bed the way I should have held that child.

We lie this way until the other side begins to pull, until the lodge asks me to return.

From the lodge, I can only beg, Let me go, Lucie.

I've seen more than you wanted me to see.

I have to do this.

I can't take you with me. I don't have that power. I don't want that power.

The part of you that's still thinking about living, reach into that.

All I know to say is we've got to play our music no matter who leaves us and no matter who fails us, no matter the memories preying on us in the small hours of the night.

Pull your fiddle out of the closet and leave me to the afterlife.

Your time will come soon enough.

How to become part earth

Dee was running toward Tell when she heard the shots that extinguished Jay's voice. She didn't hesitate. In midstride she twisted and charged off the parking lot, back onto the grass. Jay was down. She was running to him.

Dee prayed that the spirits would take her instead of Jay.

Dust rose in the air around him as he kicked and struggled. He was bellowing and furious. She prayed, Please Jay, don't send me away when I finally get to your side.

She'd been walking to death's door already and she was still so weak she was afraid she couldn't run fast enough to get to him in time. Her udder screamed in pain, spurred her on.

And then she was right on him. She stumbled over his spasming legs and her rump landed on the earth. Her head hit his shoulder and he shouted out at her in anger.

He was busy with the work of dying. Death, one of the eight teachings.

Unable to get up again, she scooted over and craned her neck until she could press her brow against his. She said, You made it, Jay. You made it to the land you dreamed about. You know that, right? Jay stopped kicking. He tried to speak but the helicopter had circled back and the sudden strength of the roar made him wince.

Dee sang his name, Jay, Jay, Jay.

Dee could hear Tell whinnying with fear. She could hear him call to Kokum for help.

Every muscle in her body screamed at her to go to her son. Her sickly teats were trying to bring milk for him. But she would not let Jay die alone.

All that begging him to love her. He had, she saw that now. She hadn't seen it then.

Dee told herself that Tell was safe. He had to be safe.

From over by the concrete and cars came the screech and caw of the magpies.

Dee did not look up. Her work was to be there with Jay as he let go of his connections to this world. Only after Jay had done this would she get her son, Jay's son, her mother's grandson. She waited, closer now to Jay than she'd ever been.

Jay's dying was so quiet.

Carter's bio sister texts

hey
gramma's okay
well she's not telling us what
the doctor said
but mom says she seems okay
just thought now that u didn't
know that right?
sorry mom's
not calling u
she been with gramma since

text me any time u want
I know what the score is
by the way
gramma doesn't have cancer

was thinking she probably told
you she had cancer?
but no
she's been telling mom that for
years now
bc she was bleeding from
the butt

mom went with her to see her
doctor a few months back
when she said she had bowel
cancer mom was so worried
doctor said its hemorrhoids

not colon cancer
says he shared the results
of the tests with gramma
already and
did she forget?
mom was mad
gramma said to mom no she
did have cancer
only she healed herself with oil
like marijuana oil
and vitamins
so her ass is
getting old or something

anyway mom will get over this
give her time

but she was sure pissed after
they said it was just aspirin
gramma cried said she thought
you'd given her the pills to die,
like she wanted
but mom lit into gramma like
crazy
me and sis never seen her like
that before

she called gramma a selfish
bitch for asking you to get her
drugs
like damn she is but shes also
like old

cursing out old people feels ten
times ruder than young ppl u
know
anyway
said gramma was lucky you just
gave her aspirin
she said she'd have given her all
the sleeping pills she needed
gramma only had to ask, to
never involve you again
never seen mom fierce like that
like some street kid but old
or urban warrior
but old
butt old
lol
gramma sat there and took it
she was like a cat who just
knocked
your glass off the table or something and the wine's all over
the
floor now but she's licking her
paws
i was there and i felt a bit like a
mouse
anyway mom says she's not
ready to talk to you yet
so whatever
you can talk to me
or text me
or whatever

MICHELLE PORTER

Geneviève's offering

Okay, so sometimes it's like Gen could drop a piece of herself into me and I'm not alive but I'm not not-alive either. It's something in between.

I don't think she knows when she does it.

It was like that the one night she came to me in the break between the rains. She was in my seat and I held her up like usual, but something was different.

She was blowing her nose and wiping her eyes and she was saying she was too old for this.

If you asked me, I said, you'll never be too old for anything.

I don't know if she heard me.

I could feel how her hands shook when she put them on the wheel. She's got a nice soft rear that was comfy on my seat. She had a pack of cigarettes that she rapped against my dashboard. She's got those long fingers and all those rings.

I got to thinking what I'd be without her. For sure I'd be dumb and silent in some parking lot, waiting for who knows what.

No time to get caught up in what-ifs because by then the crying had stopped. She had the door open. She hauled herself out and walked around, pacing. She kicked my tires and then got back in and cussed herself out.

After that she started my engine and we drove away.

I had enough gas for a lot of road that day.

Only drove a couple of minutes of road and she turned us onto some side street.

I wondered if we were heading for a pub.

My beams were on high. She was driving slow, leaning forward and squinting, and I was thinking, Does she need her glasses?

Then we were off-road and bouncing over some bit of earth and grass I never met before. My headlights reached out in long fingers and that's how I saw the river before she did.

The river was a lot wider than it used to be.

I'd never been in a river before and I sure didn't want to try now. Was I ever relieved when she slammed her foot on my brakes and we stopped a few feet from the water's edge.

She put me in park but left my engine on, grabbed her cane, got out.

That river, she was moving fast that night.

My old lady leaned on her cane and talked to it like it could hear her, which I suppose it could, way better than me. I'm just a mess of metal and gasoline. I couldn't make out the words, not with the sound of my engine and the water gushing and calling as it passed by.

My headlights were still on so I could see that she took something out of her pocket, a pouch tied closed at the top. She tossed it into the water, where it floated for a moment before it was pulled under and who knows where it went after that.

She lifted her cane, dipped the end of it into the water, and then she turned that cane around and touched the end of it to one cheek and then the other.

I swear to my manufacturer I never saw her do anything like that before.

Then she was back inside me.

What the hell, she said. Why do I want to go back to that place if Velma isn't there?

I wasn't clear on whether she was talking to me or to herself. Most times it came to the same thing.

She switched off the headlights and turned the ignition so I could rest. Then she got out, opened the back door, and climbed into my back seat. It was stained and ripped in places from the dogs but she was fine with that. Didn't realize how tense she was until her whole body relaxed and I could tell that she'd fallen asleep right there in my back seat.

I held her like that all night long.

By the time she woke up, the insides of me were almost a sauna. She was covered in sweat and the inside of my windows were dripping. The sun was already up and hot. She sat up and used the bottom of her shirt to wipe her face. She opened the door and stepped out into the morning, cane in hand. She blinked in the bright light. She went to the river, dipped her cane into it, and touched the wet end to her cheeks again. When she was back in the driver's seat, she slipped the cane into its place and she said, I have a performance to get ready for. I didn't know what she was talking about but there was no more crying and that sun was already drying me out and I could tell that something was coming.

Bison belong here

Solin moved as fast as she could along the fences, in the direction of Tell's bellowing and the scent of fear, toward the humans who held signs and chanted, Don't kill, relocate—bison belong here.

The helicopter circled back.

Huffing heavily, Solin saw humans flooding into one yard, some passing through a gate and others climbing over the wooden fence. They were calling out the same word: Calf! Calf!

Magpies shot up into the air and circled anxiously before they returned to their perches to worry at each other in harsh croaks.

Solin ran for the gate, thinking it would be the weakest spot. Could she tear it down?

Tell, she screamed. Tell!

She charged but the gate held.

Frustrated, she trampled the signs that had been dropped by humans. She tried again and again but the gate held.

The humans were screaming, Calf, calf, calf!

Between the fence slats, she saw the humans circle Tell.

The magpies all flew up from their perches and moved to the fences and the posts around Tell. One human dropped her body over Tell's in a sort of bear hug, her soft body against his little back and hump. He kicked and reared in a frenzy. The birds squawked and fluttered. The other humans backed away but the female hung on tight. Tell was bucking and charging and Solin thought he was going to break the female in half.

The helicopter dropped down to hover over Solin. The noise was blinding. She knew she was too close to Tell, that she'd brought the helicopter toward him.

Stay still, she screamed to Tell. Let the humans cover you.

MICHELLE PORTER

Tell stopped fighting then, the good baby bull he had always tried to be. He stood trembling and terrified. He called out to her, Kokum!

She knew what she had to do. She sighted a target, one of the cars, a red one, and charged. She drew on her mother's despair, on her grandmother's rage, and on their grandmother's strength. She hit the car head on. The fender crumpled beneath her forehead and she grunted and tossed her head to shake away the hurt. She took a run at the side and glass shattered and a door fell to the ground. Her head throbbed. The helicopter followed Solin to the parking lot, was circling above. She aimed for a green SUV. Smash. A black two-door. Crash. Her right horn was nearly torn off and bursts of light and pain bounced around her head. She turned back to the red car and aimed her great forehead for the back door. She felt glorious as she charged and she was sure this was what she had been born for all along. With her final charge, she leapt right off the ground. In the fraction of a second before she collided with the back window of the red car, a stream of bullets hit her side and somehow that felt glorious too.

She was up in the spirit world with her mama even before her body, her home on earth, slid down the side of the car and flopped to the ground. There was her mama. Not the haunted, glassy-eyed mama Solin had lived with on earth, but the mama Solin had believed in all these years. The mama who had been waiting for Solin on an endless grassland that had never known fences.

Carter waits for a bus

Hey Slavko
Coming to get Tucker now
Will bring him back to Calgary
Be there by dinner

I'll call in a minute

Have to get back on my bus

You on your pills?

No, on my ancestors lmao

What the hell are you talking
about?
You should delusional
sound

On the bus now

You know how you get
He's happy here, with
Baka and Deda
And me

Bus is back on the road
Be there soon

Wait
I'll call
Going outside

My phone rang.
    I answered, said, You have exactly one minute, Slavko.
    You're still depressed, he said. Go get help.
    I'm coming to pick up my son. It's time.
    You're in one of your moods. Can't you see that?
    I can hang up any time.

Don't! Look, he's happy here. My mom and dad love him. Leave him be.

I know. I know. I've thought about that too.

Maybe you should try your meds again. Do that first and then see?

I was depressed. It passed. No thanks to you.

You want to make me apologize for things you imagined I've done? Or haven't done? I won't.

Okay.

You can be just like R sometimes. You know that?

Oh, that was the wrong thing to say.

Well, Tucker will have to know.

What?

Tucker will have to know that you wrecked his childhood because of your issues.

You fucked around.

You're making shit up!

Do we need to do this again?

What I do at work isn't your business.

Because I don't want to do this again.

So you're good with that then? That Tucker will know you're insane?

I think you care too much about Tucker to mess with his head. Am I wrong?

I'll have to tell him something.

Then you tell him we couldn't get along. Period. Age-appropriate.

You'd lie to him?

What the hell? It's not a lie.

Fuck you.

He hung up. I didn't call him back.

I text: On my way!!!

I text a smiley face.

I turn the phone off.

The heat. I was sweating something awful. It was gross. The driver made an announcement and apologized that the air conditioning wasn't working. Everyone had their water bottles open. It was good to get it out, the sweat.

When I got off the bus for the final time, I found a piece of shade beneath an awning and drank the last swallow from my water bottle. I was new. I was sticky and raw. I pulled out my phone and texted for a cab. And then suddenly I was crying and I couldn't say why. Okay, you little shit, I said to myself as I searched my bag for something to blow my nose on. Go get your boy, go get Tucker.

MICHELLE PORTER

What if there's one last show?

Breakfast was on the table already when she came in from her night by the river. Pamela asked if she was okay but didn't mention her absence and Gen didn't know if anyone noticed. Gen said, Fine, fine, and then she said, I'm going to skip the morning sessions. I have to do some self-care. Pamela said, Sure, okay. She said, We can talk about this after if you like? Gen agreed and took the elevator to the second floor. In her room she took out paper and markers and she wrote out copies of two signs that she taped up and down the hallways of the first floor.

Modern and Old-Time Dance	*TONIGHT ONLY*
For One Night Only	*Geneviève Goulet*
Geneviève Goulet	*Famous Winnipeg*
and Her Orchestra	*Victor Recording Artist*
TONIGHT	*And Her Red River Echoes*
Dancing 9–12.	*Dancing 9–12.*
Everyone Welcome.	*Everyone Welcome.*
Service Men, Staff,	*Service Men, Staff,*
and Residents	*and Residents*
Free.	*Free.*

In her room, Gen pinned her hair. She put on her wig, did her makeup. Put on a girdle, took out that beaded bra she was saving up. Pamela visited and exclaimed over Gen's transformation as she checked her vitals, gave meds. No, she wouldn't be coming down to dinner. Could they bring something up?

A tray was delivered. Gen couldn't eat, but she drank some water. She slipped on her dancing shoes. Then she reached for her cane. Before the rains she'd been shaky, but now she was feeling strong enough.

Everyone was waiting in the blue room when Gen made her entrance—all the residents and all the staff who could take the time away. Most of them had heard the faint strains of a piano in the middle of the night and wanted to hear more. Seats were arranged. Gen sat at the piano.

As she began she looked into the window but the only reflection there belonged to an old woman. At first she kept looking, kept expecting Velma to step out of her light, to join first this reel and then that jig. Instead, she was accompanied by the return of loud torrents of rain and then she was joined by thunder and lightning.

She needed the music that night so she made it on her own. She played hard and she played fast, one song after another. They couldn't keep their feet still. When she paused they called for more. She was covered in sweat. They threw open the windows to get some air and the rain crashed right on in. The touch of cold on her sweaty back made her shiver.

Gen looked out the window but all she could see was the rain and they'd had that for so long nobody was afraid of too much and they were calling for another dance and another song. Gen recognized what was happening. She'd seen it before, when she was little and watching her father perform. She'd always wanted it to happen to her. If she had what they called a bucket list, this would be on it. She had become a song to the audience. She was the music in their chests and their feet. Everyone forgot about her, that she was human, that she was old and on the edge. They forgot because the music she played was solid and alive and strong. Someone did the jig and someone taught the steps to everyone else and the laughter carried Geneviève along.

There were calls for Geneviève to say a few words, to tell them a story, and as she rose to her feet she knocked her cane to the floor and her foot caught on something and she fell back onto the bench, laughing. She lost her words and buried herself in another song. She felt young again and she forgot to look into the reflection at all.

A phone rang and someone left the room to take the call and Gen kept on playing until they came back and called for quiet. Gen stopped and in the pause everyone could hear a murmuring and a soft sloshing that hadn't been there before. The river's flooded its banks, someone said. It's taken out all the roads. The thunderstorm had been speaking so loud and the river had been so quiet that everyone gasped when one of them went to the window and called out in panic that the river was in the parking lot. Everyone crowded around. Could this be possible?

Gen pulled another song from the piano, one that rose with the river and spoke to the storm, and then the water was in the building and gathering at their feet and the dancing stopped because it had to. Gen played on, low and quiet, as staff made a few phone calls and got together a plan. Pamela said, Everyone go upstairs.

Gen quit playing then and her whole body began to tremble. She struggled to stand and reached for her cane, but it wasn't there. She tried to take a step, but the heels of her shoes slipped. She was too drained to win the fight to stay on her feet and she collapsed in a heap. She was there on the floor beside the piano. Her legs shook and jerked and sometimes she was there in the room and sometimes she was somewhere else that was quiet and dry and cool, a place where time held its breath. She opened her mouth, but no words fell out. She turned her head and she saw the piano legs and she saw the cards she'd lost, the two Empresses. They were trying to rise, half floating and half sinking in a half inch of water. Gen reached out to touch them and a spasm took over her arm and her hand smacked on the cards and pushed them under. She wanted to lift her hand. She closed her eyes and tried with all her might, and still her hand wouldn't move.

Don't sink the Empresses, she told herself. She was crying.

And then she felt herself being lifted up. The arms that held her were so strong it was as if she was floating. She opened her eyes just long enough to see Gabe's face hovering above her own and then she slipped out of consciousness.

She was on her bed when she came to, and she couldn't move but she could hear Gabe walking to the door. He was so good at slipping away, she thought. She heard Norah calling her name and the sound of someone running. Then Norah was at the door, panting. She's in here, Norah screamed and a minute later Pamela was there too. She checked Gen's pulse and said to Norah, Go get my medical bag, it's under the front counter. Pamela was worrying over her, saying, How did you get here by yourself? and Why didn't you ask someone to help? Norah returned, said, Is she going to be okay? And in the hallway someone was shouting, Okay people, I need a group of volunteers. We got to get all the supplies up here, away from that water. Gen was trying to speak. She was trying to say, Carter is coming. She thought she'd said this and thought maybe they understood, but her lips had become so heavy. Gen faded out of consciousness as Pam ripped open her dress, cut the girdle open.

Carter gets an update

gramma lucie said to let you
know where she was

                                        Okay
                                        Good, I guess?
                                        Got Tucker with me
                                        on my way to rent a car
                                        Does she want to know
                                        where I am?

idk
let me ask mom
mom says no
said gramma just wanted you
to know where she was going

                                        Okay
                                        So where is she

there's a reserve
i think it's a reserve
mom says yes
near here where they brought
the bison back
a herd of them
for the People she said
gramma's going there
and she said allie has to come
with her.

                                        fuck

yeah
anyway she said it was time to
arrive

mom said you should know the
words gramma said

Is Allie going?
Did she say I should go?
Gramma, I mean

no
sorry
mom says gramma said to tell
you not to come
mom's getting ready right now
that's why I'm texting you

Gramma and Allie are going
to see the bison together?

kind of
they'll stay for a while or
something
gramma's kind of on about
learning how they did it and
organizing a group of metis to
get some land
do the same thing

Seriously?

yeah

And Allie's just up and going?
Like that?

yeah

Okay.
and you and your sister?

we got things to do here
work and stuff
but we'll go up and visit them

MICHELLE PORTER

Make sure they're not killing
each other?

hahahahaha
something like that

Okay. wow
Just a minute paying the
cab driver

okay
ur funny
we should text more
and mom says good luck

Tell her I send good luck too

and she says to send her love
to you

Got the car now
Wanna come help get
greatgramma?
Her rehab center got
flooded out

holy shit

Yeah I know right?
Not a fun trip
I'll need help with Tucker

candace too?

Don't know how we'll get her
Unless this car can float
Whatever I'll figure it out
Yeah both of you if you want

FUCK YES!
WE WANT!!!!

Okay then where you at
I'll come get you

Mamé and Lucie struggle

Lucie, you tried to follow me and now you're stuck where you never should have been, between life and death.

Let me go. There's still time for you to rise into the sky of your life.

The door here wants to open for me, but not you, not yet.

What you're looking for, you will find where you are, in life. In life, Lucie. Think on that. Don't rush to me here, don't rush away from all that you still have left. Oh Lucie.

Let me go. I'm waiting here in this lodge. Let me arrive.

Lucie, you have to cut this connection to me and to this place.

Listen—what you are looking for is not here.

Your own sky trembles on the edge of morning, wanting what must come next. Lucie, let me go. Let me arrive. Lucie, your hold is so strong. You are heavy and I can't carry you.

You've got to let morning come where you are.

You're looking for love, aren't you? Because your mother kept leaving you. Kept wanting to leave you—that's the hardest part, isn't it, for a child? All your life after, you didn't know how to stay. There's still time to learn.

I'm hearing rain again, Lucie, and I'm so hot.

The bison walked me to the river. The bison left me here so they could walk their way to earth again. Go there, go to the bison there on earth.

Carter gets a boat

Fuck if we didn't run into Jesús on our way to get Great-Gramma Gen from the floods. He was lending me a boat. Yeah, I know, right? A boat.

See, all the roads were flooded out and we couldn't get to the rehab center by car.

I'd just got home to Calgary with my boy Tucker when the Milk River flooded her banks. It was all over the news when I picked up my bio sisters.

So there we were, driving the backroads of Southern Alberta in a rental trying to find a dry road to a flooded rehab center. The rain had stopped, but the clouds were still heavy and the news promised more rain.

Carole was in the passenger seat checking the list of flooded roads against the map of Southern Alberta splayed on her lap. We were just about to lose hope when Candace squirmed and said again, I really have to pee.

Candace was in the back seat with Tucker and he was telling her how Mr. Bear was learning to play fiddle and what his favorite songs were. He was wrapping her around his little finger, stinking charmer that he is.

And I already said I'm not squatting by the side of the road, Candace added, because that's what I'd suggested the first time she told us her bladder was full.

You being serious? Grandma Gen is stranded there on the other side of the water and we have to find you a toilet? Like, really?

Hey, hey, Carole said softly, and it was enough to stop me from going on.

Carole pointed to a dirt driveway and said, We could ask to use the bathroom there.

Turned out, that was where Jesús lived.

Dark skinned and grizzled, he was set up in the shade in front of a shed, sanding the seat of a wooden chair. I parked and shut off the engine. Me and Carole got out and she asked if they could use the washroom. He nodded and pointed toward the house. In the semidarkness of the shed I saw a covered boat set on an unhooked trailer and I got to thinking.

Carole said Tucker's got to go, too, and I said, Can you and Candace take him in?

As they walked to the house, I nodded at the boat, asked, Is that a motorboat?

Yep, said the man whose name I didn't know yet.

Can I see it?

Yep, he said.

He led me into the shed, pulled back the tarp. Looked like enough room for an old Kokum in the back.

I said, Can I use your boat?

He squinted at me, said, It's a hat you need, by my reckoning.

He was right: I hadn't taken the time to put a brush to my hair since I'd picked up Tucker, that's for sure. I told him I'd take a spare cap, too, if he was offering.

Didn't take any time to get the trailer hooked up to his truck. I stopped in the house just long enough to tell everyone what was going on, that we were going to try with a boat, were they good to wait here? Carole and Candace agreed. Jesús's wife was already making sandwiches and putting out cookies. She offered me lemonade, said she's been thanking the Lord for bringing a child to their house again. I said no, that Jesús and I have to get a move on—only I didn't say his name because I didn't know it yet.

We were down the road apiece before I asked him his name. He'd tossed an old blue cap onto my lap exactly like the one that was on his head. He turned off the gravel road and onto a grassy path. We hit a bump in the earth and he told me to buckle up and that's when I asked. He glanced over at me before he said, The name's Jesús Enrique Perez, thank you.

What you leave behind

Dee lurched toward the parking lot where the protesters were screaming. She heard the roar of the helicopter returning. Magpies cawed from the fence, watching for a threat in the faces around them. The humans stood their ground, holding their signs like shields. They chanted, Bison belong, bison belong— don't reload, relocate.

Dee waited for a rush of bullets to tear into her flank and chest.

She thought how she wanted to follow Jay into the afterlife.

But the helicopter twisted away for some reason. She was no martyr.

The fact of her life disoriented her. A truck rumbled by and she stumbled to a stop, her eyes glassy and staring.

Oh, and then another high-pitched bellow from Tell and she was moving, running. Her scorching teats were leaking new milk and dripping blood onto the asphalt.

There, somewhere in the maze of fences, was Tell. The humans shouted and the humans chanted and the faint hum of the helicopter got louder as it made its way back.

By the time the helicopter was there hovering above everything, Dee knew what she was going to do.

Carter sees a vulture in the flood

Jesús didn't need to look at a map. He knew exactly where he was going.

I was lost by the second turn, and as we were leaning into the third, anxiety twisted my belly so that I had to breathe deeply and focus on not throwing up. We drove by fields planted with canola that had been coping with drought and heat stress and then too much rain and now a flooding river.

Jesús found a bend in the swollen waters of the river where we could set the boat in the water. He waded thigh deep into the flood waters and reached into the boat to open the seat where the bright orange life jackets were stored. I slipped one over my shoulders as I looked out over the flood waters to the trees a ways out. The rehab center's behind there? I asked.

Jesús nodded, which was way more comforting than it should have been, really.

He held out the keys to the boat and said, She's yours.

I'm driving?

Yes—don't know how much room you'll need.

You sure?

He grinned at me, said, You want an old man to convince your kokum to get in a boat with him?

I took the keys. Quickly, he gave me a rundown of the boat's personality, how to turn her smoothly, how to get her to move quick and how to move slow and where the emergency shit was—only he didn't use the word *shit*.

I started the motor and pointed the boat in the direction of the rehab center.

Take it slow now, Jesús called out after me.

The water was a bit choppy and as I headed toward those trees I got to thinking, What the hell am I doing out here in this boat? I could have said, I'm taking a leap of faith, but I literally did not have an ounce of faith in what I was doing. What then? Hope? Audacity? Love? Fuck if I knew.

I steered the boat through the trees and over what would have been the parking lot. The scene there scared the shit out of me. Seeing the cars just below the water, turned over and scattered as if they were toys.

The rehab center rose right out of the water.

Fear twitched at my belly again.

The river had filled the bottom of the building, lapped through the doors and windows.

Where was my great-grandmother? What the hell was I thinking coming here like this?

I'm not sure what I would have done if that woman hadn't leaned out the window on the second floor. A young woman. She waved and called out.

Helloooo, said the woman.

I didn't know what to say. I felt like an idiot. How could I say, I've come here to take a very old woman away in a flimsy motorboat a total stranger lent me?

Then another woman leaned out and said, You must be Carter?

I nodded.

The first woman said, Gen told us you were coming.

A man leaned out beside her and said, But we didn't think you'd come.

The first woman said, Gen's here and she's conscious now.

Conscious? Oh my God, I said.

The man called out, We're so glad you're here. Gen sure doesn't want to go anywhere by helicopter.

Helicopter? Oh fuck, I said.

It took them all a few minutes to decide how it would be done. They'd arrange to have Gen come out through a window on the bottom floor. Could I pull up to the window? That was when my hands began shaking.

I steered over to the window and idled the motor. I prayed to I don't know who, to the water I think. I held on tight to the side of the window frame to keep the boat as steady as I could.

My first glimpse of my great-grandmother: she's thigh-high in water, flanked on either side by young women. Maybe they were holding her up or could be she's holding them up.

There was a piano poking up out of that water and somehow they lift her onto it. They helped her to shimmy onto the windowsill and when she was sitting there with one of those women on either side she stopped and took a good look at me for the first time.

She said, That ball cap makes you look like a piece of shit. And I said, Running shoes with a dress?

Then I felt like I could reach out to her. She put an icy hand into my trembling palm.

Are we going to do this? she asked.

Fuck yeah, I said.

It was a more complicated maneuver than any of us had expected, getting an old kokum out of a flood and into a boat that Jesús lent. My great-grandmother put one foot into the boat, shifted just a bit of her weight, and then everything lurched.

Whoa, whoa, whoa, the older of the two women said.

Take it easy now, take it slow, the younger woman instructed.

I had to let go of Gen to hold the window frame, pull the boat back as close to the windowsill as I could get.

I can't hold you, I said.

Yes, you can, child, she said.

I extended my hand to her again and she patted the back of my hand before she slipped hers under, palm to palm, and gripped me so hard I winced. After she had both feet in the boat she shifted her ass off the windowsill. The boat swayed. I swore. My great-grandmother fell into the water.

There was a lot of screaming then.

I was at the edge of the boat and about to jump in after Gen when the younger woman leapt in first and almost right away they surfaced together.

What's the use of the damn boat, Gen said, spitting water and coughing. Might as well swim now.

I could see she was shivering and it took some doing, but we got her into the boat, thank you, Jesús.

I got one of those shiny emergency blankets on Gen's shoulders and one of the women handed over a small bag, said it held some of Gen's things. She said not to worry, a helicopter was coming for the rest of them. That was the first time I thought how many other people might be stuck in that building and it was like a slap in the face. I felt like a first-class asshole for not bringing something over in the boat, food or water or, I don't know, Bibles. All I had were a couple of energy bars I'd grabbed from the car before Jesús and I headed out but I wasn't going to offer those to these women. They hauled themselves back through the window and stood on the piano for a moment before lowering themselves back into the flood.

I held out a life jacket and Gen said, I'd rather die than wear that ugly thing.

You look like a half-drowned vulture in a pair of soggy sneakers, I said. You're not exactly winning any beauty contests right now.

That old woman, my great-grandmother, looked right up and into my face and her dark eyes flashed between anger and laughter and back again. She let that shiny blanket fall back from her shoulders and raised her chin, Well, I'm nearly dead now as it is. So, why not?

I got that life jacket on her and then I got that blanket back up around her because she was shivering really bad and she started talking about how she thought she was going to die right there in the boat, repeated that over and over. It was actually pretty muggy and warm out so I was thinking the shock must be bad and I wished I had something more than an energy bar.

I said, Well now, I just wish I could give you a bit of whiskey to warm you up or shut you up or both.

Her eyes went wide and she stopped her nattering and threw her head back and laughed.

I leaned over and kissed her forehead and said, I think if I ever see a vulture in a boat, laughing, I know just what it'll look like.

And she was still in shock for sure because she laughed even more, and she reached out and put her hands on my cheeks. She pressed my face against hers for way longer than was comfortable. But I stayed still as long as she held me and then when she let me go, she seemed calmer.

I figured she should eat something, so I got those energy bars from the emergency kit, opened them for her. She put them in her lap, broke them into bits, and put one in her mouth, nodded at me.

I started the motor then.

We were off. I looked over the flood water to the other side.

When—crack!—something hit the back of my head. Gen hooted. I turned around and she was rocking with laughter and I was like, What? What? and then it hit me again—only this time I looked up and saw the crow.

Thanks, Gramma, I muttered under my breath. I was swearing a streak and scanning for something to hit it with and Gen's sitting there with the blanket falling off her shoulders, her eyes all squinty with delight.

The bird circled. Another joined it. Then there were two. They were shrieking, coming at me with sharp piercing caws.

My great-gramma, she held up one hand to me as if to say, Stop. She put a piece of that energy bar in one hand and held it out. One bird landed on Gen's shoulder, ruffled its black feathers and cocked its head back and forth to get a good look at Gen before it hopped onto her arm and took a chunk, swallowed it, just like that. That bird offered a quick caw and then settled onto the boat's edge beside her. The second crow landed on her head and she just held her hand up and let it take a piece of food from her hand. And that was how it was the whole way to the other side, those two crows taking food from her hand the whole way across.

I don't think I ever stopped crossing that river.

I've been there ever since, in a motorboat with my great-grandmother and her two crows.

Perkins and Lottery cancel the show

Perkins paced from one end of the cage to another. I just feel like we need one more rehearsal before the show, he said.

Stage fright? asked Lottery.

Only when I breathe.

You're gonna be great. Don't worry.

What if they don't like us?

All of a sudden, Lottery lifted her head and tensed from nose to tail. Do you hear that? she asked.

Now you're making fun of me, Perkins said.

She jumped to all fours and pressed her face against the cage.

We could totally bomb.

Cancel the show, Lottery said.

Perkins bristled. What?

Cancel the show.

We can't just—

It's time.

You mean? Oh no. We can't just leave now. The show must go on.

Things are happening.

I got the whole band, the poodle, the terrier, the beagle, and— Perkins couldn't bring himself to identify the last dog in the band.

They're just dogs.

We're dogs!

Not in the same way they are, said Lottery. She was on her feet and pressing her nose against the cage. Could she sniff what was coming?

Sure we are. We got the hair and the ears, don't we.

We do, but—

We eat the food, don't we?

We're temporary.

We got that instinct, too, you know, to bark and to run after balls and to hump our human's legs.

I don't hump anything. Anyway, humping doesn't make you a dog, does it?

Look, I've been talking to a few of the dogs. Really talking about the way life is here. You should hear what they tell me.

You getting all philosophical now? Next you'll ask what's our purpose. You'll be saying, Lottery, I been thinking about why we were put on this earth.

Not the earth. Just the kennel.

Would you shut up? I can't smell with you yapping in my ear like that.

Okay, okay. It's just I been feeling so good being a dog here, like all the rest.

Been enjoying your dog body quite a bit from what I've seen.

My body feels so many things at once right now. Like I want to see Gen. My tail is wagging and I'm really excited. But I also want to stay with the band and I'm getting dizzy.

It's not Gen.

What.

She's not here. I don't know what's going on.

Oh my God. Cancel the show! The show's canceled, everyone! We're leaving right away! No rain checks. No refunds. Everything is canceled!

Perkins ran in circles, barking and whining. Lottery waited.

When the attendants showed up with two carriers, Perkins and Lottery walked right in with no trouble. They let themselves be carried down the corridor past all the other dogs in all their cages.

Perkins's bandmates raised their snouts and sent them off with a song: the poodle, the terrier, the beagle, and the blue-eyed husky.

Carter gets to the other side

Jesús was waiting on the other side of the flood.

He helped Gen out of the boat.

He said he'd called 911 already. All the emergency vehicles were in use, but the hospital was ready for them. He'd drive us.

We left the boat and trailer there.

In the truck, Gen laid her head on my lap. She was slipping in and out of sleep or unconsciousness, I couldn't tell the difference.

The rain started again when we were on the highway.

Gen mumbled. Bets, she said.

I pulled a clump of wet hair out of her face.

The dogs, she said.

And then she was talking about the lottery.

I had no way to comfort her.

Getting on a truck

And then a gate opened in the fence and there was Tell, a crush of humans behind trying to herd him through. Tell didn't trust the gate. He was looking wildly from the ground to the humans who were touching him as if they knew him. He was not going to go through.

From the parking lot, Dee bellowed his name. Tell couldn't see her but he kicked until the human on his back fell to the ground. Mama, he grunted. His voice was gone and he spoke so low she couldn't hear him but she could scent everything.

A line of humans formed outside the gate on either side, separating her from him. They made themselves into a fence leading to the back of a small livestock truck. Tell tried to back away. Some of the humans shouted and pointed at the helicopter, their phones raised, red lights blinking. Tell retreated farther into the safety of the yard.

Dee could barely stand on her hooves but she forced herself to move in Tell's direction. There were so many people and more vehicles were arriving. All at once the fence of people and the truck made sense to her. She understood just enough. She called out, Get on the truck.

Tell stepped ahead to the opening in the fence and looked for his mom. The people behind crowded him, risking a good kicking.

You go first, Tell. I'll follow, Dee promised.

Tell lifted his head, bellowed as loud as he could, and stepped through the gate and then through the people. One awful step and then another.

Go on, I'm coming, Dee shouted.

So long as she called out to him Tell walked.

Mama's coming after you, Tell. My little Tell. Mama loves you, Dee said.

And then Tell was on the ramp.

Mama's proud of you, she shouted as Tell walked up the ramp. Your father is proud of you. I'm coming, my little boy.

A human reached up and the door to the back of the truck closed and Dee couldn't see Tell anymore.

The helicopter drowned out the sound of the humans, who were shouting and cheering. Dee watched a human climb into the front of the truck. The sounds her son made were terrible.

There by a torn-up red car was Solin's body, lifeless as the concrete.

Dee settled down beside Solin and for the second time that day she waited for a helicopter to drop from the sky and fly away with life.

Please, she prayed as the truck moved away with her son.

Bets gets a new handler

Look, without Gen I thought I'd died.

When I came to, I was in this field and there was this little electric car idling beside me and three kids were getting out.

The sun was high and hot and had already dried most of the river out of me. I wasn't made for water, I can tell you that. I felt different, like, younger maybe, and I didn't know how I could be in that in-between place again, not alive but not not-alive either, because where was Gen?

One said, That's it. That's the car. Pretty sure.

The second said, Let's go get Jesús.

The third said, What's he going to do, Candace? Last rites?

And that last one, she had some sort of pick and she was shoving it in my driver door lock. I tried to resist but it was a little ticklish and I couldn't help but squirm and the lock flicked and she got my door open. She slid on into the driver's seat and I got a feeling that I didn't like because it reminded me of Gen and I didn't want to be thinking about her right then because I was sure something had happened to her after all this rain, after that night she slept in the back. The woman called to the other two, Get in!

One of them said, We don't have the key.

I don't want to wait, said the kid in the driver's seat.

I wasn't a car for a young person. I didn't want her hands on me. I wanted Gen.

This kid pulled a screwdriver out of her pocket and rammed it into my ignition, turned it. That got my attention. Then she used the screwdriver to pry off the plastic panels, exposing my ignition cylinder, and I wasn't shy about my body or anything but this was making me uncomfortable. Anyway, she didn't damage

MICHELLE PORTER

the steering column so that was something. I think I knew what was happening. I'd heard stories from other cars. I was being stolen. Next she took out a pair of wire strippers and cut and twisted the two brown power wires. My radio went on. It was the news, an interview with a farmer who said, I think this will be the worst crop in Western Canada in the last fifty years. My farm personally, on my north half, will be the worst crop we've had in the history of our farm. I mean, first it was the drought. We have some canola that didn't even bolt. It just stopped and the leaves, they turned upside down to shield themselves from the sun. We got a lot of rain, sure, but it was too late to increase the yields and some of it was flooded out. The damage that's been done.

I didn't want to listen to that.

I need to focus here, the kid muttered and switched off the radio.

The kid cut and stripped the starter wire and touched it to the exposed power wires and she did it so tenderly that I got a start and it was like my heart was beating fast for half a second. Oh my. I coughed and wheezed a bit sure but Do that again, I shouted. And she did. Another flicker of this electric connection between us. I was warming up to her. She did it again and there I went: I still got some gas in me. The other two climbed into my back seat and she was careful with me so we went slow over the mud and the bumps and I was just feeling like I had another chance at life and she'd given it to me, so I was always going to be on her side. She'll get a proper key made, sure, but I'll always remember this. I'd heard others talk about it, what it was like when they hotwire you, but never thought it'd happen to me. I mean, who'd hotwire an old station wagon? This kid was the only one ever. She got me to a road, oh glory be. I knew I didn't have much time left. I'm not eternal and I'm nothing on my own and I'm only what someone else makes of me. I understood myself to be a collection of parts, most of them old or used. I never thought I'd see a road again but there I was back from the dead, offered a second chance, four tires rolling on asphalt, going I didn't know where.

Perkins and Lottery decide their time isn't up

It's our old lady's car all right, said Perkins.

Is she in the driver's seat?

I don't see her at all.

But it's her car?

Can't mistake the smell.

If this is her car, where is she? Lottery said.

Oh, looks like I'm going in the back seat. Holy, there's a boy here.

A what?

A boy.

Don't tell me that. Never mind, I can hear him squealing.

He's got two handfuls of my fur.

I got the front seat.

Smell the young woman now.

Oh, I get what you mean.

Yeah, there's some of the old lady on her, Perkins said.

The boy too?

They're all related.

She's pregnant.

More kids?

Twins.

Humans don't do well with big litters. More than one and they're helpless.

Well, good thing our time with this family is almost up.

Perkins twisted away from Tucker's hands. Don't think we're going anywhere, he said.

What do you mean?

Smell the boy.

Lottery lifted her nose and caught Tucker's scent. Ah, she said, I smell it.

He stinks of the past.

It's the smell of her stories.

Our old lady's?

Yeah. Take a good whiff.

God, you're right. He's carrying a lot. Too much?

I think they call his kind an old soul.

The boy, Perkins panted, is going to need us.

Dee is a tag

One human shouted to another, There's a tag in her ear.

One of the federal tags?

Yeah, like I said, she's tagged.

One of the humans took a picture of the tag and another typed the tag number into her phone and then showed the search results to the other human who said, This one's not getting slaughtered today.

He was shouting, phone held to his ear. Inseminated, he said. Yes, inseminated. Worth quite a bit. What? No, we can't send her back. She'll probably leave park borders again and then what? What if we're not there? That's not an option. We'll truck her to the center. What, you think I'm stupid? No, the one on our side of the border. Figure out the legal stuff after that. Yeah. Possession and nine-tenths, exactly. She left the park and wandered into our jurisdiction, so we have the right. She's part of that insemination, that cocksucking insemination program. The new one. Her next calf will be something everyone will want to study. And we've got her. For fuck's sake, I'm not letting her go.

Carter opens a window

Carter got the walker from the back of my car—my Bets—and set it by the passenger door.

Get that piece of shit out of my sight, I said.

I walked up the steps of my own house, leaning on her, my great-granddaughter's shoulder. I'll say this, she's strong.

I couldn't stand the sight of that fucking walker. Perkins and Lottery got to growling whenever they saw it.

After that, Carter mostly kept it out of sight. She never even referred to it, just left it where I might use it if I needed.

The only good that ever came from that thing was when her boy raced it around the house and figured out how to do doughnuts with it.

I used it when I had to. Like when I got her boy at the piano to teach him a thing or two. He took to it quick, you know.

Take my fiddle out of the top of the closet, I told Carter. I'll teach your boy what I stole from my sister and my father, what I wasn't supposed to have.

Eventually the pain got so bad I couldn't get out of bed, but that Tucker, he had my papa's way with the bow and so I told Carter to look in my underwear drawer for the little box full of money, told her to spend it all on a violin, told her what model to get. She knew so little, she wasn't taught.

He's got my dad in his hands, all right.

I asked Velma sometimes if she was listening, but that brat was still giving me the cold shoulder. Just wait, I said to Velma. When I die I'll follow you around up there and never give you a moment's peace.

They got me one of the phones so I could do the texting and phone calls with video. Carter showed me the text part, but I told her that the only people I wanted to communicate with weren't here anymore. Okay, so I sent a text to Pamela once but it tired me out, so I asked Carter to do all that for me.

God, when the pain came over me I could've used a drink.

I'm going to die anyway. What's the harm?

Carter told Tucker not to practice at the piano when I was resting, not to scrape the bow across the fiddle. I said to her, Let him make his noise. I said, Dying is so quiet.

I knew what it meant when the parade of people began. I knew. Hardly seen any of them in years and some I'd never met and they stopped by my bedside to struggle with saying whatever it was they needed to say.

It was then I started to beg Carter for a bottle. Would you get me just one, Carter? One little bottle? What difference will it make now?

No, Carter, don't bother with my hair. Don't touch me. It hurts to be touched. Get your stupid hands off me.

Carter told me her hands have always been the smartest part of her, that I got it wrong again—now, which wig would I like?

The red one. And, sorry.

Whenever I'm ready, she said, we can make a plan.

Sure, let's make a plan for how I want to die. Sure as hell not like this, or maybe just like this. I don't know. It's even harder than I thought to do this.

A woman from the rehab center brought Elaine, the elder. Said she'd come to finish the story she started back at the center, and I told her, No, I'll finish it, I've had lots of time to think about that, and she sat and closed her eyes, and I told the rest of the story, the way I wanted it finished.

Carter was there. Maybe she'll tell you about it sometime. I don't have the time for it anymore.

They started giving me stronger stuff for the pain and I

floated in and out. When the floating faded away and the pain bled through I cried for more of the meds, demanded someone bring me a drink. Then I loathed myself.

Dying slow like this—you never had to face that, did you, Velma?

Then came a morning when I was feeling sort of straightened out.

Carter, will you brush my hair?

Braid it, please?

That feels nice.

Is the sun shining? Open the window, Carter. Let the outside come on in for now.

Get your boy to play the fiddle for me, would you?

Your hands are the quickest, Tucker, did you know that?

Bring me a drink? Oh please. Something nice and strong. Just a sip. I don't need more than that. Don't think there's time for it. Just a sip, please?

Thank you, Carter.

Carter, Carter, my girl, I'm scared.

Carter wrapped my hand in both of hers. She had trouble saying it, but she got it all out, she said, You don't need a single thing from this world anymore.

She said, Get the fuck out of here.

She said, Don't you dare look back.

Stepping onto the stage

Velma's on stage. She's just finished a song and the audience is applauding. She has her fiddle in one hand and her bow in the other. The dress she's wearing. Never seen beading like that. Fits over her hips like a lover's hand. All that hair piled up on her head. Wisps falling to soften the eyes. Sweat pouring down her face, no need to cover up any of her intensity up here. She raises a hand for quiet and the audience holds their collective breath.

She says, For the first time on this stage, please welcome my sister, Geneviève.

The audience lets it out then, whistles and cheers and calls for their favorite songs, and she looks over at me, gestures for me to move out of the wings and find my place on the stage beside her.

I don't remember walking across that stage. I raise an arm to wave to all the people and the sleeve of my dress is shiny, entirely covered in sequins.

Play, Velma commands, gesturing to the piano that has appeared to the left.

Then I'm sitting on that bench and my fingers find the keys and all that pent-up music is about to pour out, the music our papa gave us, the music our mama taught us, the music that fed our family, created our people. Velma taps her foot and the audience leans forward, anticipating. She names the next song and sets her fiddle against her clavicle. Her bow hovers above her instrument. She is listening for me, waiting for me. I begin.

Gramma Lucie texts Carter a pic

Of a clear baggie on a table. There were twelve pills in it. Twelve
beautiful white pills.
    She texted:
    I kept these ones.
    Makes me happy to keep them close.
    Just in case.
    You think I can't tell what aspirin is?
    Think I can't taste sugar?
    She added a laugh until you cry emoji.
    Nothing else.

Carter texts Gen

First thing I want to ask is
What's it like there
On the other side?
Can you tell me

We dreamed your death
We were stumbling in the dark
together

I hope you're reading your texts
from over there
Or maybe I hope you have
other things to do

Your dying was hard work for
you and me but not for Tucker
He made himself at home in
the middle of it all
You should see him playing
that fiddle now

Okay
Here goes
Nôhkom
Câpân
Gen
Just so you know
We're burning fires for you
Like you taught me

Was thinking now about how
you dreamed me into your
house
and into your death
We've got a party planned
We're playing music
Remember what you showed
Tucker on the piano and the
fiddle?
He's going to play that after the
fires burn out and everybody
gathers

I keep hoping you'll text me
back
How are the ancestors?
Going to assume no news is
good news

I dreamed of two babies
One named Jay like the bird
The other named Solin like
nothing I ever heard of
what do you think that means?

I'm learning sage, sweet grass,
and cedar

MICHELLE PORTER

Gen
Remember what you said once
about the sweat and about
traveling from earth to sky?
Is it true?

One day we'll follow you
Kawapamatin miina
We'll follow we'll follow

this dying thing
neither of us knew how
to do it in the proper way
but shit if this time you didn't
die like a fucking boss you
died like nobody's business

Mamé, finally

In the ancient lodge on the edge of the middle of everything, I am struggling. The cord that's been keeping me in the sweat frays and then breaks.

My story begins to sing itself into being. Oh, Lucie.

I'm so close to the end now. I'm leaning into the darkness ahead, slick with sweat and swollen with waiting. I can hear Bob's fiddle, the notes of a song just begun. I am here in this lodge and I am also in this cabin and I'm already tapping out a jig from a seat on the dirt floor by the far wall.

I hear the stir of people walking in. I look up and through all the dancers I catch a glimpse of a tailored coat, a long dress, red shoes. A round cheek and a high brow, first one familiar profile and then another. And now, after all this, I hear the voices of the women who have just walked in—my Geneviève and my Velma.

I never imagined it could be like this.

There is nothing holding me in this lodge anymore. I let myself be pushed on, let myself be pressed on all sides, be made into light—pure brilliant light.

Nebula's Trail.

I am already getting to my feet and I am already finishing my story.

Celestial Jig.

Finally. They're here.

Star's Reel.

Oh, and I am here.

Acknowledgments

Thank you to my mother for keeping the stories alive. Thank you to my sister who, after two years of phone calls, knows almost nothing about this book but knows in great detail how I feel about it. Thank you to Dannika and Ben for your sense of humor and your additions to the language in the texting sections. And, of course, thank you to my three daughters and my grandson for being the best reasons I can think of to tell these stories: Amara, Dannika, Elise, and Jasper. Thank you to Stephanie Sinclair for seeing the promise in an early draft and working to make sure others saw its potential too. I want to thank editor Lara Hinchberger for the space you gave me to create—nobody else would have worked so well with me. I also want to thank editor Kathy Pories for not letting me overedit my own work and for making sure I kept magic in this story. And thank you to all my Métis ancestors for living your stories so well. To all of you, Maarsii.

A
GRANDMOTHER
BEGINS
THE
STORY

Questions for Discussion

Questions for Discussion

1. The meaning of the novel's title, *A Grandmother Begins the Story*, is layered. Did your interpretation of the title change as you finished the book?

2. This novel has a number of grandmothers, each of whom takes center stage at different points in the book. How do each of the grandmothers shape the stories that are being told?

3. The stories of a bison herd are told alongside the human stories. How do the bison stories and human stories reflect, mirror, or speak to each other?

4. How do bison mothering and grandmothering reflect each other in this novel? And human mothering and grandmothering? Why do you think the novel was written this way?

5. There are very few male characters in *A Grandmother Begins the Story*, but the main male characters play a pivotal role. How do they affect the outcome of the stories of both the humans and bison? Why does the Englishman have no name? Do Jay's final actions change your perception of him and his relationship with his son?

6. Some of the characters speak from the Spirit World. How does the Spirit World contribute to the novel's meaning? Is this Spirit World different from the one you've believed in? What do you think of the roles of death and dying in this novel?

7. If there were a definition of hope at the beginning of this book, what might that be? What is the role of hope in the novel's outcome?

8. The women in the book are members of one Métis family. How do each of the women struggle in different ways with their identity and the long-term impacts of intergenerational trauma?

9. Geneviève and her sister Velma reconnect through music at the rehab center. How does this relationship help them better understand their own life stories?

10. Carter is asked to help her grandmother kill herself. What do you think of the role of anger in her character's development? What is it that makes Carter begin to care enough to get her life together?

11. How does Dee's life story interact with Carter's? Why is Dee angry? What do you think is going to happen to Dee after this book ends?

12. Which of the characters don't get to speak very much? Why do you think their voices were not given more space? If they could speak, what might they say?

13. There are a number of stories told in the book: Solin tells a story to the calves; the elder Elaine tells a story to Geneviève; Geneviève finishes Elaine's story. Why are these stories included in the novel, and why don't readers get to hear Geneviève's ending?

14. What does this novel have to say about dealing with difficult family relationships? Specifically, with the often-challenging relationships between mothers and daughters?

15. What did the non-human characters contribute to the novel? Would it be the same without those voices?

© BOJAN FÜRST

MICHELLE PORTER is the descendant of a long line of Métis storytellers. Many of her ancestors told stories using music, and today she tells stories using the written word, including the memoirs *Scratching River* and *Approaching Fire* (shortlisted for the 2021 Indigenous Voices Award), and a book of poetry, *Inquiries* (shortlisted for the Pat Lowther Memorial Award for Best Book of Poetry in Canada). She holds degrees in journalism (BA), folklore (MA), English (MA), and geography (PhD); has been published in literary journals and magazines across Canada; and has won numerous awards for her poetry and journalism. She teaches creative writing and Métis Literature at Memorial University. Porter is a member of the Manitoba Métis Federation and she lives in Newfoundland and Labrador. *A Grandmother Begins the Story* was shortlisted for the Atwood Gibson Writers' Trust Fiction Prize in 2023.